A Puhaka Books Selection

puhakabooks.com

A Jack Wesley Novel

Be Prepared To Bleed

W.B. Martin

Also by W. B. Martin

The Jack Wesley Series

> Trouble Leaves Too Slow
> Shoving Back the Shadows
> Forever Now
> Only Pretty Lies
> Shaking Off Futility
> Pleasure Smiles
> Chasing the Black Bird
> Too Stupid To Survive

Other Libertarian Novels by W. B. Martin

> German Golfers Who Changed the World
> Sweetness in the Dark
> Endangered Species

Young Adult Novels by W. B. Martin

> Cubo Zoan
> Vincent van Gogh Likes Cats

To the Memory of:

Gregory R. Gale

A promise kept

Printed by permission of
Puhaka Publishing

Printed in the United States of America

Edited by T. Johns

Cover Layout by Morwenna Rakestraw

Version 2.1

Print ISBN 978-1-940554-26-6
eBook ISBN 978-1-940554-27-3

First Edition February 22, 2019

#9 in the Jack Wesley Thriller Series

Main Characters

Jack Wesley - Age 58, Eugene, Oregon police department detective, retired to Jackson, Wyoming, divorced and re-married, two children with first wife, currently living in Missoula, Montana.

Ed Wesley - Jack's older brother, lives in Jackson, Wyoming, Chief of Staff to U.S. Senator from Wyoming

Carl Wesley - Jack's son, age 33, business manager, married to Stacey, has two children, JJ, age 5 and CJ. age 2, currently living in Missoula, Montana

Inez Wesley - Jack's daughter, age 31, school teacher, fiancee to Eric Reiner, major in the U.S. Air Force, currently living in Colorado Springs, Colorado

Kotone Wesley - Jack's estranged second wife, Japanese-American, triathlete, banker, age 37, current whereabouts unknown

Katarina Vanderzanden - Dutch friend of Jack, age 26, single, retired champion figure skater, currently lives in Hilversum, the Netherlands.

Sir Graham Elphinston - Australian friend of Jack, married to Fatima, retired New South Wales Police Inspector, currently lives in Sydney.

LaMarcus Lewis - Jack's former African-American sniper team partner in the Marine Corps, age 61, divorced, retired captain of the Cambridge

Massachusetts Police Department, currently lives in Thailand.

Misty Duran - Jack's friend, age 40, widow of retired owner of hedge fund, currently living in the British Virgin Islands

Valentina Tosi - Jack's Italian friend, married, age 30, former intelligence agent for Italian AISE, currently living in Rome, Italy.

Gregory Roberts - Jack's next-door neighbor in Missoula, age 60, retired British SAS

Karma Somda - Jack's next-door neighbor in Missoula, age 52, retired British Gurkha Regiment.

Daniel Vasquez - Son of Ernesto and heir to his deceased father's Mexican drug cartel, currently living in Las Vegas, Nevada

Chapter 1

Missoula, Montana

The warmth of the autumn sun brought some relief to the Bitterroot Valley of Montana. The high mountains to the west still held the early white dusting that had arrived yesterday to announce that winter would soon come to Missoula. Classes at the university were in full swing as students with their backpacks walked by on their way to campus a few blocks away.

The leaves of the trees along the quiet residential street still held on while their color change portended their eminent fall to earth. The light breeze coming up the Clark Fork River rustled the dry leaves. Soon leaf piles coupled with the delight of children jumping into them would line the street. But for now the last vestiges of summer held on while the Craftsman-style homes lining the street awaited the harsh Montana winter.

One soul fought for warmth reading on his front deck. He would take every opportunity to sit and enjoy the end of the outdoor season even if it meant being wrapped in polar fleece for comfort. To him every moment outdoors was to be cherished before being forced into the confines of artificially heated houses. He had lived through a number of

Rocky Mountain winters now, and while they beat the rainy winters of the Pacific Northwest that he had endured for most of his life, he still wasn't content with the long dark winters.

Jack Wesley had settled into life in Missoula because of one reason, his grandchildren. Actually four reasons, as he included his son and daughter-in-law in that equation. But being near JJ and CJ were reason enough. Now aged 5 and 2, they had enough personality to keep Jack happy for extended periods, which happened frequently since they lived next door to Jack.

Jack glanced over to his right at a similar house for activity. Stacey would be leaving soon to pick up JJ from his all-day Kindergarten, CJ strapped in his car seat in the back of the Pathfinder. But all was quiet. Jack scanned the street for the daily return of the local school kids from the neighborhood grade school two blocks away. But with no sign of school having been released, Jack knew he had a few more minutes to relax.

Today was the day he would watch his two grandkids while Stacey went shopping. He enjoyed at least three weekdays with CJ as Stacey had a part time job and Jack was glad to help out. Otherwise, CJ went to day care one day each week. Today was Stacey's day off.

He found his place in his crime novel and continued reading. But his attention was distracted by the high whine of a car engine. The noise barely registered but Jack had heard it before and he knew what was coming. It happened too often on his quiet street, or at least what should have been a quiet street.

Lined with 1930-style bungalow houses, his street was three blocks from the University of Montana campus. The Craftsman houses were all similar with a covered front porch, hip-style roof and a single-car driveway leading to a garage just off the back of the house. With three bedrooms down one side of the house, the other side held the living room in the front with the kitchen/dining room toward the back. One bathroom squeezed on the back finished off the small 1200-square-foot house.

The style dominated the street with slight variations as individual personalities had altered each one over the decades. Jack liked the intimate feeling the houses offered. During the summer the front porches provided families a neighborly setting as people watched their kids play on the tree-lined sidewalks. And with each house having a long single driveway, cars didn't dominate the scene as in many American neighborhoods with their large, overwhelming two-car garages and driveways up front. At least all but one house on his street held the pattern. His next door neighbor to the left had what Jack estimated to be a 1970's style house with the garage up front with two bays. A fire had consumed the original house, Jack had learned, and the two-story modern house stuck out noticeably.

But all that was forgotten as the whine of a high-revving engine took on a more noticeable sound. Jack had seen the fast and furious wannabe before and had even called the police to report the danger it presented. But nothing seemed to have been done to slow the Japanese rice burner down.

Jack Wesley, retired police detective, put his book down and picked up his phone. If the police hadn't done anything over the three weeks this had been going on, then he decided that maybe a video on his phone might persuade the authorities to do something.

He clicked on his camera and aimed it down the street toward the growing noise. He could hear the gear changes as the car built up speed through the thickly settled neighborhood. Then followed the down shifts as the car reached the corner onto his street. Accelerating quickly, the engine hit extreme revs with the custom exhaust blaring out. Jack caught a glimpse through the trees of the lowered Honda Accord as it hit third gear. He had reported that the driver typically went by his house doing at least fifty miles per hour and today was no exception.

The Honda flashed by parked cars and continued its acceleration. From the corner of his eye Jack saw something. Holding the camera on the moving car, he shifted his eyes slightly to a large truck tire that was rolling down his neighbor's driveway. The heavy metal wheel added mass, and as the tire hit the flat sidewalk it bounced slightly over the driveway ramp off the street. Hitting the street pavement, it bounced again with perfect timing just as the Honda reached the same spot. The lowered front end caught the wheel mid-hood, which knocked the tire from vertical to horizontal. Now acting as a flying disk it smashed through the car's windshield jamming the glass into the passenger compartment.

The car continued down the street, but the driver was no longer in control as he was pinned to his headrest by the heavy-weighted wheel. Deploying airbags saved the driver's life as the exploding bags directed the tire up toward the roof liner, thus preventing the driver from being decapitated. But with the driver incapacitated, his jerking movement caused the Honda to swerve and slam into a tree across from Jack's house. As the car crumpled, the energy released by the crash flipped the car to the right as it tried to twist itself apart.

Jack lowered his camera and dialed 911. Neighbors came running out of their houses, alerted by the crash, and as one man reached the wreck he leaned into the car. Jack stood up as he talked to the 911 dispatcher and soon sirens were heard from the emergency response. He hung up as the first police car arrived followed quickly by an ambulance and fire truck. Letting the paramedics do their job, Jack walked to the end of his driveway and put his phone away. Standing and watching the scene, a man walked up beside him.

"Hell of a thing," the man said.

Jack turned to the voice and recognized his next-door neighbor. "Sure is."

"Good thing there weren't any kids out in the street playing."

"Yes, good thing," Jack responded.

Jack had met the man when he had moved in a little over a month ago, as Jack was also new to the neighborhood. He had gone over to say hi. But no other conversation had taken place, and Jack now wished he'd been a bit more neighborly. The man seemed to be a quiet type, so Jack hadn't pushed. *All in due time* he had thought.

"I'm bloody amazed the authorities hadn't done anything before this," the man offered.

"Yeah, I've called the police a number of times and nothing. It just continued. And with all the little kids around here, too."

"No respect. Young people today have no respect."

Jack turned to face the man and held out his hand. "I'm sorry I haven't been more neighborly. I'm Jack Wesley. We meet the day you moved in. Greg isn't it?"

"Greg Roberts," the man replied. "And no, Jack, I should have been more neighborly. It's just with unpacking and getting sorted out, time just flew by."

The paramedics were carefully pulling the driver out the car door. The firemen had had to force the door open and were now working on the passenger's door. A short back brace had been slipped in behind the driver and his head and upper body strapped to the brace. As the driver came out the paramedics laid him gently on the ground where a full body brace had been placed. His entire body was now strapped down to protect any potential spinal injuries.

As they examined the driver, two emergency personnel were working on the man's girlfriend. She screamed as the men checked her for injuries. An inflatable leg splint was placed on her left leg after her door was forced open. The two were soon placed into the ambulance and driven off to the hospital. One police officer stepped over and looked into the car. With his leather gloves for protection from the sharp metal and broken glass, he yanked on a large object. Two firemen moved to help as the large truck wheel and tire were extracted from the car. Two of them rolled it onto the sidewalk and let it fall, the tire slamming the concrete with a bang, causing some of the onlookers to jump.

An officer with sergeant strips stepped over the tire and asked, "Anyone see what happened?"

The people in the crowd all offered that no one had witnessed the accident.

"Who called 911 then?"

The sergeant looked around as a number of people held up their hands. He started going from one to another asking if they had witnessed anything or had just called after the accident.

Jack stood and watched the sergeant work through the hand raisers. Finished, the sergeant turned. "Anyone else call?"

Jack raised his arm slowly. The sergeant swiveled around the crowd and finally noticed Jack's arm raised. He walked across the street flipping his notebook to a fresh page.

"Name?"

"Jack Wesley."

"And you called it in?"

Jack nodded that he had.

"Did you witness the accident?"

Jack hesitated slightly. Things were getting complicated real fast. The truck tire that had caused the mayhem had come from the driveway of the man standing next to him. While the punk that had terrorized his neighborhood certainly needed to be put out of commission, Jack wasn't sure a truck tire through the windshield was the right answer. But he did like the neighbor's style if he had caused it. Jack had dealt with punks all his life as a policeman in Eugene, Oregon. And after retirement he had dealt with even more of them. Bad boys deserved to be put down and Jack was inclined to provide the force to put them down. So he hesitated to step too far into being a witness. The sergeant stared at him for an answer.

"Sort of," Jack said.

"Sort of what? Did you witness the accident or didn't you?" The police sergeant showing his irritation.

"I saw the crash when he hit the tree. I was coming out my front door just as the Honda hit the tree," Jack lied. He glanced slightly to the left. His neighbor had a stone face. The sergeant noticed the head movement.

"Who are you?" the sergeant asked, looking at Greg.

"I'm the neighbor. I live right there."

"You a witness?"

"No, officer. I was in the house when I heard the crash."

"OK. Then Mr. Wesley, can you tell me what you saw."

Jack described the car hitting the tree and coming to rest lying across the street. The officer wrote his notes as Jack talked.

"Any idea how that truck tire got into the front seat?"

Jack hesitated again, then lied again. "No idea."

Jack saw the look he got from Greg but tried to conceal any sign that he sure as hell knew where the truck tire had come from. The sergeant looked at Jack and then at Greg.

"You positive about that, mister?"

"Asked and answered, sergeant," Jack said.

"You a wise guy?" the sergeant asked. One of the patrolmen walked up to the group.

"From the black marks on the hood it sure looks like they hit that truck tire. If they were going as fast as some have said that could have killed them both. Like having a deer come through the windshield doing seventy," the patrolman said.

The sergeant turned back to Jack. "So no idea how a truck tire came to be in the middle of the road mister smart ass?"

"How do you know how fast they were going? I don't see any skid marks," Jack asked.

"The other people offered that this kid drove doing fifty through their neighborhood regularly. From the impact, and damage to the tree we can estimate his speed. And no skid marks because he never hit the brakes since he had a truck tire on top of him."

"Well, I called about this punk a number of times and you never did anything about it," Jack said. "I have grandkids living right here and this asshole zooming down the street didn't make things very safe. And you not doing anything about it didn't help."

"So you took things into your own hands, then. Roll a tire out into the street?"

"You won't find my fingerprints on it. I didn't roll any tire out but if the punk had been going the required speed on this street I guess he could have avoided it. And if you have any other questions, it will be in my lawyers office."

"Got something to hide then."

"No, thirty years on the force. I know cops aren't your friends." Jack pulled out his wallet and flipped it open to show his retired law enforcement card.

The sergeant eyed the credentials and then the person holding them. "I'll do that if we have any more questions."

"Excuse me, sergeant," Greg interrupted. "How badly injured were they?"

"They'll live. The driver was lucky."

Greg continued, "So will the driver be cited or something?"

"You English or something? The way you talk ,I was thinking."

"British actually. From Wales, part of the British union. Just interested how you Yanks handle law and order here. I'm new here."

"Well, don't you worry about any citations."

"Considering the bad job you did stopping this driver before this happened makes asking about citations a reasonable question, sergeant," Jack interjected.

"I'm not liking you one bit, retired law enforcement or not. So just mind your own business."

"This street is where I live so this is my business. What if my grandkids had been crossing the street and were now pinned under the car dead. Not my business?" Jack was getting worked up.

The Missoula police sergeant fixed a stare at the two of them before he turned and walked back to the accident scene. The patrolman followed behind.

"Are all your police like him?" Greg asked.

"Some. I guess. Pointing out how they didn't do anything beforehand about this street racer doesn't sit well. No one likes their screw-ups pointed out," Jack offered.

The crowd dispersed as the wrecker hauled the Honda away, the truck tire still sitting on the side walk. The police had left so the tire seemed to be abandoned to the neighborhood. Jack and Greg stood on the side walk as the wrecker turned the corner and disappeared.

"Can we go to your house, Greg?"

Greg acknowledged the request and led Jack up his driveway through the garage into the house.

They passed a vintage Mini obviously being worked on in the garage, a newer Toyota parked next to it.

"Project car?" Jack asked when he was seated on a bar stool in the kitchen. Greg offered Jack coffee and when Jack mentioned English Breakfast tea, Greg's eyes lit up. As he brewed tea a short dark man walked into the kitchen.

"Oh, Karma Somda, I'd like you to meet our neighbor, Jack Wesley."

Jack shook hands with Karma as the man returned a slight bow.

"And yes, Jack, the Mini project is mine. Keeps my retirement interesting getting parts for it here in America."

Jack wasn't sure how to approach the subject but he felt that he needed to. He pulled out his phone and brought the picture file up. Holding it up to Greg, he hit the play button. Greg and Karma both watched as the video caught the tire rolling down the driveway and smashing into the car, the car slamming into the tree.

Greg stood in the kitchen and calmly sipped his tea. Karma made no facial expression to indicate what he was thinking. *Two very cool characters* Jack thought.

"Well Jack, you have your evidence right there that you certainly didn't roll the tire down the driveway on that bad boy," Greg said. Karma stood eight inches shorter than the Welshman, but showed no emotion. Jack was getting more suspicious of these two as the minutes clicked by. He knew the tire had come from Greg's garage, so one of them was the culprit.

"You claimed you were in the house when the accident occurred," Jack said.

"True. And Karma can be my witness. But remember that the garage counts as part of the house," Greg said.

"Technically yes," Jack said.

"But you didn't offer the video to the police or mention its existence. Being former law enforcement, aren't you sworn to uphold the law?" Greg asked.

That was the issue Jack focused on. While he had evidence of a crime, he wasn't all that concerned about implicating his neighbor. The fast and furious driver and his girlfriend had been dealt a lesson in life. Jack wasn't sure that anyone needed to know who had provided the lesson.

He looked once more at the video of the accident and then hit the delete button. He held up his smart phone so Greg and Karma could attest that the video no longer existed. Both smiled back at Jack as Greg picked up the tea pot.

"Another cup, Jack?"

Chapter 2

Phoenix, Arizona

"Do we know anything yet?" the man asked. As the head of a criminal organization, the man expected answers. When none were offered by the other men around the table, the leader exploded.

"I want some answers. This shithead who killed my father has lived too long already. He dodged us in Wyoming and then disappeared. Now we have information he has been spotted in Montana."

A short dark man with a black mustache ventured into the tirade. "But boss, we have our spy across the street and he is sending us information."

"Too slow. I want this man dead in a week. Do you hear me? A week. And I won't accept any failure this time."

The eight men around the table nodded agreement. It would happen in a week, this they knew. Daniel Vasquez knew how to get what he wanted. As the son of Ernesto, they knew the ruthlessness and brutality bred into his body. Most had worked for the family since Ernesto had risen to control his own organization in Las Vegas. That they had not prevented the boss from being violently murdered had set the wraith of the son on them.

That a hit team that had already gone to Wyoming in the dead of winter and had all been killed raised the stakes. And when the target had disappeared seemingly from the face of the Earth, that had been the clincher. For a year the man had vanished, only to finally re-appear in Missoula, Montana sitting quietly in his house. Already a team had been organized and was on its way from Las Vegas. All the while their money-making business of drug running, prostitution and loan sharking was suffering. The boss turned his intense gaze onto Alfonso. The underling squirmed in his seat at the glare.

"Tell me it is done."

Alfonso swallowed hard. Making the boss unhappy could prove fatal. He carefully weighed his words. "Boss, I have a two-man hit team leaving Las Vegas as we speak. It will be over in three days, I swear."

"You had better swear. A year is too long for that pig to live. And do we know the where-a-bouts of the black bastard? He dies too."

Alfonso blanched at the mention of the black man. No sign of him had surfaced and that would only enrage the boss more. "No sign of him, boss. We have every resource on it. But nothing."

"And you have told our team to try to find an answer to that question before they kill him in Montana?" Daniel asked.

"They have been told. And, as per your instructions they need to videotape it all. And if possible, they are to make it slow and painful," Alfonso offered.

"The slower and more painful the better. They will be paid extra if they impress me. You told them that, right?"

"Si," Alfonso added.

"Good, good. Now where are we with bringing in our next shipment from Sonora?"

* * *

At that moment Jack Wesley was standing at the altar of the Air Force Academy Chapel beside his daughter, Inez. The minister looked over the gathering and asked, "Who gives this bride away?"

"We do," Jack answered as he stepped back and sat down next to his ex-wife. She smiled slightly at the response.

But Jack had noticed the broad smile on his daughter's face at what he had just said. They had discussed the response beforehand and Jack had offered an olive branch to say 'we do' instead of the more traditional 'I do'. Jack knew the traditional father giving away the bride had been replaced by a more politically correct version of inclusiveness. If it had been up to him he would have screwed the inclusiveness, but he knew it was important to Inez.

The daughter who had left long ago with the ex-wife in the divorce was back in his life. And Jack would suffer any indignities to keep it that way. Even including his ex-wife in the formal proceedings sitting next to him while Inez married her love. And he would even suffer sitting in church next to the ex-wife while her boyfriend sat on the opposite side of her. Jack took a big breath and tried to relax. It would be a long day.

But he was ecstatic at his daughter's choice. Eric was a major in the U. S. Air Force and was stationed at the Air Force Academy as an instructor. Jack hadn't known Eric long and didn't know his life history, only that he was from Wisconsin and had flown C-131 transport planes for his regular job in the Air Force. Beyond that, Jack hadn't been told much.

Sitting behind him was his son Carl, Carl's wife, Stacey, and one grandchild, CJ. The oldest grandchild, JJ, was in a miniature tuxedo standing behind Eric holding a pillow with two rings on it. Standing with Eric was a brother officer as best man. Having lived in Colorado Springs her adult life, Inez had a local friend standing with her. Neither of them had wanted a big wedding, so no other attendants were present except for someone's young daughter being flower girl. *I think the matron of honor's daughter* Jack thought.

Jack was just glad his daughter, at age 31, was finally getting married. And married to what seemed to be a great guy. *Not like some of the drips she brought home* Jack thought. Soon the couple kissed and turned to greet the applauding crowd. Jack turned as sixteen fellow air force officers lined both sides of the aisle beside him. At a command, each drew their sword and held it aloft. The happy couple walked arm-in-arm under the swords followed by the attendants. Jack winked at JJ as he passed, trying not to hold the flower girl's hand.

The officers sheathed their swords and marched out of the chapel. Two officers soon returned to release the guests one row at a time. Jack reached down and picked up CJ as Carl and Stacey fell in behind, his ex-wife trailing behind with the boyfriend. Everyone headed to the reception located next to the chapel.

At the reception hall Jack noticed that his name was on one table place marker. He strolled around the round table and realized his ex-wife would not be with him. That brought a smile to Jack. Carl and Stacey came over and took their spots next to Jack at the same table, CJ and JJ taking their place with them. The ex-wife was seated closer to the groom's family which suited Jack just fine. Jack looked over and saw her approaching.

"Hi, Mom," Carl said. He gave his mom a kiss. The two grandkids gave their grandmother a hug as Stacey kissed her cheek.

"A nice wedding, don't you think, Jack?" the ex-wife looked at Jack as she asked her question.

"Yes, very beautiful," Jack offered.

"We raised a great daughter."

Jack noticed the consolatory attitude in the phrase 'we' and nodded his head. He had been a career-minded policeman bent on advancement. That meant getting a college degree to supplement his Marine Corp veteran status that had got him onto the force. To make detective meant a degree and lots of overtime. He knew he had sacrificed his family life too much in striving for the gold shield. And when his wife left for Colorado with his daughter, he knew he had to make things right.

Carl, two years older, had stayed in Eugene and Jack went to work to mend the relationship. It took a lot of angry outbursts in martial arts training between the two to get his son back. That they both earned their black belt in the process was a bonus. And then the years spending time with Inez to earn his way into her life. Although mostly long-distance with her in Colorado, Jack felt good about their relationship now.

"Yes, we raised a beautiful daughter together," Jack finally answered. And he meant it. He would always feel resentment towards his ex for walking out on their marriage. But it had been enough years so he could put most of it aside, especially on such a special day. The ex turned and walked back to her boyfriend and her table.

A tug on his arm caught Jack's attention. Inez and Eric stood next to him as the band started to play.

"This is Eric's and my dance together. Dad-daughter dance comes next. Are you ready?" Inez asked.

"Aways and forever," Jack answered which was always his response to his children whenever they asked.

"And parents have a dance coming up too, don't forget. So play nice."

"When have you ever known me not to play nice?" Jack quipped.

The parents soon joined the bridal couple on the dance floor. It was a little stiff between Jack and his ex-wife not only because of their past, but also because Jack was not a smooth dancer. The two kept a proper distance between them and Jack avoided stepping on any toes, at least physical ones. He did manage to step in it when he asked about the boyfriend.

"So your boyfriend enjoying himself?" Jack looked over toward where he sat at the table, a scowl emanating.

"You know his name is Larry, so please use his name," the response came back.

"Sorry," though he didn't really mean it. "Is Larry having a good time?"

"He is being supportive which is a damn sight better than you did most of our marriage."

Jack decided he would let things go so that Inez could have her day. His answer was brief.

"Good man, then." Jack lied and tried a little swirl on the dance floor. His ex, startled by the sudden change in rhythm, attempted to keep up.

"Been practicing, have we?"

"Just getting better in my old age. Retirement has a way of bringing out new skills I never thought I was interested in."

"Or just trying to keep up with those younger women?"

Jack settled back to the slow dance and took the comment in stride. His ex had certainly seen him with at least one younger woman. Did she know about the others? Had Inez found out from Carl and passed that information on? And did the ex know that he had eventually married again? A marriage that still existed in name only, as Jack's wife had chosen to leave him. The only reason it wasn't a second failed marriage was he hadn't been served papers for a divorce. So maybe somewhere out there he still had a chance.

The thought of two failed marriages kept Jack quiet the rest of the dance. He looked up as the music stopped and his ex-wife withdrew from his arms. Jack retreated off the dance floor as the next honorees got ready for their turn with the bride and groom.

Sitting down at his table, Jack pushed his chair back away from the crowd. His thoughts were elsewhere and he was enjoying a quiet moment alone with his thoughts. The grandkids were with Stacey's parents at another table while Carl and Stacey danced, leaving the table empty. The solitude suited Jack's frame of mind.

Jack's thoughts focused on his second wife, a wife who seemed to attract trouble. They had met after she had killed someone who had attacked her. That it had been ruled self-defense but didn't help the psychological damage that Jack had witnessed. An intense relationship had eventually won through the scars, but that initial intense time had ended with them both going separate ways.

A reunion of sorts took place when the woman's sister needed help. That had rekindled the spark for a brief time. But it was Carl and Stacey's wedding where things had come together for the two of them and they had finally been married.

But trouble soon followed for his new wife, and Jack had to rescue her once again. The compound scars had been too much and she had disappeared on him. His pain continued as Jack missed her. The music continued as the happy couple swirled past. *If only I had another chance* he thought. *I could make it right between us.* A melancholy mood swept over him as he stared out over the hall, gazing at nothing.

"Penny for your thoughts," a voice beside him said.

Startled out of his trance, Jack turned to find his daughter sitting down next to him.

"Oh, hi honey. Don't mind me. Just an old man sitting here with his thoughts. Go back to your party."

"Come on, it's time for the garter toss."

"I'm married, remember," Jack said.

There was a notably lull in the conversation at his statement. Inez knew Jack's wife from Carl's wedding and a brief encounter in Colorado. But Inez hadn't been involved in all the troubles that seemed to come between Jack and his wife.

Jack perked up. "But Larry isn't. I'll come watch and see if he gets lucky."

"Now Dad, remember what I told you. And I suppose you want me to hit Mom with the bouquet, too."

"It has been a lot of years that they've been shacked up together. It might spur them on to do the right thing."

Inez grabbed her Dad's arm and pulled him to his feet. Together they stormed to the head table where Eric waited patiently. As they reached the chair provided for the garter removal, Inez let go of her father's arm, but not before whispering in Jack's ear, "Jack Wesley, you are a trouble maker."

"He isn't there." Alfonso rushed into his boss's office.

"Who?" Daniel asked but already knew the answer from the sweat on Alfonso's face.

"Jack Wesley. He's gone. Our source called to say he left two days ago and they just figured it out."

"Permanently gone? Or just visiting somewhere? It is the holiday season," Daniel said although he himself didn't pay too much attention to the holiday season. Just more tourists coming to Vegas to extract money from.

"Temporary, it seems. The source talked to a neighborhood kid. Seems he was hired to keep the walkways shoveled. So he will be back. I haven't been able to get ahold of our team there yet."

Daniel glared at his underling from the news he was being told. He couldn't do anything about the man leaving, and Alfonso had been on top of things. He would let him live another day.

"Check with me when you know more," Daniel said and went back to checking his accounting books. Alfonso knew when he was dismissed and quietly withdrew himself.

Chapter 3

Sydney, Australia

The Randwick Office of the New South Wales Police Department was quiet for a Friday afternoon. An upscale neighborhood of Sydney, Randwick held the University of New South Wales. Located about 5 kilometers southeast of downtown Sydney, the police typically had an easy time of it. Only if the students were demonstrating could things get out of control. Otherwise, the normal load of thefts and assaults filled the docket.

Chief Inspector Nigel Elphinston sat at his desk and read the days report. Having spent too many years on the night shift, he was still getting used to his new schedule. He had grown accustomed to having his mornings to workout along the Bondi to Coogee Coastal Trail while using his afternoon for sleeping. He had never met anyone to marry, but didn't blame his police work and its schedule for his lack of commitment.

But today was his last work day for three weeks, as he was going on holiday. The advantage of seniority was being able to pick the better times for leave. And being gone over Christmas summer break was the choicest time of all. That he would be spending it on a push bike excited him more. He loved an active lifestyle, even if he didn't have someone to share it with on a daily basis.

He would be joining his uncle and uncle's friends on the bicycle trip. When his Uncle Graham Elphinston had finally moved back to Australia after many years living in Europe, Nigel had relished getting to know his uncle again. That they had a common bond of the New South Wales police between them added to their common interests. Meeting the friend that had been with his uncle when he received his knighthood would finally offer some answers. His uncle was very tight-lipped about the whole affair except to acknowledge his nephew's key role in it.

Nigel put down the report and straightened his desk. It was time to head home to his apartment near the Royal Randwick Mall and grab his things. His uncle would be by to pick up him and his bicycle this evening.

The next day found the two men standing in the early morning at the immigration exit for international visitors. They awaited the arrival of their American guests. A steady stream of people walked through the open doors into Australia proper. Many were met by relatives with embraces and kisses. Some just wandered out into Sydney on the start of holiday. Graham perked up as he saw a familiar face.

Pushing a luggage cart with a large box on it, Jack Wesley emerged to a warm welcome from his old friend Graham. The two embraced and shook hands vigorously. Soon Carl, Stacey, Inez and Eric walked up pushing luggage carts. Introductions were made all around as Nigel met his cycling companions.

"So this is the wonder bike?" Graham asked patting the large box on Jack's trolley.

Jack had mentioned bringing their own bicycles down-under, but Nigel had offered that it was easier to rent them for the three-week trip. Renting avoided the airline charge for the large luggage and the problem of assembling the bicycles once in Australia. All but Jack had agreed that renting sounded much easier.

Jack rode a recumbent bicycle, so a rental was not an option. And Jack was not about to spend three weeks on an upright bike. So Nigel had arranged a work party with some mates, all accomplished cyclists. They would meet up at Graham's house and help assemble Jack's recumbent.

"Yes, Sir Graham," Jack half joked with his friend. "My lower parts are past the age of sitting on one of those little saddles."

"Bloody hell, mate," Graham said as he smiled. He and Jack had a running joke about the knighthood Graham had received from the Queen. They were the only people who knew the whole truth about how Graham had received it and the role Jack had played. A few knew some of the story, or at least thought they did. Jack and Graham were content to keep the whole story to themselves. "Should have been you."

"Americans can't receive such an honor. Looks better on you anyway," Jack said. The others looked on. The rest of the group certainly knew the formal story of why Graham had been knighted, and each waited to see if they were about to learn more.

"Well it does get me free beer at the pub so I guess it was worth it." The two men laughed as Jack pushed his trolley out the airport exit. A passenger van pulling a small enclosed trailer waited at the curb. Graham directed everyone to place their luggage in the trailer and helped Jack load his bike box.

Graham climbed into the front passenger seat as the six others all grabbed a seat. Other passengers filled the remaining seats in the airport shuttle and when full, the driver climbed in. Taking addresses from each passenger, the driver worked out an efficient route to deliver each to their destination. All the other passengers announced a downtown Sydney location while Graham provided his location for the group.

Determining his route, the driver turned to Graham. "Right, we'll drop you and your mates off at Coogee Beach first then."

Standing on the sidewalk after being deposited at Graham's house, Jack surveyed the neighborhood. Coogee Beach sat off to his right down a small hill, a commercial center of shops lining the promenade. Graham's house, about eight houses up from the beach, faced the ocean. It appeared that it was an older house that had been remodeled recently. Most of the neighborhood looked like it had undergone a major upgrade. All were large substantial brick houses that prosperous professionals from Sydney coveted.

"You sure you have room for all of us, Graham?" Jack asked. He didn't want to impose on his friend. From the size of the house it seemed a stupid question. As Jack glanced to the side he realized the house had three levels and certainly held enough room for all.

"Fatima wanted this huge place so I bloody well need to fill it up sometimes."

Graham's wife came out the front door, walked to Jack, and gave him a hug. Her dark complexion radiated out a golden glow. *Her Mediterranean heritage thrived in the Australian sun,* Jack thought. With introductions, everyone headed into the house as Fatima led everyone to their rooms. Soon they were back in the living room enjoying the cool breeze coming in through the open sliding doors. The view out onto the Pacific Ocean entranced everyone as Fatima offered cold drinks on the deck. Settled under the two umbrellas, the party sipped and relaxed, the long flight forgotten as Australian hospitality took over. A doorbell broke the mood and three middle aged men along with two women walked in as Nigel opened the door.

"Jack, these are my mates who volunteered to put your bike right. Just relax and we'll get started."

As the two women newcomers took drinks and sat down, Jack joined the bike crew heading to the garage. Graham's car had been backed out of the two-car garage to make room for a workshop. Soon the box was opened and Nigel had the recumbent hanging from the ceiling so they could work on it. Soon the front and rear wheels were attached.

The crankset on the recumbent was taped to the long tubular frame. Jack carefully undid the tape and swung the crankset around to the front of the bike. He shoved the crank tube into the frame tube after making sure the chain was straight. He moved the crank back and forth until the mark on the crank tube met up with the frame tube. He tightened the bolt to hold it in place.

While regular bikes adjusted for riders by adjusting the seat height, on a recumbent the crankset was adjusted. And if the crankset was moved, the chain had to be adjusted for length which required shortening the chain.

With the crank tight, the pedals were turned around and tightened in place while the handlebars were straightened. All had been removed to accommodate the cardboard box Jack had obtained from the local bike store in Missoula.

Jack's recumbent was an under-seat steering model and the Australians took in the strange bike. With the crank out front on a long tubular frame, the riders legs and feet were out in front instead of the traditional upright bike with pedals below.

As one of the helpers picked up Jack's contoured fiberglass seat, a quizzical look came over their faces. The seat more resembled a car's bucket seat then any bicycle seat they had ever seen. Jack took the padded seat and placed it in position on the recumbent. The others all saw the attachment points, grabbed wrenches and soon had the seat in place. Just the cables needed reattachment so the shifters and the disk brakes worked properly. When finished, Jack knew what was coming.

"Ok, I think we need to go and test ride this thing to make sure we've got it right. Who's first?" All four hands of the volunteers went up. Soon they were down on Coogee Beach Promenade as Jack knew a flat straight area was required for first-time riders.

Nigel was first and Jack instructed him on how to climb onto the recumbent. Nigel took hold of the low handle bar and stepped over the long tubular frame in front of the handlebars. He slowly backed himself down onto the seat. Leaning back, he placed his head on the headrest and placed one foot up onto a pedal. Jack stood behind him holding him steady. One stroke on the pedal and Nigel placed his other foot on the opposite pedal and cranked away slowly. Jack jogged behind keeping the recumbent upright. With his hands down by his side and his rear end lower than his feet, Nigel wobbled noticeably down the promenade. Jack caught his breath as he ran up to a stopped Nigel

"How do you turn this thing?" Nigel asked.

"Carefully and with a wide area at first. Until you get used to the balance differences it's a bit unsteady."

"Bloody hell, you say. I keep wanting to drift to one side."

Nigel stood up and physically turned the bike around in place. He sat back down as Jack held on. A wobbly ride back to the others gave Nigel a perspective on recumbent riding. Each one took a turn as Jack gave up his running-along-behind duties to the younger ones.

Carl stood beside Stacey as the Australians all remarked that they would remain upright bicycle riders. They each thanked Jack for the experience as Jack thanked them for help on assembling his bike.

"I bet you won't miss pulling your trailer," Carl offered.

"No, son. And having Graham drive the sag wagon sounds good. Just carrying enough for the day made me excited about this trip," Jack said.

As the group all chatted about the upcoming bike tour, one of the two women who had joined them spoke up.

"No one said you were going on a bike tour."

Jack remembered she had been introduced as Deidre. A woman in her mid-forties, Deidre had blond hair, blue eyes, stood about 5' 7" with a good build. She looked to have a few pounds extra but her breasts overshadowed any growing midriff. The other woman was called Angie. In her thirties, shorter than Deidre and less well-endowed, she also had the blond-hair blue-eye complexion. Both were your typical Australian beachgoer, at least to Jack.

Angie added, "Is this trip open? I want to go too."

Everyone turned to Nigel and Graham, as they were the hosts. Graham looked at Jack for help. None came.

After a long quiet spell, Graham said, "If it's OK with my friend, Jack, I guess we can fit two more in."

Jack, who wanted to help his friend, added, "Before you two decide to join us, do you even know where we are riding? And have you been conditioning yourselves? We plan on covering about 75 miles a day."

"How far is that?" Deidre asked.

"About 110 K," Nigel offered the conversion to kilometers for the locals. "We will be riding the coast road to Melbourne and then following the Great Ocean Road. Plenty of hills on that one."

"Nige, we've ridden 150 K before. You remember," Angie said. "And Deidre and I ride together all the time. She's a strong rider."

Jack noticed the 'Nige' comment and assumed that there was something between Nigel and Angie. Or at least there had been something there at one time.

"I don't see any problem with two more along if Graham can handle the extra gear," Jack said.

"Well, let's go check. He's on cook duty and is probably ready for us to eat now."

The three bike volunteers were invited to join in as everyone headed back up the hill to the house. Jack pushed his recumbent along behind cursing that he had forgotten his stick today. But he did have it for the trip so that he wouldn't have to bend down to steer the low handlebar.

Chapter 4

Missoula, Montana

Greg Roberts stood at his window and observed the street in front of his house. He had been trained to observe while not being observed himself. Many years of plying his craft had taught him well. The car that had been there yesterday was back again today. And the driver and his passengers were sitting in the same spot.

Karma Somda walked into the living room and was careful not to walk in front of the window. He slid up behind Greg as his friend moved slightly to offer the shorter man a clear view.

"They are back," Karma said.

"Yes, same car, same two inside. Same Nevada license plates," Greg replied.

They both stood carefully using the wall as a block to any outside observation. The late afternoon darkness was settling over Missoula. With the short winter daylight, the car had returned just as the darkness settled in. With the cold temperatures outside, the car's exhaust emitted a small cloud as the driver let the engine run for the heat.

The front passenger door opened and a man stepped out followed by the exhaust plume stopping. The driver stepped out of the car and closed his door gently. The two stepped onto the sidewalk, their stance a little unsteady from the frozen snow that had not been removed.

Walking towards Greg's house, they scanned the neighborhood as they went. Being the dinner hour, no one was on the street. Neighbors had arrived home from work in the dark and quickly settled inside the warmth of their homes, leaving the street deserted.

As the two men walked in front of Greg's house, Karma disappeared from the living room. Greg knew he would acquire them from the side window in the attached garage. The window faced the Wesley home next door, with Jack's single driveway in between. The two men turned and walked up Jack's driveway.

"They are heading up the driveway, just like yesterday," Karma whispered into the small microphone attached to the ear unit. He and Greg had often used such communication devices in their work, so they were comfortable wearing them.

Greg stared at the now-empty car. He added, "I'm slipping out the side door." Two bursts of static told Greg that the message had been received.

Greg checked that the Sig Sauer 9 mm in his holster on his back was racked and loaded. He shoved it behind him and pulled his sweatshirt over the gun. He quickly walked to the door that led outside on the opposite side from the Wesley house.

He circled around his backyard coming up on the rear of Jack's garage.

Announcing quietly that he was behind Jack's garage, Greg waited for the soft response of his friend. Jack's single car garage was circled to the rear as Greg came around. Karma had quietly stepped out from the back of Greg's house and moved to the front of Jack's garage. Greg and the Karma met just as the two strangers came into Jack's backyard.

The two men reacted at once, each pulling a knife. They widened their stance in the snow and lowered their bodies as to take on a charge, the knives ready in front. Karma stood beside Greg and smiled.

"So what are you two doing here?" Greg asked.

"None of your damn business," the one on the right said. Greg marked him as the leader.

"Well it is my business. You're trespassing. This is private property."

"You don't live here, asshole," the leader challenged.

Greg estimated him at 5' 10" and about two hundred pounds. Just slightly shorter than Greg but much taller than Karma. But everyone was taller then the Gurkha. The men had a similar complexion to Karma but not the facial features. *More Mexican*, Greg thought.

"No, but my neighbor asked me to watch his property for him, so that sort of makes it my business."

"Well I don't give a shit who the hell you are."

"Why don't we call the police so they might find out who you are and what you're doing here," Greg said.

Karma's smile had widened as he stood staring at the two adversaries. Greg touched elbows with his friend as they stood side by side. The message was acknowledged.

"My friend here thinks you are up to no good. So you'd better answer my questions or he'll get mad. He isn't friendly like me."

The Gurkha widened his stance. His British combat boots scrunched the icy snow. His fatigues rustled slightly at the motion and he pulled his tunic down with a snap. Greg knew he was ready.

"Screw him and that shit-eating grin he has on that freak face of his. I'll cut his heart out and stomp on it, the little brown bastard."

"I wouldn't piss him off, friend." Greg was enjoying this. It would help to get some information out of these two, but he probably already knew more than these guys did. He knew who had sent them and why. He knew many things about these two. And he knew that they were expendable.

"Look, asshole. We sure as hell aren't going to answer any of your shithead questions, so step aside."

"And if we don't step aside, then what?" Greg asked.

"You'll be bleeding out in the snow. And we'll walk right over your corpses and drive out of town."

"Well, if all you got are those little things I'd think twice about threatening anyone with a knifing." Greg nodded at his friend and in a flash Karma's left hand lifted the tunic while the right hand extracted his kukri. His grin grew larger as the large Gurkha knife flashed into fight position.

A kukri knife is the feared weapon of the Gurkha soldier. Lying somewhere between a large knife and a small sword, the kukri had a heavy steel blade with a bend in the middle. The bend made the cutting edge act as hook to hold and tear at its victim. For over a century many enemies of the British Empire had learned the lethal combination of the small mountain people and their blades. Greg moved to one side and backed up a bit to give Karma room.

"Now, I'd advise you men to put your knives on the ground slowly, back up, turn and put your hands against the side of the house. I'll call the police and you'll live another day."

The two men acted as one. They leaped at Karma, who dodged to their left while swinging the kukri low, catching the outside man's leg in the rear.

In a scream he fell to the ground, grabbing the gaping wound in his calf. Blood squirted out onto the white snow.

As Greg backed further away from the fight, the remaining man turned to lunge again at his antagonist. Karma dodged again to the left and swung his right arm in an upward motion across the man's back. He lurched forward while trying to reach his wound in reaction. Karma hit him in the back of the head with the butt end of the heavy knife. The second man collapsed in the snow.

Karma walked over as Greg pulled out his cell phone and called the police. They watched the two thugs laying in the snow as sirens soon broke the cold night air. The first police car half slid into the driveway and stopped, its headlights illuminating the scene.

The driver's door was flung open as the officer drew his weapon and crouched behind the door. A second patrol car arrived soon after, followed by an ambulance. Greg and Karma were already leaning against Jack's house with their hands placed high on the wall.

A third police car arrived and an officer with sergeant's stripes came up behind the two. With the other officers standing nearby the sergeant conducted a search.

"What's this?" he asked as he came upon Greg's handgun. The sergeant pulled up his sweatshirt and pulled the Sig out with a thumb and one finger. He dropped the clip and unchambered the round. A patrolman offered a plastic evidence bag to place the items in.

Behind them the other patrolman had gathered up the two knives as the emergency personnel worked on the two injured men. The sergeant stepped behind Karma to frisk him.

"Front waistband, sergeant. Large knife," Greg offered so there weren't any surprises.

The sergeant lifted Karma's tunic up and retrieved the kukri. He whistled as he held it up for the patrolman to see. A large evidence bag was produced and the kukri was slipped inside.

Now in handcuffs, Greg and Karma were led to the first patrol car and placed in the back seat. They sat while the two men they had struggled with were placed on stretchers and loaded into the waiting ambulance. Sirens sent them off to the hospital while Greg and Karma found themselves in a holding pen at Missoula police headquarters.

When Greg was offered a phone, call he dialed the number that had been given him when he had entered the United States. Ten minutes later the police chief received a phone call. Ten minutes after that Greg and Karma were back out on the street, the Sig safely in Greg's holster and the kukri secure on Karma's waistband. The police even offered to take them home.

Chapter 5

Bateman Bay, New South Wales, Australia

The journey from Randwick to Bateman Bay was 285 km, which the group of eight cyclists had covered in four days. Now stopped at Corrigan's Beach Reserve, the trip was settling in for the riders. The younger riders who had conditioned themselves for the trip could be found out front each day.

The younger riders who joined the group late, the two Australian women, were bringing up the rear. At least Jack had found company at the back of the crowd. His recumbent was slower going up hills and they had hit their share of hills over the first four days. On the flats Jack could get his bike to a respectable speed and would leave the women behind only to fall to the rear on the next set of hills.

The terrain had been hilly with what the locals call bush. Forests were what Jack called them and they aided in keeping the heat down with the shade provided on the roadway. The local rivers that emptied into the nearby sea provided the open flat country as the small valleys held farms and small communities.

And always last was Graham in the sag wagon, or what the locals called a 'Ute'. In the Australian vernacular a 'Ute' was a sport utility vehicle. But the one Graham had did not resemble any Jack had ever seen.

The front cab was an old Toyota Land Cruiser seating two with no air conditioner or much else for comfort. The back had even less. Where a normal Land Cruiser had seats and a body, Graham's loaner was styled for the Outback with a flat wooden deck with short side rails. Four metal corner posts held a frame for a canvas top. Along the top rails there had been welded racks that could hold six standard bicycles. Jack's recumbent and one other bike could be thrown on the flat bed along with the luggage and camp gear.

That would only happen if the group didn't ride their bikes. With the bikes loaded it meant a tight fit for eight people along with their gear. Luckily the riders didn't anticipate needing a lift over the next three weeks. Having their gear carried for them was enough of a job and Graham was up to the task.

Finally, Graham had made a banner which announced 'Bicycles on Roadway Ahead' and tied it on the back of the Toyota. He then added an official Australian diamond shaped road sign that showed a cyclist and a car with an arrow between the two. The graphic had the lettering of '3 m' added to remind motorists of the three-meter separation required by Australian traffic rules. Finally Graham had added a light bar with yellow strobe warning lights to the top for added visibility.

While no one heading south along their route could claim they hadn't been warned of bicycles on the road, there had still been too many drivers cutting close to the riders. Getting through the port city of Wollongong had been the worst. The heavy traffic with no side street options had the riders all swearing.

But the ride into Bateman Bay had been along a quiet road off the main highway. A resort town for weekenders from Sydney, Bateman Bay was a typical Australian seaside town. They had passed through town and had taken a spot at Corrigan's Beach Reserve, south of the center. A short walk across a quiet street held a small protected ocean beach. With the afternoon free due to the short day's journey, they all took the chance to relax at the beach.

"Dad, are you doing OK?" Carl asked as he walked up to a seated Jack. Graham had folding camp chairs on the Ute and Jack had headed immediately to the beach with one. The others had stayed in the camp setting up tents and getting organized.

Jack turned toward his son from staring out over the Pacific Ocean. "Sure, son, why do you ask?"

"It just seems that you have been sort of distant since we started this trip."

"Well, it's hard to keep up with you and your sister, if that's what you mean."

Carl and Inez with their spouses had the young fit legs to chew up the miles in a hurry. Nigel had ridden the first three days with the power group, as Jack had labeled them in his mind. Today Jack had noticed that Nigel had hung back and had seemed focused on Angie. The two had ridden together as they had come down Beach Road from Ulladula.

Carl looked at his dad with a look of frustration. "That's not what I'm talking about and you know it. Like tonight, you just walked off while everyone else got camp ready."

"I'll set my tent up later. I just wanted to sit and watch the ocean by myself. Is that a crime?"

"No Dad, you can be alone as much as you want. But the last couple of nights you've seemed stand-offish. I just wanted to know if things were OK."

"Just thinking son. You know I've never ridden with this many people. I'm a solo rider or at most one companion."

Carl let that comment settle for a bit as he sat in the sand next to his dad. Then he asked, "So are you thinking about your last riding companion?"

"Stacey? No, son," Jack said. Carl's wife had been his cycling companion a few years back before Carl joined the party. That Stacey had ended up marrying Carl added to the father-son issues. Issues that were never talked about. Jack was happy for his son's choice in a wife and purposely didn't bring up his and Stacey's past time together.

"You know what I mean Dad. Are you thinking about . . .?"

Carl was interrupted by new bodies on the beach. "Are you blokes going swimming or just sit there?"

Deidre and Angie walked up to the two men. Dressed in thong-bottom swim wear with a T-Shirt on top, both Australian women placed their towels down by Jack's chair. Pulling their T-shirts over their heads revealed the naked breasts underneath. Jack looked up and confirmed that Deidre had a nice set of breasts but with a larger back side to go with them. With the single thong barely covering anything, her extra weight had obviously all settled in her breasts and rear. Not that some men didn't admire those two attributes which now headed towards the water.

Angie. being shorter and of smaller build, had well-proportioned female parts. The small breasts fit her body well and as she walked beside Deidre her rear in comparison held firm. Jack had noticed the differences in his days of riding behind the two Australian women. Dressed in cycle shorts and perched on their bicycle seats, Jack had spent time drafting behind each and admiring the view. Now he had almost an unobstructed view and he stared at the two.

Carl cleared his throat in an exaggerated manner. "So, as I was asking, are you missing . . .?"

"Kotone? Is that what this is all about? Am I missing my wife who has disappeared on me? Is that what you want me to admit?"

"Dad, we've talked about this and you know that whenever you and Kotone are together, it seems bad things happen. I'm sorry, but its the truth."

Jack knew his son was right. Trouble and Kotone just seemed to walk side by side. But that was part of his dilemma. Was it Kotone that attracted the trouble, or was it the two of them together? If it was her problem, then he wanted to be there to protect her. He had done that many times and would gladly do it again.

But if was the two of them together that caused the problems, then he wanted to stay away. *Keep her safe by not bringing trouble her way* Jack thought.

Nigel walked up and broke the mood. Following along were Inez and her husband. They each placed folding camp chairs down and placed towels in them. Dressed a bit more modestly than the locals, they headed for the water. Stacey arrived and Carl joined his wife in the surf, leaving Jack once again alone with his thoughts.

As he stared at the swimmers, he noticed each couple separating from the group and enjoying their own small piece of ocean. Nigel and Angie were soon together leaving Deidre swimming alone. Deidre soon walked out of the surf and up to Jack, dropping down onto the sand. She twisted and laid down on her back, her breasts sliding slightly to each side of her chest.

Jack stared down at the tan blonde. With the others all coupled up, that left Deidre and him as the odd couple. And then there was Graham who seemed happy to be providing the support for the group. With his wife at home in Sydney Jack didn't think he was up for a little romance on the trip. *And I'm not sure I am either* Jack thought.

"So Nigel said you are married," the blonde said. Deidre sat up, turned to face Jack and crossed her legs yoga style. She started bending forward as if stretching.

"I guess separated is more the term I'd use." Jack watched the display that was being presented as her two breast jiggled with each lean forward. The front of her thong stretched across what was hidden beneath. As her tendons on the inside of her thighs drew taut, her thong revealed much of what was underneath.

"Oh, so am I. My husband is a real wanker. The only good thing I got from him was my two kids."

"Sorry to hear that. Good marriages are rare these days it seems." Deidre was very nonchalant about her workout in front of Jack. Jack watched as she turned onto her hands and knees and started arching her back. With her rear facing him, the thong once again left little to the imagination. Deidre, for her age and having given birth to two kids, was in good shape. *Maybe three weeks on a bicycle will take that extra twenty off her* Jack thought.

But Jack was distracted from the workout by his thoughts of his marriage. With Kotone's leaving, Jack had not been faithful. *But if I've been abandoned was it still infidelity?* Jack thought. And it wasn't a legal separation, he was still fully married. His wife had chosen a physical separation when she had walked out the last time. Jack had not seen or heard from Kotone in two years. A long time to be alone and wondering if he still had a wife.

People had told him to seek legal help and file for divorce for abandonment. But he abhorred the thought of another divorce. His first marriage had ended badly when his wife had left him. That his second wife had left with no trace bothered Jack. He would continue to hope that Kotone would show up and they could try to live their life together again.

"Boy my legs are stiff."

Deirde's comment caught Jack day dreaming. He focused on his beach mate who was now standing while bending over in front of him stretching her legs. Her arms would slide down her legs and grab the back of her knees as she faced the ocean. The view refocused Jack onto what stood in front of him.

"Your legs get tight, Mr. Wesley?" Deirdre asked.

"Please call me Jack. Don't make me feel any older than I am. Trying to keep up with the young people on this ride is bad enough."

Deidre laughed a loud reply. "Oh Jack, you aren't old. What are you, barely fifty?"

Jack laughed, "Hardly, I'm pushing sixty."

The comment stopped Deidre in her stretching. She turned and stood in front of Jack. She thrust her hands onto her hips. "No bloody way. Sixty? I was figuring you to be five years older than me, max."

"No. At my fifty-eighth birthday it got me thinking. Might be time to settle down. I'm getting too old for these adventures. I even have two grandkids."

"Well, you are way ahead of my husband. Between the cigs, Fosters and womanizing, at 45 years old he could never do what you're doing. He eats most of his meals at Makkas and has the belly to prove it."

Jack looked at Deirdre in a quizzical way. She noticed his stare and asked "What?"

"Makkas?"

"Oh, that's McDonalds to you. Just like Hungry Jack's is Burger King to you."

Jack nodded his acknowledgement of the English language interpretation. Jack hadn't traveled much in the world but his grasp of Australian English had been going badly. The famous quote that the British and the American people are separated by a common language was even more so with Australian English.

He was discovering that Australians used slang words for common terms. With the accent down under along with different words, he had been lost a number of times when a local had spoken to him. The most embarrassing incident occurred the one evening they had spent touring around Sydney.

While strolling the central quay near the Sydney Opera House Jack had been approached by a young woman. She had asked him if he wanted to get a 'root on'. Not sure what a 'root' was but assuming from the woman's dress and demeanor that it would cost him money to find out, he had declined. Later, asking Graham only elicited a large laugh. It seemed a 'root' was the local term for having carnal knowledge.

Jack noticed the rest of the crew coming in from their swim. Deidre recognized the same so grabbed her T-shirt and pulled it down over her head. She took her towel and excused herself to Jack. As she headed back to the campsite, Carl walked up, the others strolling in out of the water after him.

"Gee, Dad. I didn't mean to break up the yoga lesson that was going on, but I'm starving."

Chapter 6

Leongatha, Victoria, Australia

Leongatha lay about halfway on the cyclists' three-week trip. It had been seven days since leaving Batemans Bay and the eight cyclists had established their pattern. Two days out of Batemans Bay, they had crossed out of New South Wales and would now spend the rest of their time in the State of Victoria.

The capital of Melbourne lay about 135 km to the northwest. While Melbourne rivaled Sydney with its 5 million residents, Leongatha was far enough away to maintain its small city charm. The seat of the local shire, or county as Americans knew the term, Leongatha was a moderate city with a population of 30,000 residents. Set in low rolling hills with farms in this fertile part of Australia, Leongatha provided the basic shopping needs of the surrounding area.

Their tour had left the ocean two days ago as the only through road headed inland. In fact, the road since Batemans Bay had missed the ocean, typically passing through forest preserves of immense size, the sea only seen in a few locations.

Crossing the Snowy River had elicited comments by those familiar with the famous Australian movie, while a tour by Ute to Wilson Promontory National Park had been a highlight.

Spending a day off the bicycles and on the beaches gave each rider a welcome break.

But Jack had noticed the couples thing continued to grow. The newlyweds kept to themselves which was to be expected. Carl and Stacey, already with two kids, were more social. Nigel and Angie had become quite an item as Nigel began sharing his tent with the young blonde. Which left Diedre alone in her tent.

Jack continued as a solo camper with his tent. And Graham had avoided the whole issue sleeping alone. Riding and sleeping had become very much a couples time, while at the rest stops, as well as dinner and breakfast, the group gathered together.

Thrust together by default, Jack and Deidre spent their days riding and conversing about their lives. Jack continued to learn about Deidre's life as they rode each day. Mostly talk of her children which were younger than Jack's grown children.

Camped at Leongatha Apex Caravan Park, it, like all campgrounds in Australia, had a common kitchen. Along with a rec room with a TV, laundry and bathrooms, the park was very comfortable for the travelers. Many caravans, or travel trailers to Americans, were parked in their spaces. While located about an hour's car trip from the ocean, the campground filled up during the Christmas break with the overflow of campgrounds at the beach.

That had been a consistent problem. Full campgrounds was universal at Christmas time for all parks near the beach as Australians enjoyed their summer break. Luckily Jack had planned this trip ahead of time and Graham had done extra good work getting reservations. While it tied them to a tight schedule of riding each day, not having to camp along the road was a good thing.

That Sir Graham Elphinston had called to reserve a campsite certainly helped. And Jack noticed the deferential treatment Sir Graham received at every stop. He was quite famous in Australia for his heroics in London. Jack smiled each time Graham looked at Jack and shook his head at all the fuss. Jack was glad for his friend's recognition and was just as glad his own part in the heroics was unknown.

"Stacey, could you cut up those carrots?" Carl spoke up as he stirred the pot over the gas-fired stove.

Jack sat and watched dinner being prepared. Meals each day had been divided into two groups. Jack's two children and their spouses would shop, cook and clean-up one day. Jack joined the Australians on the opposite day. Graham, as their driver, was duty free, although he often joined in. This way there was an American food night followed by an Australian food night. Jack attempted to keep up with his fellow Australian food preparers. Today had been his day off. But not feeling like reading his book alone in his tent, he was just enjoying watching his family spend time together.

He jumped as a steam whistle sounded close by. The shriek of steam through a confined space took him to movies of old steam-powered factories. The sound rose in pitch and then dropped only to rise again. Jack stood and looked out the window for the factory nearby. But all he could see was a mixture of houses and trees. No industrial site was visible.

As the whistle continued, the others all stepped out the kitchen door wondering where the factory was that seemed so determined to warn whoever of whatever. But a more careful scan showed no sign of a factory. As the noise built in volume Jack happened to look up as a large flock of white birds flew by. As they disappeared behind some trees the noise lowered. The birds swung around back over the campground and the noise grew to a loud shriek.

"It's the damn birds," Jack finally realized.

The birds came around again and the noise built to an earful. Then they would disappear and the noise dropped to a reasonable level. But as they continuously circled over the campground, the extreme whistle noise modulated up and down.

"They do have some wild birds in this country," Stacey said as she went back inside to finish dinner.

The colorful birds they had seen drew comments each day. All along their journey they had been amazed at the beauty and noise of the large variety of native birds. Graham did his best on keeping up with the names of each bird so the tourists would learn a bit about his country.

But it was the more deadly creatures that had drawn the most attention. On their first night camping Graham had explained the necessity of assuring a tight seal on each tent's zipper to keep out unwanted guests. The campgrounds located in the heavily wooded area added to the excitement with the snake warning signs.

Each sign was simple. A picture of a snake on a placard with a 'Warning' written across the top. Jack had been the first to notice the sign, and since it didn't offer any more information, he wanted to know just what the warning meant. Jack had seen a pair of fishermen putting fishing gear away in a campsite near theirs and asked what the signs meant.

"Well mate, you don't want to get bit," one of the fishermen said.

"Well, yeah. I grasped that from the sign. But can you tell me more?" Jack wanted details.

The two fishermen stopped their meal prep and looked at each other. They both turned to Jack and one offered again, "Trust me, you don't want to get bit."

Jack was getting frustrated with these two. He pressed for more details.

"Well, suppose I do get bit, what then?"

The two again looked at each other before replying, "You don't want to get bit."

Jack gave up getting any answers from the two and headed to find Graham or Nigel. Nigel appeared first so Jack told him of the snake warning sign in the kitchen and the answers the two locals had provided. Nigel looked long at Jack and said, "Jack, trust us, you don't want to get bit."

Jack was ready to explode in frustration and Nigel recognized he needed to offer more.

"Jack, of the top twenty most poisonous snakes in the world, eighteen are native to Australia. The top five are all Australian. The Inland Taipan is the most lethal snake in the world, but luckily it lives up north in Queensland. But the others are beauts all on their own."

Jack pressed. He had heard about the many things that could kill in Australia, but wanted to hear how the locals explained the deadly things they lived around each day.

"So, if I get bit?"

"Well you need to get a shot of anti-venom fast."

"How fast?" Jack asked.

"Fifteen minutes or so."

Jack thought about that answer and imagined a map in his head. Where they camped was a least an hour's drive to the nearest town of any size. He didn't say anything, but his facial expression told Nigel all.

"Like I said, you don't want to get bit."

Ever since that conversation Jack had avoided walking in the forest or tall grass. And each night he made double sure that his tent zippers were closed tight.

As Jack stood and watched the flight of birds finally shriek off to the west, he marveled at the strange sights, sounds and threats Australia held. He returned to his place supervising the food prep when he heard loud yelling. Sensing trouble, Jack turned and headed towards the sound. As he came around the corner of the kitchen the toilets appeared. Outside the female entrance was a highly animated Deidre arguing with a man.

The man wore a long beard and hair, and by his leather jacket and boots Jack easily placed him in the biker category. Combined with the level of dirt and grease on his clothes, Jack knew trouble. At a loud 'bitch' and shove on Deidre's shoulder Jack stepped into the mix.

"Back off asshole," Jack yelled at the man.

"And who the bloody hell are you, mate?" Jack received a menacing glare as he stepped beside Diedre.

"Just back off, shithead." Jack moved Deidre into a position behind him for protection.

"What, Deirdre? You getting the root from this Yank? Ha ha, Johnny would love that."

Diedre fought to get around Jack. "Screw you Sid. You bloody wanker. Tell Johnny to sod off."

The two danced around with Jack in the middle keeping them separated.

"Oh, he'll just love to hear from me where you are," the man called Sid said.

"Tell the bloody bastard whatever you like. He doesn't own me."

The arrival of Nigel changed everything. As soon as his Chief Inspector credentials were displayed, Sid backed off, but not without one final insult.

"Johnny will be glad to hear you're going with the redundant set now."

Jack knew that redundant meant retired in the Australian venicular and glared back. Sid turned and walked away, joining his three mates who had been standing nearby. Jack watched them walk towards their campsite.

"Thanks, Jack. Sorry you had to be in the middle of that." Deidre said.

"No worries. I assume they're mates of your husband?"

"Yes, he has some beauts. And Sid is definitely the asshole of the whole bunch."

As the rest of the bicycle riders arrived to see what the commotion had been, Jack took Deidre's arm and led her back to their campsite. All nine gathered around the Toyota.

"OK, it seems we have a bunch of stunned mullets camped nearby that have an issue with us," Jack offered.

"I'm so sorry about this," Deidre said.

"You have nothing to be sorry for. They are the ones with a problem. But we do need to be careful with them around. So group rules. No one goes to the restroom alone, and preferably any woman will need to be accompanied by a male. Is that understood?" Jack asked.

The group nodded their agreement. Hopefully they would be getting on their bicycles tomorrow and riding west away from Sid and his fellow bikers.

Chapter 7

Las Vegas, Nevada

The famous Vegas Strip lay thirty stories below as the sun set over the Nevada desert. The light display grew in intensity as darkness descended on the city. Two men stood on the hotel balcony and took in the sights. The younger one held a drink in his right hand and took a sip as the older man stood waiting. A much younger woman sat on a living room couch inside the sliding glass doors. The two men turned away from the open door and talked in a low voice.

"And why are you bothering me here?" Daniel asked.

"You said that as soon as I had word I should tell you."

Alfonso was nervous. Although the evening was still warm from the hot afternoon sun, Alfonso felt the sweat running down his back. He was always nervous when he was around the boss. Violence and death were workplace hazards in his line of work. And it wasn't always the competition that met with the violence. Alfonso knew that his fellow cartel co-workers risked an untimely demise if the boss was not happy with the work.

When word arrived that the hit team sent to Missoula had been put in the hospital by the targets neighbors, Alfonso feared the worst. Daniel had exploded with rage at the news and Alfonso knew that the two hit men would not be long for the world upon their return to Las Vegas.

Alfonso had seen it before. Unsatisfactory workers would be sent to the cartel's base in Mexico, never to be seen again. Just south of the U.S.-Mexican border, a compound had been built. From that base the drugs and prostitutes were staged for their journey to Las Vegas and final distribution across America.

"So tell me some good news," Daniel said.

"You remember that this Wesley guy had left Montana for a trip to Australia. We learned that from our source in Missoula. And we knew that his family went with him."

"Yeah, yeah. You're wasting my time here." Daniel turned and looked at the woman patiently waiting on the couch. Alfonso knew from the woman's attire what he intended.

"We have heard from our source in Colorado Springs, and we have the shit on when his daughter returns and where she will be."

From the smile on Daniel's face, Alfonso relaxed just a bit. After the two hit teams sent out to kill the murderer of Daniel's father had failed, it was decided to set a trap so the Wesley character would come to them.

The two men talked quietly for a few minutes discussing the latest news. A decision was made and as Alfonso turned to leave, Daniel grabbed his arm to stop him. Alfonso shuddered with dread.

"And don't screw this one up," Daniel said.

Alfonso didn't need to say anything. He nodded his understanding and his arm was released. He left quickly as the woman finally rose from the couch and brushed by him as she walked out onto the balcony. The smell lingered in his nostrils as he stepped onto the elevator. Alfonso knew he had to get this right or it would be the last thing he would ever do.

* * *

As the second largest city in Australia, Melbourne sits at the head of a large bay. With the Yarra River flowing through the city before entering Port Phillip Bay, Melbourne's water features added beauty and open space to the high rises located along its banks. While certainly not comparable to Sydney and its stunning harbor, Melbourne had a different type of charm.

Jack was relieved that Nigel and Graham had worked out a cycle route that took them south of the city. Leaving Leongatha, the riders had taken a ferry to French Island. Located within the bay, the charm of riding across the island keep them away from the heavier traffic on the mainland. A second ferry brought them back to the mainland and a night's stop at Merrick's Beach. The motorcyclists had followed them out of town but had turned right at the intersection leading into the city. Graham had confirmed that Sid and his crew had continued to Melbourne by lingering at the intersection.

The next day found them on the Sorrento-Queenscliff ferry crossing the mouth of the bay. The narrow opening leading out to the open ocean of Bass Strait was notorious for its riptides. Australia had even lost a Prime Minister near Queenscliff from the bad rip. His body had never been recovered. Jack sat with Inez and stared out at the water contemplating losing a national leader in the water they were crossing.

"I'm sorry we haven't been riding with you every day, Dad."

"Inez, don't worry about me. You younger people need to set your own pace. I have plenty of company back at the end of the pack."

Now into their second week of cycling, Nigel was a permanent fixture along with Jack and the two Australian women. Nigel and Angie continued to share a tent while Jack was content to be a solo sleeper, although the opportunities for companionship had certainly been there.

After their run-in with Sid and the bikers, Diedre had been staying even closer to Jack than she had been. And she had made it very clear that if Jack wanted intimate company, she was available, even bringing the subject up in private conversation between the two of them.

Jack felt bad spurning Deidre. She was certainly attractive and after two weeks conditioning her extra weight had been reduced. The change was noticeable and others had commented about it. Deidre had accepted the compliments gracefully and Jack noticed that she avoided many of the treats the others bought along the way. *Yes, she was certainly looking very nice,* Jack thought.

He couldn't put an answer to why he remained by himself. Each day on his recumbent his mind wandered as to the source of his aloofness where companionship was concerned. When he was drafting behind Deidre or Angie, which happened often as the four riders rode as a small peloton for energy conservation, his mind became very focused.

The two women riders wore their Lycra cycle shorts well and sitting down on his recumbent offered a revealing angle up at the two. Their upper thighs and rears pumping up and down kept Jack's mind focused on the women's attributes.

But it wasn't enough to invite Deidre into his tent at night. He had spent many nights on his adventures with different women since his retirement. Beautiful women who, thankfully, had accepted his affections. While Jack had warm feelings for all the women who had shared their bed with him, a couple of them he truly loved and missed greatly.

That loss seemed to carry him to the point where he wanted to avoid more of it. Deidre would be another loss, since Jack knew he would head back to America soon. Jack didn't want to add to the recreational sex attitude he sometimes felt about himself. Some men didn't care at all, but Jack felt uneasy. There were too many women in the world who had been a part of his life and now weren't. A certain loneliness had settled over him on this trip even though surrounded by friends and family.

"Eric and I will try to do better on the Great Ocean Road," Inez said.

Jack broke out of his trance staring at the passing water as the large ferry's engines thumped its vibration through the deck.

"Honey, trust me I'm doing fine," Jack said. "Ride with your new hubby and don't worry about me. We have a fun group that has a good time riding at the back. You and Carl take it out front. The four of you seem to be enjoying yourselves."

"Couldn't be happier, Dad. I know our official honeymoon starts when we get back to L.A., but I think this trip will be the one we remember."

Jack knew from what his daughter spoke. While a typical three-week trip to Australia would satisfy anyone's honeymoon wishes, spending those three weeks sleeping in a tent with seven other people nearby wasn't quite the same. The others always tried to give the newlyweds space, but sometimes the size of the campsites precluded much separation.

Jack knew that a final week at a resort on Catalina Island off Los Angeles awaited the new couple. There they could enjoy soft beds, quiet dinners and plenty of time for just the two of them.

"Your resort stay will be special, trust me," Jack offered.

"I know, Dad. But Eric has commented how his family would never do something like this. Their idea of a family get-together is dinner around the TV watching football."

Jack smiled at the family reference. Jack knew that it was only recently that he and his two children had started doing things together. While a long time back they had had family trips, after the divorce and with Inez heading to Colorado with the ex-wife, they had drifted apart. Jack had worked hard getting both his kids back in his life. *There was a time when even sitting and watching football together would have been wonderful,* Jack thought.

Jack knew he was a lucky guy. Two wonderful children all grown up and now married. And to have children that wanted to spend considerable time together with him was the best. He knew Eric only got a month's leave each year from the Air Force and if he was willing to spend three-fourths of his time with his in-laws spoke volumes.

"Dad, could I ask you a question?" Inez asked.

Jack was taken aback by the statement. He had certainly learned over many years that when someone said they wanted to ask a question, it usually was a bombshell.

"Of course, honey," Jack said. He waited for what was coming, not sure what was on his daughter's mind.

"Did you want kids?"

Jack sat up and looked at Inez. "What? What kind of question is that?"

"Mom said you really didn't want to have kids."

"Well, she's wrong. The two most important days of my life were the days you and your brother were born."

"But you were gone all the time," Inez persisted. "It seemed like you didn't want to be around us."

"Let's back up a bit and re-educate you from your mother's view of life, shall we?" Jack said. "If you recall, I was a patrol officer with the department when you kids were born. Your mother quit her job when she had your brother so she could be at home with him. And then you came along right after."

"But you were in school all the time. I remember you studying hard at the dining room table and us kids being chased off so you could concentrate."

"All true. I didn't have an education except for high school when I came out of the Marines. Good for an entry level job in police work, but if you wanted to advance up the ladder, a degree was required."

Inez asked. "But couldn't we live on what you made as a patrolman?"

"Sure, but not the lifestyle that your mother grew accustomed to. If we had wanted to live out in the River Road area and send you kids go to public school, yes. And oh, only have one car and make sure it's an old one. And those sports teams you and your brother wanted to play on, you would have had to settle with Kidsports only."

"Really?" Inez asked.

"Honey, you and Eric are just starting out together. You both have good professions. But soon you'll want a house to buy. Then children show up and you find out most of your salary after taxes goes to day care, so why bother? You might as well raise your own kids. So you are out of work until your kids are in school."

"But Eric and I have talked. We're going to do it differently," Inez said.

"Every couple has those same ideas. But America sucks you in. Bigger houses, newer cars, nicer vacations. It all adds up."

"So you took all that overtime for us?" Inez asked.

"Did you see me collecting old cars with the extra money? Or expensive artwork on our walls? No, it went to your Mom to make our home as comfortable as possible."

"But it would have been better to have you around more. Carl and I could have done without."

"You say that now, but you remember your friends who went to public school. I'm sure they told you some of the things that went on there. I wanted you two to get a good education along with a lesson in morality that a Christian school could provide."

"And I remember your comments all the time as to what police business you had at the local schools," Inez said.

"Well I never told you everything. Just enough to make you aware," Jack said.

"But you hated Eugene. Why did you stay?" Inez asked.

"Your Mom wouldn't move. I wanted to move to Idaho or Montana, but your Mom wouldn't budge. I figured in a more conservative place we could send you to the public school. We would have saved a lot of money."

"I remember the arguments. I'm sorry, Dad."

"Not your fault," Jack said "I just tried to make it work as long as I could. When your Mother went back to work when you were in school, her not having an education limited her job options. Her salary helped, but not enough."

The two sat quiet as the loud clanking of the ferry continued its crossing. Each contemplated what they had just discussed before speaking again. As it grew obvious that a certain tension had developed between them, Inez spoke.

"I loved our vacations."

Jack was relieved at her comment. "Yes honey, we had fun vacations. Mostly thanks to Uncle Ed."

"Well, as much as I loved staying in his amazing house, the trip over and back to Jackson was even better."

"It was?" Jack asked.

"Of course. Camping and fishing while we crossed Oregon and Idaho. What could be better? Mom was happy. I had my time with you. Each year I looked forward to our trips."

Jack remembered those trips. Two little kids. Fishing the rivers of Eastern Oregon and then Idaho. More fishing around Jackson Hole. It had been great, the ex content to see her family together as long as they had the travel trailer and she didn't have to rough it.

"Well, I'm glad you have those memories, honey," Jack said.

Inez slid her arm under Jack's arm and clasped his hand. She squeezed hard.

"And now we are making new memories. My Dad and I."

"And Carl, too," Jack added. They both laughed at the comment.

"Oh yeah, him too."

"We are a lucky family. We are very blessed," Jack offered.

Inez leaned and placed her head on Jack's shoulder. Jack moved his arm around his daughter and pulled her close. The two sat and enjoyed the moment. But deep down, Jack couldn't get the dead Prime Minister out of his head.

Chapter 8

Bell's Beach, Victoria, Australia

The name had literally rung a bell in Jack's head, but he couldn't place it. Bell's Beach was stuck in his mind for some reason, but for the life of him he couldn't put a reference to it. Graham came to his rescue when they reached the caravan park on the beach.

"Endless Summer, mate," Graham said.

"What about it?" Jack asked.

"The movie, Endless Summer. The young people don't remember. But in 1966 two blokes came through here filming surfers. They were going around the world to all the surfing spots. South Africa, New Zealand, Hawaii, you know. Well, Bell's Beach is where they did the Australia surfing bit."

"Oh, I remember now. Was this the place with the backwards wave?" Jack asked. He was young when the movie had come out but had seen the movie a few years back.

"No, no. That was a Kiwi beach. Raglan. On the North Island of New Zealand," Graham said.

They had drawn a crowd by now to their discussion and Eric asked, "What's a backwards wave?"

Graham was stumped as the group all looked at him for an answer. "Do you remember, Jack?"

As the only other person who had been alive when the movie was released, Jack remembered that Raglan was unique for a backwards wave but couldn't recall what a backward wave had been in the movie.

"I don't remember. A wave you surf back out as well as in maybe," Jack said.

"Well, I guess we all need to watch it the first chance we get to see. And now that we've been to the famous Bell's Beach we can see how its changed since the 60's," Carl said.

Their surfing discussion was cut off as a loud group of motorcycles pulled through the campground. Deidre knew instantly that surfing was the least of their problems.

"Oh no," she exclaimed.

"Sid again?" Jack asked.

Deidre stared at the gang as they passed by their campsite. One revved his engine to a high pitch and the others joined in. Unlike American bikers that tended to ride Harley Davidsons, these riders all road crotch rockets, as they were affectionately called. The major Japanese motorcycle makers all competed as to who could make the fastest motorcycle. With low clip-on handlebars, these motorcycles were the antithesis of the 'hog-stye' American bikes. Capable of lightening-fast acceleration combined with high speed, this type of motorcycle had become the scourge of most of the world in the hands of criminal riders.

Racing through traffic at breath-taking speeds, out-running any law enforcement attempting to stop them and performing trick riding on public roads had all led to confrontations with everyday drivers. Videos of gangs of bikes surrounding a hapless driver and his family were constant themes on social media. And when one driver ran over a biker to escape, the police had arrested the car driver.

The six motorcycle riders all joined their leader in revving their engines to an ear-splitting decibel. Jack and his group covered their ears in response. Soon the owner of the caravan park arrived in his golf cart, the motorcycle riders all idled their engines.

"OK you blokes. We won't be having any of that. I warned you." The owner pointed the gang to the campsite that had been assigned. He turned to Jack's party. "Sorry folks. That won't happen again."

Deidre was the first to ask. "I know our party booked our campsite some time ago. How did those assholes get a space? I know beach caravan parks are reserved months in advance."

The owner raised an eyebrow at the crude language. "Well, one of our campers had a family emergency and had to head home. The bikers arrived right after and grabbed the cancellation. They were lucky." He climbed on his golf cart and putted back toward the main office.

Jack was the first to talk. "Deidre, what are you thinking?"

"That was my husband that was leading those assholes. Sid obviously called him. Besides the two that were with Sid, two more came down from Sydney with my husband. And knowing him, he probably sent one of them in here with the carrot or the stick approach. Found a camper to threaten and then probably offered a thousand dollars to hit the road. And if they didn't take the money and scram, bad things would happen to them."

"Your husband has that kind of money to throw around?" Jack asked. He hadn't gotten Deidre's life history, only that she and her husband were separated.

"Actually, he's filthy rich. Or at least his family is. They own the four largest motorcycle dealers in Sydney. Each one of the four sons owns one of the dealerships. My husband's dealership happens to be the largest located in North Sydney."

"He's a business owner acting like this?"

"Actually the family hired a manager for him. The other brothers are all normal people, but Johnny is no good. The family covers for him all the time."

"I haven't asked, but why aren't you divorced yet?" Jack knew he was getting personal, but Deidre had brought her family problems into his family.

"When we married twelve years ago I was assigned fifty percent ownership in the dealership. When things went bad, the family decided to reorganize the company and put all four dealerships into a holding company. My stock all of a sudden shrank to a minority ownership. My lawyers have been fighting over ownership issues for a year now."

"And your husband's family has deep pockets and lots of lawyers to tie things up, correct?" Jack had heard it all before. That Australia and America shared English Common Law only reinforced the two countries' similarities. *Assholes everywhere* Jack thought.

And now they had a biker gang to worry about. Jack pulled everyone together to remind them of the enforced rules from Leongatha. No one was to go anywhere alone and all women would be accompanied by a male. Deidre offered to leave and take the train back to Sydney but was voted down unanimously

Nigel assured everyone that his status as a Chief Inspector with the New South Wales Police would mean no trouble. Jack wasn't so confident. But he would leave it to the locals to take care of things.

The next day the local connection worked just fine. The road from Bell's Beach to Wye River constituted the start of the Great Ocean Road. Built by returning World War I veterans from the killing fields of France, the road had been a make work project to put the men to work. The result was a spectacular scenic drive along the Southern Ocean.

This part of the Australian Coast was notorious for shipwrecks due to the strong currents and rough seas. That combined with a coast constituting many headlands made a rugged project for a road. It had been completed in 1932 and had been a tourist attraction ever since.

Two constables in a Victoria Police car showed up as the group of bicyclists shoved off for their daily ride. Along with Graham in the Toyota Ute, the police with lights flashing escorted the group the entire 58 km to Wye Beach.

Arriving at their campground, Jack noticed both Nigel and Graham thanking the constables. Jack and the party all waved thanks as the two drove off. They returned the next morning for the short 29 km ride into Apollo Bay. Graham and Nigel again chatted briefly before the car headed back toward Melbourne.

The bicyclists set up camp along a tide water river at Apollo Bay Recreation Reserve. A rain squall could be seen approaching their site so everyone hurried to erect tents and store gear. Retreating to their tents Deidre asked if she could join Jack. The two leaned against their sleeping bag stuff sacks as the first gust of wind shook the tent. Soon sheets of rain pounded the nylon rain fly as the two riders waited out the storm.

"Jack, I should leave. I'm ruining your family's holiday. Jesus, we even had a police escort the past two days."

"Deidre, I asked Nigel about that. It has nothing to do with your husband, although it seemed to have worked as we haven't seen him and the boys since we left Bell's Beach. No, the police were here to escort us through the traffic. When they heard Sir Graham was part of our group the local police turned out."

"Really? Graham has that much pull?"

"Sir Graham is quite the national hero it seems. Saving the Queen of England and the Commonwealth and all the other titles she has seems to be popular here."

"But we haven't been part of all that since forever. Australia dropped the whole British thing years ago."

Jack shrugged. Australian history and politics were a blur to him. "Well, enough people seem to think it's important. And I won't complain. Riding the past two days with police escort sure kept the drivers following the three-meter separation rule. I like that."

"And I enjoyed all eight of us riding together."

With the police escort, Jack had suggested that they all ride as one peloton. With the police car leading and Graham following they had had little trouble with cars and trucks cutting too close when they passed. The two that had been stopped and cited pleased Jack.

After dinner in the common kitchen the group walked down the main highway, crossed the tidal river and walked the short distance to the ocean beach. Driftwood gathered had Nigel starting a bonfire. Everyone sat on the sand and listened to the surf pound the beach as the fire flickered light over the scene. Jack knew it didn't get any better.

The morning brought a gentle breeze as Jack laid half awake in his tent. Sleeping solo he stretched out under his sleeping bag as the cool ocean breeze gently rustled the tent.

A scream followed by a louder scream shook him out of his repose. He pulled on his Big Dog shorts and a T-Shirt as he quickly unzipped the tent door. His rain fly was unzipped as he scrambled into his flip flops and ran towards the scream. Carl and Nigel were just ahead of him as Graham emerged from his tent. They turned the corner of the main building holding the restrooms to see three bikers tossing Inez between them.

Deidre jumped on the back of one of the three thugs and got thrown to the ground for her trouble. Eric lay in the doorway of the men's room not moving. Carl ran headlong into the nearest thug and the two fell to the ground. Nigel pulled out a police baton and chopped the back of the legs of the second thug. Jack squared up with the one called Sid.

Sid lunged at Jack. Having a black belt in Tae Kwon Do, Jack was grateful when the bad guy always provided an opportunity to use his skills. He dodged to his left and slammed the passing head with his right elbow. Jack quickly spun around and whipped his leg into the left knee of the staggering opponent. As Sid fell to his knees from his left leg collapsing, Jack swept in and landed another elbow to Sid's temple. The man collapsed unconscious.

Jack spun around and saw that Nigel had his thug on the ground immobile. Carl, also having a black belt in Tae Kwon Do from the father and son training they had taken, had subdued his thug. Jack raced to Eric who was being held by Inez. Graham showed up holding his cell phone.

"Police are on their way," he offered.

"I think we need an ambulance also," Jack said as he pointed to a very drowsy Eric. Inez inspected the back of his head where blood was seeping down onto his shirt. "Inez, what happened?"

"Deidre and I grabbed Eric to use the ladies room. These three were waiting when we came out. One of them clubbed Eric in the back of the head."

"Which one?" Jack asked.

Deidre pointed at Sid and Inez nodded agreement. Jack looked and spotted a length of wooden board lying near Eric. He noticed a spot of blood on the board as he picked it up. He walked over to Sid, rolled the unconscious thug over and smashed the board across Sid's nose. The sound of gristle and cartilage breaking was heard over the groan the man emitted.

"Jack, you can't do that," Nigel said.

"Oh no?" Jack retorted. He saw his friend Graham reach out and grab his nephews arm. Jack walked over to the other two thugs and proceeded to smash the board into their faces also. The one who had been conscious that Nigel had restrained fell over on the grass. Jack threw the board down in disgust and walked back to where Eric had risen to his feet. Inez propped up one side of the pilot and Jack took the other side.

"Let's go find you some ice," Jack said. As he helped Eric back to the campsite, Jack noticed the glare Nigel gave him as they passed. Graham stood stone-faced but continued to hold his nephew. The dual sirens of the police car and ambulance broke the serenity of the campground.

Chapter 9

Apollo Bay, Victoria, Australia

The morning start to their day's bicycle ride was delayed as the local Victoria Police took statements from all involved in the altercation. When it was evident that the police were going to question Jack longer than the others, Jack asked the constable if there was a car hire shop in Apollo Bay. Discovering that there were two companies offering car rentals, Jack loaded his recumbent into the back of the Toyota and told Graham to get everyone moving.

"I'll rent a car and catch up," Jack said.

"Are you sure you don't want me to stay? We can get everyone headed out and I'll be able to catch up later," Graham said. Driving the 'Ute' would allow Graham to catch the riders later in the day. They had discovered that although not fast, with a top speed of about 45 mph, the 'Ute' would have no problem out-distancing the bicycle riders. "You might need a little local help."

"You've got the cell phone and two-way radios if there's no cell service ahead. I'll contact you if something happens that I need help on." Great Otway National Park lay to the west of Apollo Bay and with its mountains plunging down into the sea it offered the most spectacular spot on the Great Ocean Road.

But they had noticed that some spots away from the big cities did not have cell service. And Great Otway Park was both remote and rugged, and the two-way radios they had purchased in Sydney would have to cover for the lack of cell service. The radios had been used to keep track of the cyclists as they pedaled along with one set with Graham at the end of the group and usually Carl with the second set at the lead.

As Jack took the radio from Carl, his son showed concern. "Dad, I'm not sure it's good that we leave you alone here. That Johnny character and his two friends are still around. You don't want to be caught by yourself if they are looking for trouble."

"Son, it's OK. Get everyone through the ride ahead. Stick together. I heard you've got some big climbs ahead before it flattens out near the Twelve Apostles."

Jack waited by the Victoria Police car as seven cyclists passed him headed to the main highway. They turned right, crossed the tidal river and disappeared around a hill. Graham pulled up in the Toyota and Jack waved him off. The diesel 'Ute' clattered off heading west.

The Victoria Police constable motioned Jack into the back seat. The short trip to the police station in Apollo Bay gave Jack time to collect himself. If

Nigel and Graham had not elaborated on how the three thugs noses had all been broken then Jack wasn't about to add to the story. As the Inspector on duty questioned him, Jack stuck to the defense of his daughter and her husband as well as the Australian woman riding with them.

Five hours later Jack was released and given a ride to the car hire shop. A medium-size car was selected and Jack pulled out his credit card and driver's license.

"You want full coverage on this?" the customer service representative asked.

"Yes please." Jack quickly read over the contract to make sure any damage to the car would be covered by the additional fee charged over the daily rate.

"And how long would you be keeping the car?"

Jack figured things in his head. "I need to drop it off in Melbourne in four days."

"There'll be an extra charge for that."

Jack agreed to the extra charge for returning the car to a different location. Handed the keys and his contract, Jack walked out to the small parking lot of cars. He located his car in the numbered spot marked on his contract and hit the button to unlock the car. The lights flashed once and the car chirped.

Now, let's see if the bad boys are still where we want them Jack thought. He drove back to the Victoria

Police Station and noticed six motorcycles parked in the parking lot. *Good, still here.* He found a parking space on the street across and down a block. He switched off the car, lowered the windows and sat back. The smell of salt air drifted in off the nearby ocean. The afternoon sun filled his back window as the day wound down.

While Jack sat in the station's lobby between questioning, he had noticed the three thugs from the fight arrive at the police station. Assuming they had been treated for their injures at a local clinic, they had been placed in a room for questioning across from the room Jack occupied. The window in the door let Jack keep up with the inspector as he moved from one room to another and then disappear into the station, presumably to call higher-ups for instructions.

Jack knew the involvement of Sir Graham and Nigel had raised the profile of the whole event considerably. And Jack had counted on that connection keeping anything from sticking to him. When he was released, he knew that Graham had gotten to his nephew. The Chief Inspector of the New South Wales Police would have said something if not for his uncle's intervention.

When the rest of the bikers had shown up, Jack knew he needed to know what was going to happen. Johnny had been absent from the mornings fisticuffs as well as his two friends. Sid and the other two had been dispatched to do Johnny's bidding. As time reached mid-afternoon a very expensive car pulled up to the police station. A man in a suit with a briefcase stepped out and hurried into the station.

The lawyer Jack thought. *Or solicitor down under, I think.*

Deidre had warned Jack that her husband would use the family connections and have a high-powered lawyer out of Melbourne take care of things. A half hour later the lawyer emerged with six leather-jacketed charges. They stood on the sidewalk discussing something before Sid and the two injured bikers climbed on their motorcycles. Jack lowered himself below the steering wheel as the three riders came up to the intersection in front of him and turned left. Jack watched as the three stopped at the next intersection before turning left onto the main highway.

Heading east toward Melbourne Jack thought. *That's good. Three down, three to go.* The lawyer shook Johnny's hand and opened his car door. He soon passed Jack before heading east back to Melbourne. *Now what are you three going to do?* he thought.

The three remaining thugs seemed to be discussing something. They pulled on their helmets and climbed onto their Japanese motorcycles. The electric starters whined the engines to life and the three riders all raced their engines. Jack started his rental car and waited.

Johnny and his two friends pulled up to the intersection, turned left without stopping and gunned it the short distance to the main highway. Jack pulled the gear lever into drive and the Japanese sedan crept forward. As soon as the motorcycles turned right, Jack knew where they were headed. Trouble lay west to the right while home lay east to the left. These three were going to find more trouble. Jack stepped on the gas and turned toward the main highway. He made a quick right turn and glimpsed the three motorcycles disappearing over the rise west of downtown Apollo Bay.

If they wind it up there is no way I can keep up Jack thought. As soon as he was clear of town he floored the rental. The automatic transmission kicked down as the revs in the engine kicked up. He winced at the noise the sixteen valve engine made as he attempted to catch the motorcycles. He flew past the RV park and hit the bridge over the tidal river where they had camped.

Rounding a curve he noticed the three motorcycles up ahead, a straight stretch of highway separating him from them. Assuming they had slowed down, Jack kept the sedan floored across the straight stretch. Whatever the three were doing they definitely were just easing along. Jack knew it was now or never. He knew the road climbed into the Otway Mountains just ahead with the road clinging to the mountainside.

He had seen pictures of the Great Ocean Road as it went through Otway National Park and it was spectacular. Curvy roads, hills, scenic ocean vistas, all hot buttons to three males on motorcycles. They would crank up the speed as soon as the straight section ended and the curves began. It was the macho thing to do.

The sedan flew down the straight and caught the motorcycles just as the road approached the first curve. Jack could see the road climb and twist up ahead before the trees blocked his view. He kept his foot hard on the accelerator and pulled to the right into the passing lane. The rental car flew past the three startled bikers. Jack took his left hand off the steering wheel long enough to give the three a universal one-finger salute.

With tires squealing Jack fought to keep the car on the road as he drifted around the corner. Luckily no one was coming and as the road twisted to the right in completing the 's' curve, Jack's tires screeched as he drifted back into the left where he belonged. The car slowed from the effects of the curves it had just fought through as well as the hill it was now climbing.

Jack looked in his rear view mirror just in time to see all three motorcycles reach his back bumper. The acceleration of the motorcycles had easily caught the struggling car through the curves. Jack knew there would be no out-racing these three. The bikes acceleration and maneuverability easily out-classed the sedan. But Jack was holding an ace and he intended to use it.

The road leveled out but swung into a tight turn toward the mountains. Another tight turn and another hill brought them out of the small ravine and back onto the mountain slope where it dropped into the ocean. Jack didn't have time to admire the view to the south as the three motorcycles clung to his rear bumper.

As they completed the tight right turn, Jack saw the short straight stretch before the next ravine would throw them again to the right. He knew that Johnny and the boys would make their move here. As soon as the thought left him, one of the motorcycles flew by the car on the right and quickly pulled in front a short distance ahead. Johnny and the other one still hung on his rear bumper.

Suddenly the bike's brake lights flashed on and the motorcycle slowed in front of Jack. His right side mirror caught a second motorcycle accelerate up to position just off Jack's driver's car door. A quick glance placed Johnny still hugging his bumper in the rear.

Slowly the speed dropped as the motorcycle in front blocked the road. The motorcycle on the right slowed with them blocking Jack's escape into the passing lane. The bike to the rear stayed with them blocking the rear.

Jack had always been amazed when he had seen videos of this same thing. Bikers would surround a car and force it to stop. Then they would typically pull the driver from the car and assault him, usually for some offense the car driver had caused like getting in the way of the bikers. Jack had always laughed at such videos and now he would show why such events were hilarious.

The blocking tactics being used against him only worked on drivers who were afraid to get their car damaged. But Jack had made sure he had purchased full coverage. His car outweighed a motorcycle by a factor of five and that was his ace. The only risk he faced was getting a motorcycle stuck underneath and losing traction. Jack didn't intend to lose traction. He did intend to use his ace right now.

The brake lights flashed again as the front blocking motorcycle continued his slow stop, Jack flattened the accelerator to the floor and held tight to the steering wheel. The sedan hit the blocking motorcycle with its left front fender and pushed the rear tire of the bike off to the left. The accelerating car then plowed into the motorcycle in the side throwing it and its rider into the roadside ditch.

Jack glanced right and saw the other blocking motorcycle scramble to get out of the way of the car as Jack swerved towards it. The biker was too late as the car flattened the motorcycle against the side of the driver's door. Jack rode the second motorcycle right across the opposing lane and dropped his right side tires off the pavement. The motorcycle and its rider hit the gravel. The rider tried to brake but Jack hit the brakes to keep the car tight to the motorcycle.

The second bike lost control in the gravel and dropped out of sight. Jack saw the rider disappear from view, so Jack went back to full acceleration. He watched the side mirror as he swung the car back into his travel lane. The second motorcycle had flipped with the rider flying through the air, landing in the gravel before summersaulting to a rest.

Jack now focused on the last rider. Johnny was now alone behind the car and had dropped back as his two mates had fallen. Jack hit the brakes hard and the sedan's anti-lock brakes shuddered to a stop. He shoved the car into reverse and floored the accelerator again. Twisting around in his seat Jack took a bead on his last target. He saw Johnny suddenly realize what was happening.

The lone rider hit his brakes hard and stopped. Finding first gear, Johnny leaned to the right to turn around and escape. Jack caught him before he could twist the throttle on the bike. The rear bumper of the car caught the rocket bike just on the back wheel and flipped the motorcycle around. Jack flew past the stunned Johnny who now found his antagonist behind him.

Jack hit the brakes, threw the gear lever into drive and floored the accelerator. The car's transmission groaned at the strain placed on it. The car's tires chirped as the four-cylinder engine strained at the abuse it received.

Johnny struggled to get his motorcycle to move before he glanced around and noticed his back wheel bent from the initial impact. He raised his gaze up from his back wheel just in time to see a 2,500 pound Japanese import side-swipe him, crushing his left leg and foot. The impact of the hit threw the motorcycle off the road, rider and bike rolling into the roadside ditch.

Jack once more slammed the brakes and the car shuddered to a stop. He banged the gear lever into park and climbed out. He walked back to Johnny laying in the ditch. Close by, his motorcycle was smoking from the gas leak the impact had caused. A flame ignited on the hot engine and quickly followed the drop to the source.

Reaching the downed rider, Jack bent down at the helmeted Johnny. Jack looked around quickly, and not seeing anyone, he took his two hands and placed them on the two bottom sides of Johnny's helmet. The biker moved at the intrusion just as Jack twisted his arms in a quick jerk. The crackling sound and the twitch of Johnny's body told Jack what he needed to know.

Jack unsnapped the helmet clasp and removed the helmet. The eyes were still open and Jack felt the neck for a pulse. Finding none, he reached in his pocket and retrieved a small flashlight he kept on his key ring. Shinning the light in Johnny's eyes there was no response. The nearby burning motorcycle exploded as the gas tank finally let go and Jack dropped to the ground. He crawled away from the flames and walked back towards the other two riders.

As he reached the rider that had blocked his door side, a passing camper van pulled up and stopped. An elderly couple stepped out with a cell phone in their hand.

"Call an ambulance," Jack yelled. The second rider was moving and Jack jogged back to the first rider he had shoved out of the way. He was moaning in the grass near his crashed motorcycle. Jack walked back to the camper with the elderly couple standing nearby. *I think they call these things caravans down under* Jack thought.

Chapter 10

Catalina Island, California

Two Harbors held the northern moorage for pleasure boats that ventured across the channel from Los Angeles to escape to Catalina Island. Laying a short distance off the mainland, tourist boats out of San Pedro would deposit day trippers further south for an excursion off shore. Hundreds of beachgoers took the trip each day to the small community of Avalon.

But Two Harbors was off the tourist path. Only accessible by boat, no charter companies serviced the north end of Catalina. Only private craft found their way to this secluded spot. And once moored, there were few services available. On-shore showers and toilets and a small store were about the extent of the place. A couple of private homes filled out the area as most of Catalina Island was privately owned by the descendants of the Wrigley Chewing Gum fortune.

Now a nature preserve, the island had numerous trails for the adventurous set. But the three men who had arrived two days previous hadn't moved any muscles on any of the trails. Sitting under the covered veranda of a small resort on the western portion of Two Harbors, they had been content to sit and drink each day.

While not typical guests, the three men didn't do anything to stand out. Quiet and keeping to themselves, they seemed to be waiting for something. While the more typical guests usually came in pairs and were normally energetic, the staff at the resort didn't pay the three much attention.

There were other guests enjoying their honeymoon or looking for solitude and did not worry about the three. But today the three actually stood up after breakfast and took a walk along the beach to the south. With no other people on the beach, the three men stopped in a secluded spot.

"Tomorrow we head back, are we ready?" one asked. He was slightly taller than the other two and wore a beach hat over his bald head.

"Good, we can get off this damn island. It's driving me crazy here," the man in long pants said. The others were dressed in typical beach resort fashion. This man had stayed dressed as if he was going to work the entire time.

"You are getting paid well to sit here, just remember who's paying you," the man with the hat said.

The complainer shuddered but stood mute. The implied threat had had its effect.

"That's better. You two expect no problems getting to Tijuana once we have our target?"

The third man finally spoke. "No problem. We make the run all the time. That's why you hired us."

The man in the hat knew they were experienced seaman. At least experienced in the Tijuana to Southern California trip. He wouldn't want to cruise the Pacific Ocean with them but the one-hundred-fifty-mile run down the coast to Mexico was different. Except for the heavy shipping lanes around Huntington Beach and San Diego, there was not much that could go wrong.

"And the U. S. officials won't bother us?"

"They worry about stuff going north. They don't worry about much going south. We've done it for years and have only been stopped once heading south. And that was when there was that big murder investigation."

"So we hijack the shuttle boat tomorrow and then kidnap our target. What about the crew and any other passengers that might be on board?" the man in the pants asked.

"Expendable, but keep it clean. We don't want to have a huge mess to clean up when our targets arrive. We don't want to spook them," the man answered as he took off his hat. He wiped his scalp with a handkerchief before placing his hat back on his head. "OK, let's go back, gets some drinks and enjoy our last day in paradise," he chuckled as the three turned and started back toward the resort.

* * *

Parting at Tullamarine International Airport had been difficult. As Melbourne's main airport, the Americans had all arrived with their bags ready to fly home. Their trip had been cut short when Jack had called Graham and told him of the car accident. Jack had waited for the authorities to arrive at the accident scene while everyone at camp quickly packed up.

With the Toyota 'Ute' loaded, the drive to Melbourne through the night had been quiet. The three who were squeezed in the cab couldn't hear much over the diesel noise. The five in the bed of the 'Ute' were wrapped up for warmth against the cool night air. Combined with the wind on the tarp overheard conversation had been limited.

They had arrived at their hotel two days ahead of their reservation and luckily found five rooms available. Jack had shown up in the late morning driving a much abused rental car. While not under arrest, Jack's passport had been taken and he was told he couldn't leave Melbourne.

Much argument had ensued the next two days over whether everyone would stay in Australia until Jack could travel. But he would have none of it. He knew Inez and Eric had their honeymoon booked and they needed to get home for that.

And he knew Carl had a job to get back to in Montana while Stacey had the kids to take care of. So the recumbent had been boxed up and added to Carl's luggage. All had been checked through to Montana as Jack sent everyone on their way. Graham's assurances that he would stay with Jack had gotten everyone to board the plane. Angie and Nigel had caught a flight back to Sydney, leaving Graham the task of returning the rental bicycles. Luckily the company had a store in Melbourne.

Deidre sat beside Jack in the Toyota as Graham gave them a ride back to their hotel where Jack had shared a room with Graham. With her husband dead and Jack at the scene, it wasn't a time to be sleeping with the widow.

Avoiding the temptation that Deidre had presented to him for the past three weeks had grown harder as her extra pounds disappeared. Even as she grew more appealing, something held Jack back. He had been with other women over the past few years. But in Jack's mind he was tired of it all. He missed the commitment that one woman could provide, and while he did have a wife somewhere in the world, he longed for that commitment.

He was older now and his priorities were shifting. Physical satisfaction was important to him but a personal connection had grown more important. And while he had grown close to Deidre over their time together, he knew he was heading back to America and she would remain in Australia. At least he hoped he would be heading back to America.

"Jack, you and Deidre relax. I'm heading down to the Victoria Police Centre on Flinders Street and see if I can get a feel for your situation," Graham said.

"Graham, I've seen all of Melbourne I want to see over the last four days waiting for everyone's flight."

"Then go watch the tele," Graham offered. "But I'd stay out of sight from the prying eyes of the press. You know, widow and suspect boyfriend enjoying the high life together."

Jack knew that Graham hadn't approved of Deidre staying with them. *To much chance that people would put two and two together and get five* Jack thought. But he knew that Deidre was in shock. Even though her husband had been no good, his untimely demise changed her world. And Sydney suddenly became a hostile place with Johnny's family starting to throw their money around.

The call from the divorce lawyer had added to the shock. With Johnny's death Deidre was now the sole owner of the largest motorcycle store in Sydney. At least she would be once the lawyer had finished with his lawsuit against the family over their shady business reorganization. He was convinced all of it would not stand up in court.

The two walked across the hotel parking lot to where it overlooked the Northwest Expressway. The traffic noise drowned out the nearby street noise. Speaking for the first time about what had happened, they checked that no one was nearby.

"Jack, did you have anything to do with my husband's death?"

"Deidre, the three bikers tried to stop me so they could do what ever to me. I simply used my car to protect myself."

"And you didn't go looking for them?"

"As I told the police, they caught up to me on the highway going out of Apollo Bay. They tried to stop me. I learned from Reginald Denny not to let people stop you. It probably won't be good for your health. They suffered the consequences."

Deidre looked at Jack. "Who the hell is Reginald Denny?"

Jack explained that in the 1992 Los Angeles Riots a large crowd had blocked a main street in LA. They were terrorizing drivers, pulling people from cars and assaulting them. Reginald Denny had been a truck driver who chose to stop his Kenworth semi loaded with sand instead of putting down the hammer. He was pulled from his truck and brutally beaten. The assault became famous for the aerial video feed the news chopper provided of the thugs dancing over Denny and dropping cinder blocks on his head. The man lived but was severely brain damaged.

"I am not a victim Deidre. Especially to three thugs who choose to try to stop a car with a motorcycle. That's about as effective as taking a knife to a gun fight. Ain't going to happen with me."

"I'm just still in shock by it all Jack," Deidre said. "I'm sorry. I just don't feel up to heading back to Sydney."

"I understand, but I think it better if you stay at another location so we aren't seen together. Graham said he'd take you to a place out in Moonee Pond when he returns."

"If that's what you want Jack." Deidre stared down at the traffic as it crept by, snarled by an accident somewhere.

Jack wasn't sure what he wanted right now. The woman beside him had made every attempt to entice him into bed and he continued to resist. He hadn't killed her estranged husband so as to free her for him. It was because of Inez and what the thug had done to her and Eric. *Or was it?* Jack thought.

He just had an overwhelming feeling that he didn't want any more entanglements. There were too many in his past already and a certain guilt went with them. Women he had loved and lost. Women he would have gladly settled down with, but for one reason or another that was not to be. One more partner just didn't appeal to him, no matter how beautiful or willing. He just didn't have it anymore.

Chapter 11

Missoula, Montana

Carl shoveled the snow away from his Dad's garage doors so he could open them. Being a 1930's vintage house with separate garage, the doors swung out on large hinges. While the neighborhood kid had kept the walkways shoveled while they had been away, the driveways were piled deep with the January snows of Montana.

A call to a friend with a pick-up and plow had improved the parking in both driveways, but a little hand work with a shovel was needed to clear both Carl's garage doors as well as his Dad's doors. Swinging one door open, Carl muscled Jack's bicycle box into the garage and leaned it against the wall.

The recumbent had been boxed up in Melbourne and Carl had added it to his luggage for the flight home. As Carl swung the door shut and relocked the clasp, a voice behind him startled him. Carl turned to see the neighbor Greg walking up the driveway.

"Good trip?" Greg asked.

"Yes, being in summer weather felt great," Carl said.

"Well, good on you then. From your face you got some sun. Where's your Dad?"

Carl and Stacey had returned the day before and were finally feeling like they belonged in the Mountain Time Zone. Jet lag always seemed to be worse returning from a trip as the routine of home life settled in.

"There was a bit of a problem in Australia that my Dad got wrapped up in. He is staying on a little longer to get things straightened out."

"Well, nothing serious I hope."

The conversation stalled as Carl wasn't about to elaborate on his Dad's troubles to the neighbor, and Greg seemed reluctant to ask for more details. Finally Greg broke the impasse.

"Had a bit of a dust-up here while you were gone. You'll hear about it soon enough from the other neighbors," Greg said.

"Trouble? Here? What kind of trouble?"

"Seems as if I caught two fellows where they weren't supposed to be. I think you blokes call it casing a joint. My friend Karma took care of them when they took exception to our calling the police."

"Well thanks, then. I know you and my Dad had worked out you watching the houses for us. I appreciate that. And thank your friend for us."

"I will. No troubles really. I think Karma enjoyed himself," Greg said.

Carl looked at the neighbor a bit askance at the comment as Greg turned and headed back inside. The cold Montana air cut any lengthy conversations off even with the brilliant sun shining. Carl walked back to his house to get ready to drive to Missoula's airport. *Stacey's parents are flying in today with the children from Colorado. Things would be back to normal soon* he thought. *Or would they?*

With Jack still in Australia, Carl had a nervous feeling about things. Walking up to his front door the look on Stacey's face sent a chill down his back. And it wasn't a chill from the cold. Something had happened. And from the look on his wife's face, something bad had happened.

"What?" Carl asked. He shut the door and stared at Stacey.

"Inez and Eric were a no-show at the resort."

The four had all flown together from Melbourne to Los Angeles. The non-stop flight was a sixteen-hour endurance contest. The last Carl had seen of his sister and husband had been after Customs. Carl had placed his luggage back onto the conveyor for the flight to Missoula by way of Salt Lake City. Inez and Eric had gathered their bags and had headed to the exit to grab a cab to a hotel near Marina Del Rey.

Located next to Los Angeles International Airport, Marina Del Rey held a large boat basin for the L.A. area. Inez and Eric would meet their shuttle launch there for the trip out to Catalina Island. Inez had said they had a night on the mainland before they would head out to the resort the next day. That they hadn't arrived yet was not good news.

"Did the resort call us?" Carl asked.

"We were the emergency number the resort had. And it isn't just Inez and Eric. Their boat is missing, too."

"What? The resort's boat is gone? How can that be?"

"The resort said the boat left Two Harbors on its regular run with three guests headed back to L.A. The launch never checked in from Marian Del Rey as is the policy. The resort checked and the boat docked as it normally does and left again. The neighboring business confirmed that," Stacey said.

"But it never made it back to Catalina? Has the Coast Guard been called?" Carl asked.

"A Marine Alert has been put out and the Coast Guard is conducting a search. But no sign of the launch has been reported yet. What are we going to do?" Carl saw the strain in Stacey's eyes. Tears formed as she relayed the information. The newlyweds were missing. Jack was stuck in Australia and they were in Montana, everyone a long way from Southern California.

There was a knock on the door and Carl spun around to see a familiar face in the front door window. He opened it to Greg standing next to Karma, the smaller man holding something.

"Sorry to bother you folks, but Karma made a Nepalese dinner for you. Something to get you settled back in America," Greg said as he looked past Carl, focusing on Stacey's strained expression. "If we've come at a bad time, I'm sorry."

Carl stepped back and opened the door for the two men. Greg and Karma stepped inside as Carl shut the door.

"No, its fine. Thank you for the dinner. It was very thoughtful of both of you," Carl said.

But the tears were now flowing down Stacey's face and all three men stared at her. Stacey reacted by covering her face and running from the room. Carl turned back to his neighbors, who stood quiet.

"I'm sorry, we just received some news that has Stacey upset," Carl said.

"Well, excuse us then. We'll just pop dinner in the fridge and be on our way then," Greg said. Karma walked swiftly past Carl into the kitchen. The refrigerator door opened and closed and the Gurkha returned. As the three men lingered in the living room, Greg spoke first.

"If there is anything we can do to help. We are 'experienced at solving problems', I think is the polite way to say it," Greg said and Karma's face smiled at the statement.

Carl stood and looked at the two offering help. With Jack not available, Carl felt the burden of being the man in charge. His children were due soon along with his in-laws. The incident while they were gone that Greg had talked about had already been described by one of the other neighbors whom Carl had seen yesterday. Carl knew about the knife fight and the two thugs going to the hospital. The neighbor had added that these two had been returned by the Missoula Police soon after like nothing much had happened. And now the offer of help.

"I'm not sure what kind of help I need right now," Carl said.

"Why don't you tell us what is happening? We know your Dad is being detained by the Victoria Police involving the death of a motorcyclist there."

Carl was stunned. *How do they know about that?* he thought. He looked at the two without asking.

Greg offered more. "Let me just say we are very well connected. If you need help, you only have to ask."

"Please sit down. I guess we need to talk," Carl said.

Once seated, Carl started with Jack's predicament. While describing the events as they happened down under, Carl didn't elaborate on the death. Only his Dad knew the real story and Jack had been careful not to tell anyone what really had happened out on Great Otway National Park.

Greg and Karma listened carefully but Carl sensed they already knew the entire story. They nodded politely as Carl told them what had happened up to flying out of Melbourne. Carl looked at his neighbors.

"That fits with the story that has been presented to us," Greg said. "But since you left, your Dad has been questioned several times more by the police. Sir Graham has remained close by so he is in good hands."

"But how do you know all this? Who are you?" Carl asked.

"Not important right now. The problem is this Deidre woman. The dead man's estranged wife. She is lingering in Melbourne, luckily not at your Dad's hotel. The police have been observing the two to see if there is any collusion between them"

"There is none I can assure you," Carl offered. "I spent three weeks with both of them and while Deidre certainly was willing, my Dad wasn't."

"Our latest info is that your Dad will have his passport returned soon and he'll be able to fly home."

Carl sat back, relieved at the news. *But how do these two know all this?* he thought. Before he could ask, Greg spoke up.

"But there is more news from the look on your wife's face that we don't know."

"My sister and her husband are missing. Along with the hotel launch they were traveling on," Carl said.

Greg looked closely at Carl and then stood. "Come on, Karma, we have some work to do." The two neighbors opened the front door and were gone before Carl could even start to ask who they were again. With the information they had already provided, they were connected somewhere. Carl was just glad for the help.

* * *

Inez woke with a start, her head hurting. She struggled to move but her body continued to fight her effort. All she remembered was taking the cab ride to the dock and meeting the captain of the hotel launch. She and Eric had been escorted onto the boat while one of the crew members stowed their luggage. Fresh cold drinks were offered by a third crew member. And that's where her memory stopped.

With supreme effort she rolled her head to one side. The bulkhead of the boat blocked her view. With more effort she twisted her head to the other side. Eric lay next to her asleep. She was relieved for the moment that they were together at least. *But why am I so groggy?* she thought.

Pulling from deep inside her she rolled off her back onto her side, looking at Eric. He was laying on his back fast asleep. Or was he? Inez struggled with her left arm and brought her hand up to Eric's face.

She felt for any breath on her fingers and felt none. She looked at his chest and saw no movement.

Panicking, she stretched her fingers onto his neck and found where his carotid artery should be. She searched for a pulse but could not find one. Her anxiety spiked and the added adrenaline gave her strength to prop herself on one elbow. She pulled one eyelid back and looked onto Eric's left eye. The pupil was fixed as it stared at the deck above.

Tears filled her eyes as she tried to hear a heartbeat. She placed her ear on Eric's chest and listened carefully. The boat noise precluded any careful search for sounds and Inez slapped Eric's face. No reaction. She screamed as she had never screamed before in her life, a blood-curdling scream that brought a man to the cabin door. Unlocking the door, the man stepped into the small state room and looked at Inez. Then he looked at Eric.

"Quick, my husband isn't breathing. He needs medical care right now," Inez screamed.

The man placed his hand on Eric's neck, checking for a pulse. He then leaned over and checked Eric's pupils. He turned and left the room, locking the cabin door.

Inez was in shock at the man's disregard of her pleas. She screamed louder but no one came. Finally exhausted, she slumped onto the berth and cried. Tears flowed down her cheeks as she stared at her dead husband. *What is going on?* she thought.

Chapter 12

Melbourne, Australia

The dock at St. Kilda stretched out into Port Phillip Bay. St. Kilda was the original seaside resort for Melbourne and over the years it had transformed into a bedroom community for the sprawling metropolis. But one thing remained the same from those day, the street cars continued to run throughout Melbourne. While almost all the world's cities had ripped out their street cars in the 1950's when buses took over, Melbourne had resisted the change.

Now recognized for their charming convenience, Melbourne's street cars offered an extensive network of public transportation. Jack Wesley was tired of the street cars and couldn't care less about their history. He sat on the park bench on St. Kilda's pier only because his friend Graham Elphinston had told him to be there.

His forced indenture to the Victoria Police continued as they drug their feet on the investigation of Deidre's husband's death. At least Deidre had finally headed home so that temptation had been removed. Jack knew the police would be watching for any connection between the two, and with her leaving he hoped that things would begin to move in his favor.

When the news from Missoula had arrived early this morning Jack's only concern was getting home as fast as he could. Carl's call and email had brought the bad news of Inez's disappearance. With no sighting for two days, the Coast Guard had called off the search for the missing boat. The Marine Warning to other boaters to be on the lookout for the hotel boat continued.

But Jack just wanted his passport and a flight out. He looked up from his park bench and saw Graham approaching. He stood and walked to his friend.

"Well Graham, what's the decision? Do I get my passport back?"

"I spoke with the Commissioner this morning. They will wrap up the investigation tomorrow and issue their findings. I've been told you will be cleared of any charges in the report and the death will be listed as an accident," Graham said.

"Thank you my friend."

"Jack, it took some persuading to get you out of this. Your fingerprints were on the dead man's helmet. With a broken neck, that could be looked at as . . . "

"My fingerprints were there because I took the man's helmet off to see if there was any medical help I could offer," Jack said.

"Yes, as you told the police many times. But it is very easy to snap a man's neck by twisting his motorcycle helmet. And the tire marks on the highway show you ramming the dead man on his motorcycle while going backwards."

"I stopped after the accident and put the car in reverse to back up to help. He ran into me."

"Again a logical answer that you gave the police. But the whole Deidre thing keeps coming back into the equations."

"Motive and opportunity, I know. Basic police work. Well the opportunity was certainly there. But no motive. Deidre and I never acted on anything. She just became a friend on a bicycle ride, nothing more."

"And that's what probably saved you. Having a New South Wales Chief Inspector along to confirm that there was no love interest between you two helped," Graham said.

"I wasn't sure where Nigel stood on this. So he backed my story?"

"I had to talk to him, Jack. With the incident at Apollo Bay and the wooden club to the faces of those three added to the three others being run down, he was adding three and three together and coming to too many coincidences. Deidre or no Deidre."

"Thanks Graham. I owe you one," Jack said.

"You and I know what really happened in London. I know you earned the knighthood instead of me that night. You turned a nightmare into a tragedy. That will never be forgotten. And Jack, I had to call London to remind them. A call came back to the Victoria Police that ended any further investigation. You will receive your passport, but the Australian government will tell you that you are not welcome to come back."

"Suits me fine. If Australia wants to be like America on being afraid to lock up the bad boys I'll pass on coming back. And with their gun ban after that shooting in Tasmania, they deserve what they get."

The two friends stared at the harbor without looking at each other. They had been through much together and knew neither one would change. They accepted that the lives they had saved was the basis of their friendship.

"Jack, I know about your daughter. I'm sorry. I know how concerned you are and want to get back to America as soon as you can."

"Thanks, Graham. Its been torture not being able to do anything sitting here."

"I've taken the liberty to book a reservation for tomorrow. The government wants you on a flight to L.A. tomorrow evening. They will escort both of us to the airport where you'll be handed your passport," Greg said.

"But Graham . . ." Jack started to speak.

Graham interrupted. "My friend will fly down and collect his 'Ute'. So I'm free to go with you. And I think you are going to need some help. I've made a few contacts. I hope you don't mind."

Jack wasn't sure what contacts Graham had but Jack's only concern was the news that he would be heading home tomorrow. Inez's trail was getting cold as they sat half a world away. It was time to move.

The sixteen-hour non-stop flight felt like sixteen days to Jack. While he was finally moving, the Boeing Dreamliner he flew couldn't move fast enough. Graham had been quiet the whole trip, which suited Jack fine. He had to think. No news of Inez's location had arrived before they had left and now most of a day was being burned up in the air.

The question as to who would meet them at Los Angeles had been answered before they got on the flight. Jack had wanted to call Carl and have him fly down from Montana. But Graham pointed out that Carl needed to be in Missoula for when the bad guys called, if they did.

He argued that whomever had arranged the abduction, Jack might be the main target. The abductor would have to inform Jack where to go to be hopefully exchanged for Inez and Eric. And Carl's phone was the only one that they could assume would be known.

By the time they had landed, cleared Customs ,and collected their bags, Jack was about to burst. Seeing his two neighbors waiting outside immigration only added to the anxiety. Somehow

Graham had contacted Greg and Karma, and Jack still didn't know the connection.

Graham walked up to the two men and introduced himself. Karma grabbed Jack's bag as Greg stumbled slightly grabbing Graham's luggage. Graham noticed the wince on Greg's face and pushed the younger man's hand away, keeping his luggage.

"Jack, good that you're back. We've been in touch with Carl," Greg said.

"What's the latest?" Jack asked.

"They found the boat," Greg said.

"They did? That's good news. Where?" Jack pumped out questions. His frustration showed in his face.

"Tijuana. Tied to a dock down there. No sign of your daughter or son-in-law."

"Mexican officials saying anything? The boat crew answering questions?"

"No boat crew. Seems the boat was docked late last night and everyone was long gone by the time anyone noticed the boat was important. We contacted the FBI office to see if they can get any cooperation out of the Mexican officials."

Jack knew he had to make some phone calls. Greg offered that they had hotel rooms booked nearby and the four men all loaded into a rental car for the short trip. When Jack was settled into the room he placed his first call. Carl answered the phone in Montana.

"Son, what's the connection between Greg and Karma and Graham?"

"I don't know how they know Graham. But they offered to help when they heard about Inez. And they knew all about what had happened in Australia."

"What's with that?" Jack asked.

"And Dad, you need to knew. Those two cut up some bad guys who seem to have been looking for you. From their description of the two I'm afraid of what we're dealing with."

Jack sat quiet. With Inez and Eric missing and now the boat they were supposed to be on discovered in Mexico, he dreaded what was coming. If true, things would be very dangerous for everyone involved. Carl spoke before Jack could go any further with his idea.

"The two arrested outside your house - you need to know that Karma sent them to the hospital when they pulled knives on him and Greg. Seems you don't want to threaten a Gurkha. But I checked the arrest record on the two. They were both Mexican nationals with Las Vegas, Nevada driver's licenses."

Jack stared blankly at the news. The dread he had been feeling grew in intensity at the news of the Mexican connection. With Inez possibly in Mexico, it was all adding up to Ernesto. Or at least Ernesto's son, Daniel. Ever since Ernesto had died in a fiery houseboat explosion outside Las Vegas, Daniel had taken it upon himself to seek retribution on Jack. Retribution for what Daniel perceived had been Jack's role in his father's death.

That Ernesto ran a prostitution and drug operation as part of a cartel out of Mexico added up to continued trouble for Jack and his family. While Jack had been found innocent of a run-in with Ernesto during an altercation in a night club in Las Vegas, Jack knew the son carried a grudge to even up things for his father's death. And Jack had had a target on him ever since.

And now Inez and Eric might be in the crosshairs. Before he went to war with Daniel and the cartel, Jack needed to know more about the three men offering help. Especially the two who were new to him. But first, Jack had to make one very important phone call.

Chapter 13

Los Angeles, California

Jack found Karma sitting on the hallway floor in the motel outside his room. The Gurkha rose as Jack approached. He bowed slightly.

"Karma, I need to talk to Greg."

"I'm sorry, Sahib. Mr. Greg is resting now. Very bad to disturb him."

The door across the hall opened and Graham stuck his head out. "Everything OK here?"

"Oh yes, everything very OK here," Karma offered.

"I need to talk to Greg as soon as he's awake," Jack stated.

"Very good, Sahib. I will tell him"

The door behind Karma opened and a squinting Greg stared out. "I heard voices. What's up?"

"Greg, we need to talk," Jack said.

Jack noticed the man had one eye closed and showed a pained look on his face. He stepped back and motioned everyone into the darkened room. When Jack walked over to open the blinds, Greg stopped him.

"If you don't mind, can we talk in the dark?"

Jack turned back and pulled a chair from the small table in the room. Greg sat down on one of the beds while Karma sat on the second bed. Graham sat down next to Jack in the remaining chair. With his eyes adjusted to the darkened room, Jack sought some answers.

"My son said you knew about my situation in Melbourne before he knew about it. Can you explain that to me please?"

Greg looked at Graham first and then back to Jack. He continued to keep his right eye shut as he sat on the bed. A squint out of his left eye indicated that all was not right with the man.

"Jack, can we just leave it that Karma and I are just good neighbors willing to help you out?"

Jack studied the man and then turned his gaze to the small Gurkha. Karma sat stone-faced with no hint of anything. Jack turned slightly and looked at his friend Graham. Graham held a blank look also. *Three very cool characters* Jack thought.

Jack said, "Before I came over here I placed a call to my brother Ed. Ed is the Chief of Staff for the Junior U. S. Senator from Wyoming, and as such can make inquires in the power salons of Washington D.C. I expect a call back from him to let me know who you two are. Want to save me the hassle of the phone call?"

Neither of the three men offered an answer as they continued their quiet repose. Greg's pained look continued. Jack sat and waited for his brother's call. Greg laid down on the bed and closed his other eye. Karma and Graham sat in the dark.

Jack's cell phone buzzed, startling everyone. Seeing that it was from his brother, Jack hit the answer button. Jack held the phone to his ear and awaited his answer. His stone face revealed nothing as he sat and listened.

"That's it?" he asked. The phone went dead. He placed the phone back in his pocket and focused on the others. "Seems you three swing a lot of weight in Washington. My brother went through his friend at the CIA and all he would offer was you could be trusted. No other comments."

Jack knew there was more but his brother was unwilling to share it with him. He knew his brother well enough to grasp when things were not being forthcoming. Jack would just have to trust his brother.

He already knew Graham from their adventure in London, so one third of the equation was settled. The other two thirds would be based on Ed's recommendation and what appeared to be a connection between the Missoula neighbors and Graham.

Greg sat up on one elbow and opened one eye. "Good. Then we can get on with finding your daughter."

"Yes we can. And thank you for your help," Jack said. "I guess the first place to start would be the dock where the hotel launch picked up Inez and Eric."

Since Greg seemed to be incapacitated, Jack and Graham left Karma in charge and took the rental car off to Marina Del Ray. First locating the address for the dock on the internet, it was a short ride from their airport motel to the marina.

Parking the car, the two walked across the large lot and down onto the floating dock. Along the dock were signs announcing various commercial enterprises that ran their operations off the dock. Mostly fishing charter companies, Jack looked for the Two Harbor Resort sign. They found the sign beside an empty slip near the end of the dock. Jack looked around at the neighboring businesses. Noticing a fishing charter company's boat tied to the dock, Jack and Graham approached the deck hand.

"Is the Captain aboard?" Jack asked.

"Down below in the engine hold," the crew member offered and pointed to the wheelhouse.

The boat, about fifty feet in length, had three decks topped off with an elevated bridge under a Bimini top. Jack stepped onto the boat and walked through the lower wheelhouse. A companionway led down into the main salon. Jack turned back toward the stern and found the engine room door open. He stuck his head in and called for the captain. A grizzled overweight man in blue jeans and a white captain's hat stuck out his face from around the engine.

"Yeah, what you need?"

"Mind if I ask you a couple questions?" Jack asked.

"Buddy, I'm busy here. Got a charter going out in an hour."

"It won't be long. It's about the Two Harbor's launch disappearance."

"Oh that. Strange deal that one." The captain stepped around the engine wiping his hands on a cloth. He glanced at Graham standing behind Jack. He refocused on Jack as Jack spoke.

"My daughter and husband were supposed to be on that boat."

"Sorry to hear that. Hopefully they'll find them soon."

"Were you here when the launch set off for Catalina?" Jack asked.

"No, my day off. But Denny was working that day. He might have seen something."

Finding out that Denny was the deck hand they had passed topsides, the three men all climbed the ladder back onto the main deck. Denny looked up from his boat-cleaning job and the sudden appearance of the captain.

"Denny, these fellows are asking about the Two Harbor Resort boat on the day it disappeared.

Do you know anything about that?" the captain asked.

"Si, Captain. I was working that day right here. I see the boat come in and load everyone on board."

Jack noticed from the answer that the man was Hispanic and very dark from being out on the ocean constantly.

"Did the authorities talk to you?" Jack asked.

"No sir. No one talk to Denny," Denny said.

"Did you see anything out of the ordinary?"

"No sir. The boat docked at the usual time. And left at the regular time with the passengers aboard. Nothing unusual about it."

"And you see the launch every day, do you?" Jack asked.

"Not every day. But I see plenty. Depends how the fishing is going. If no fish, I clean the boat. That's when I see the launch," Denny said.

"And everything was like it always was on that day?"

The answer did not come immediately. Jack noticed Denny was thinking about his answer. Denny finally spoke "No sir. There was a difference that day. The captain of the resort boat was new. I knew the regular captain real good. He hires me some times to clean his boat for him. Make it real nice for the resort guests."

"The day the boat disappeared, it had a new captain?"

Denny nodded his agreement. "And new crew members. I never see either of them around here before."

Jack thanked Denny and the captain and stepped off the boat. He turned to Graham as they walked up the dock. Pulling his smart phone out of his pants pocket, Jack searched for a phone number. Dialing the Two Harbors Resort, he asked for the manager. The answer stopped him cold.

* * *

Inez struggled to get free as she lay on her side. Her hands and ankles had been duct taped. A strap of tape pulled her ankles up behind her legs so she couldn't move her legs. A piece of tape had been placed over her mouth and a cloth hood tied around her head. While she couldn't see anything, she could still hear and smell.

After she awoke from whatever drug they had used on her, she had discovered Eric's dead body lying next to her. Still on the boat at that time, she was soon drugged again. She awoke in her present state and as far as she could tell she was in a moving vehicle. When she tried to roll she discovered her confinement was a tight space. Assuming a car trunk she had carefully rolled each way to confirm a small space. And with the road noise she heard she knew she was traveling somewhere.

She just didn't know where she was since her time frame had been interrupted by her unconsciousness. But the smells that made it into her space let her know she was near an agricultural area. Inez recognized the farm smells as they seemed to pass various agricultural activities.

Recognizing manure smell as well as pesticide spray, Inez recorded each passing. Whether it would ever help her once she arrived at her destination, she had no way of knowing. But it kept her mind focused away from the sheer terror that wanted to overwhelm her.

She knew she had to hold the terror back if she was to survive. But it was a challenge to accomplish as the journey continued. Tears would flow as soon as she stopped focusing on the background noises and smells. She would redouble her mind to her task until the tears stopped and anger took over. Anger at what her captives had already done and anger at what the future held.

Chapter 14

Missoula, Montana

The Montana winter continued unabated as the Clark Fork River succumbed to the cold and froze along its banks. Flowing through Missoula, it would take a more severe cold snap to freeze the entire river. Only where the water settled quietly did the cold hold its grip long enough to produce ice.

Carl and Stacey had attempted to return to their lives but it wasn't working. Distracted by the continued disappearance of Inez and Eric they struggled to hold their lives together. The grandparents had left for home and the daily routine of two young children kept their minds off other things.

Trying to return to their jobs and concentrate on work failed them, their bosses understanding the situation. Their friends in Missoula had rallied their support, but the longer the unknowns went on the more desperate things became.

Carl talked daily with his Dad still in Los Angeles. News that Jack had found out from the resort that their regular crew had left Two Harbors that eventful day gave them something. That the regular crew never made it to Marina Del Rey added to at least some answers.

Jack further dug up that there were three resort guests heading back to L.A. that afternoon. And all three were described as Hispanic and not the typical resort guest. The manager of Two Harbors did not offer more of an explanation for the statement, and Carl knew his Dad had worked hard getting an answer. Political correctness had overtaken any further discussion of the three men. The potential of being tagged a racist in today's society because the three men were Hispanic kept the manager quiet. That had been two days prior and Jack's investigation had made little new headway. Stacey broke Carl's concentration as he sat in his living room.

"Carl, there's a phone call for you."

Unlike many of their friends, Carl and Stacey had a land line. The phone had been left by the previous owners with the explanation that cell service could be sporadic, especially in the winter storms. Carl wanted to keep the land line because it gave them a local number. Stacey's cell phone continued to use her Colorado number while Carl's Oregon number remained on his phone. The land line made them locals.

Carl walked into the kitchen and picked up the phone. Being attached to a cord to the wall, he stood by the kitchen counter while Stacey stared at him.

"Yes, this is Carl."

"Listen carefully if you want to see your sister alive."

"What, who is this?" asked Carl.

"Shut up and listen. In two days you will have that gangster Dad of yours standing in front of the Bodega on Route 2 and Pancho Villa Road in San Luis Rio Colorado in Sonora."

Carl raced to find a piece of paper and something to write with. He scribbled frantically.

"Hold on, I'm writing."

The man on the line stopped talking then repeated the address. "You got all that?"

"Yes. But is my sister and her husband OK?"

"Shut up. Your gangster Dad is to come alone if you want to see your sister again."

"I want to talk to her. Put her on the phone now."

Carl repeated the demand but the dial tone announced that the call had ended. Carl hung the phone on the cradle and slumped onto the counter. Stacey placed her arms around her husband.

"What is it? Is Inez and Eric safe?"

"I don't know. But they want my Dad."

The first call made was to Jack to tell him about the demands. The call lingered as something was discussed on the other end. After a long break Carl mumbled agreement and hung up. Carl then opened up the computer and loaded up the airline web site. He wrote down the flight and time as Stacey looked over his shoulder.

"Yuma? What's in Yuma?" Stacey asked.

"No one at the moment, but it's close to this town in Mexico we just got directed to. I'll meet my Dad there tomorrow. They're driving over tonight."

"What are you going to do?"

"Find my sister and Eric first. And then take care of those who took them."

"Carl Wesley. Don't be like your Dad and risk your life. Remember you have two little kids that need you."

"Stacey, I'll take good care of myself. But this is my sister."

The couple went quiet. Stacey knew the Wesley family very well.

* * *

The City of Yuma lay just north of the U.S. - Mexican border in Arizona. After crossing California in a straight line due to the Gadsden Purchase of 1853, the border turned south along the Colorado River before turning east again along southern Arizona. This area had been part of Mexico until the Union Pacific Railroad decided to run their rail road track to San Diego. A forced land sale, the Gadsden Purchase had made sure that the track remained within the United States.

When the land grab was added to the Colorado River water, 'El Norte' had affected major change in this corner of Sonora. Located between the Sea of Cortez and the border, Sonora struggled along with what the 'gringos' had left them. The Colorado River seldom ever flowed to the sea due to the Americans redirecting the river water to the demands of Arizona and Southern California. Little remained as it crossed the border into Mexico.

San Luis Rio Colorado was a dusty agricultural town just south of Yuma. It made do with what water it could find to grow the crops that sustained the area. But what really sustained the area was shipping items north, back to America. Drugs and people were the main products that Mexico supplied to its rich neighbor.

Yuma had always been a frontier city. The U.S. Army located a fort nearby in the early days to protect the overland stage coach. It continued its role as a frontier town with the Marine Corps having an Air Station in Yuma.

The taxi from the airport took Carl to the address he had been given. The guard at the main gate onto the air station directed the driver to a Quonset hut by the airfield. Carl stepped out into the mid-day sun. The warmth of Southern Arizona was relief from the cold he had left earlier that day in Missoula. Carl recognized the face that walked out of the Quonset hut door.

"Uncle Ed, What are you doing here?" Carl certainly knew the entire family had been contacted about Inez's kidnapping but to see his dad's brother in person startled him. Carl knew Ed was a powerful figure in the Nation's capital and he was impressed that Ed had made the trip out West.

"And where else would I be with your sister missing?" Ed asked.

The two hugged as Ed directed Carl into the Quonset hut. The World War II relic continued to serve as Ed closed the door. Carl's eyes adjusted as Ed led him into the building. Stepping from the corridor through another interior door the two stepped into a hangar, a large helicopter sat in the middle with its tail hanging out the open doors. Jack stepped over to greet his son. The two held each other extra long as the gathered men stood a respectable distance from them. Carl recognized Graham from Australia and Greg and Karma from Missoula sitting by the helicopter. Two Marines in flight suits sat with them

Ed spoke first. "We are all here now, we can head out."

Before Carl could ask where they were headed, Ed grabbed his small duffel bag and directed him to a waiting helicopter outside the Quonset. A match for the one inside, the two Marines climbed into the cockpit and started the engine. As the rotor slowly began to turn, the rest of the team climbed into the back and cinched their seat belts.

Various luggage sat in between the two seats that faced each other. Ed motioned for Carl to put on the headphones. The others all pulled head phones over their heads as Ed said, "We need a place a little less visible. Won't take but a few minutes to get there."

With the rotors shaking the helicopter violently, the pilot lifted off. The pilot tipped the chopper slightly forward and Carl felt the lift as they moved forward. Gaining elevation, the view out the open door grew as the helicopter gained altitude. The wind noise combined with the rotor made conversation difficult even with the headphones on. The men all sat and stared out the doors.

The Sonora Desert stretched out in all directions, and Carl looked south to see if the border could be seen. The haze and dust blocked visibility the twenty miles to Mexico. But closer in, the view changed from the City of Yuma to open desert. Soon the desert was covered in vehicle tracks, the kind of tracks armored vehicles make.

The helicopter flew over more Quonset huts lined along paved streets. A mesa came into view ahead of them and Carl saw an airport laid out on top of the mesa. The pilot slowed the chopper and began a slow turn to come into the airport. Hangars of various sizes lined one side of a taxi way and the helicopter flared up to stop. Dropping down onto the ground, Carl felt the skids absorb the landing. The pilot dropped the engine to idle and the passengers each grabbed a bag and unloaded.

Ed led them into an empty hangar and once in the shade, dropped the bags. The idling chopper gained revolutions and lifted off. Carl watched the big helicopter sweep forward and bank right, headed back to where he had come from.

"Ok," Ed started. "We are on the Yuma Proving Grounds. And this is Laguna Army Airfield. We should be away from prying eyes up here on the mesa.This is home base until this is over."

Carl soon found out that it was his Uncle Ed who had made the decision to move to Yuma. Carl had been the last to arrive. The four who had driven through the night had arrived by rental car from L.A. Flying in soon after, Ed joined Jack as the two brothers shopped and stocked the small kitchen in their hangar.

Cots had been set up inside the hangar but Carl was mystified. There were many more cots than the six of them required. Carl knew when to keep quiet. He would be informed of what was to happen when he needed to be. Counting twenty six cots for the six of them, it was obvious that visitors were expected. *But who?* he thought.

Chapter 15

San Luis Rio Colorado, Mexico

Amidst the fields along the Colorado River that separated Sonora from Baja California sat numerous farms. One in particular held several buildings with a concrete wall surrounding the buildings. Inside the walls sat houses with the typical garages and shops associated with any farming operation. The walls leant this one farm a unique position among the other farms in the area. A position that stated this one farm had goods of considerable value ensconced inside.

When Ernesto established his business in Las Vegas many years ago, drugs and prostitution had been his main interest. Since that day the market for smuggling humans across the border drove a bigger and bigger share of his revenue stream. And with Ernesto dead, his son Daniel moved up to take over the business.

Often described as a cartel, Daniel's business was far from the cartel he knew. The major drug cartels that terrorized northern Mexico were many times bigger than his operation. Tied to Las Vegas exclusively, Ernesto had grown his crime syndicate by paying off the bigger cartels when needed. And if payoffs didn't satisfy, then Ernesto was not above violent confrontation on a selective basis. He had mastered the art of applying violence when necessary without antagonizing the big cartels to the point that they would eliminate him altogether.

Daniel had learned from his father. Ruthless when he needed to be, generous to the right people, and survive on the edges. Daniel knew never to step into territory ruled by the big cartels and was content to continue his father's work of catering to a select group of wealthy people in Las Vegas.

The walled compound was Daniel's base of operations in Mexico. Drugs would be stored there for their journey north. On other days, illegal immigrants were loaded into semis for the trip north. Some to work the varied jobs American said they couldn't do and others to be turned into prostitutes. All paid well and San Luis Rio Colorado served a valuable purpose.

As Inez awoke from her sleep she recalled the needle that had been stuck in her arm when the car truck lid opened. Now awake she opened her eyes to a darkened room. She moved and realized that her legs and arms were free along with the tape that had covered her mouth. She struggled to sit up as she moved her sore joints.

"Como estas?" a voice asked.

Inez knew a little Spanish from teaching school in Colorado Springs and recognized the greeting asked her health. But her knowledge just about stopped there. She turned around to see a young woman sitting against the wall. They were in a room about twelve feet on each side with only a bucket on the corner for fixtures. Besides the bucket and the two women the room was empty. And with no windows, the only light was the little that flittered in through the cracks in the walls.

"I've felt better. Do you speak English?" Inez asked.

"No entiendo, senorita."

Inez pointed at herself and said her name twice. Then pointed at the woman. She had to repeat the motion twice before the woman realized what was being asked.

"Si, si. Carmen," the woman pointed at her chest in response.

"Well, Carmen. Nice to meet you I guess," Inez offered.

"Si, si. Miss Inez."

"Now if you could only tell me where I am and what's going on," Inez said softly to herself.

"Si, si. Carmen," the woman responded.

Inez nodded that she understood and moved to a place beside her new roommate. Inez placed her back against the wall and lowered her head to her drawn up knees. *Time to wait,* she thought. But her bladder suddenly announced that there would be no waiting.

Inez looked around the room and settled on the bucket. She stood up grasping the wall for her unsteady legs. She walked to the bucket while leaning on the walls. Looking down she realized from the contents in the bucket and the smell what the bucket was used for. Her bladder wasn't going to hold on any longer. She unclasped her pants and stepped to straddle the bucket. The other woman looked away to offer some privacy.

* * *

Of the two-day demand that Carl had received, one of those days was already used up. Phone calls had gotten things in gear, but Carl had no idea just how many wheels were turning. At dusk, he got his first inkling of what was about to happen.

Off in the distance the distinctive sound of helicopters could be heard. Since they sat in the middle of the Yuma Proving Ground, the noise of helicopters was certainly common enough. But this noise grew stronger and Carl walked out of the open front of the hangar to see what was approaching.

Coming in from the west, the setting sun caught the two UH-1 Iroquois transport helicopters with the sun backlighting them. Famous in the Vietnam War and affectionately called Hueys, the two machines approached the air field, lights blinking from their bellies.

One and then the other flew in along the runway as if each pilot was familiarizing themselves with the various buildings. Carl looked around and noticed they had the only building showing lights. The interior lights in the hangar carried out into the desert evening twilight.

Maneuvering around the back of the building the first Huey came back over the runway and banked left to line up with the hangar. The bow of the machine flared up as the speed dropped and, once stopped, the pilot lowered the copter onto the tarmac. The second machine swung in and settled beside the first as uniformed men unloaded off the first. Soon a large group of troops carried gear into the hangar to find an available cot.

Jack approached his son at the front of the hangar. Just before the light finally gave up on the mesa, a twin-engine transport plane swooped by and quickly lined up for landing. With its bright landing lights on, it settled onto the runway and taxied over to where the two helicopters sat. It pulled up, aimed at the hangar and then gunned its right engine as it pivoted one-hundred-and-eighty degrees. Now aimed back at the runway, the pilot switched off the engines. The side door opened and a ground crew stepped out and placed wheel blocks on the main tires. The plane's flight crew joined the others in the hangar. A single man walked over toward Jack as

Carl noticed his Uncle Ed approaching. All four men met by the open door.

"Glad you could make it," Ed said.

The man from the plane said. "I grabbed a ride over from Marine Corps Air Station after I flew commercial to Yuma."

The new man looked at both Carl and Jack and then looked at Ed. The motion was obvious to all.

"Mike, I want you to meet my brother, Jack and his son, Carl."

The three men shook hands upon being introduced. Carl noticed his Dad look carefully at the man called Mike.

"Mike. As in, owner of a canal boat in France Mike?" Jack asked.

Carl wasn't privy to the whole story, but he knew that his Dad had done something spectacular in Europe four years ago. That there had been a canal boat involved that was owned by a mysterious owner had been expressed in confidence. That that owner now seemed to be standing in front of him meant one thing to Carl. *My Uncle Ed knows some powerful people in Washington D.C. and it would appear he is pulling in all his favors to rescue my sister* Carl thought.

"Yes, unfortunately I had to sell her last year. Just wasn't using it enough. Too busy at the company," Mike said. "So, who's arrived so far?"

Mike looked hard at the gathered men and made a quick evaluation. "OK, the Aussies are here. Any sign of the Air Force yet?"

"No Air Force types yet," Ed said. "But they are on the move and will be here in the morning. Just enough time to get Jack set up and on his way to Mexico."

"What? My Dad isn't actually going to meet these guys?" Carl asked.

The three others looked at him. Greg walked over briskly and Mike turned to greet him. The two embraced with much backslapping.

"I'm glad you're here, Greg," Mike said.

Carl was confused as everyone seemed to know each other. But he dwelled on his Dad going to Mexico to meet the kidnappers.

"I don't think my Dad should be going to Mexico. That's what these guys want. He'll be dead as soon as they get their hands on him," Carl said.

"Son, it's the only way. We have to find where Inez is being kept," Jack said. The other three men all nodded agreement.

"We will be watching the entire time, and as soon as we get the signal, we will send in the cavalry and rescue both of them," Ed said. "And we know Daniel is still in Las Vegas?"

"Confirmed this afternoon. Nothing will happen until he gets to Mexico. He'll want to be there," Mike said.

"For my Dad to die," Carl said.

Jack took his son by the shoulders and walked him into the hangar where they could alone. He turned to face his son.

"Carl, it's the only way. I've talked it over with Ed and he assures me that they will know where I am at all times. And these guys that just showed up are very capable to come and get me."

"Who are these guys anyway?" Carl asked. He could see Sir Graham over with the contingent that arrived by helicopter. He was shaking hands as he chatted with the troops.

"Just between you and me, and never to leave this room. This operation is definitely off the books as they say," Jack offered. "Graham is meeting the Australian SAS special forces. They are here in Yuma training with the Marines in Long Range Patrols. They fought together in Kandahar, Afghanistan, and train together regularly."

Just as Jack was about to explain who else was involved, Graham walked over. He took Jack by the arm and led him toward the Australian troops. Carl fell in behind.

"Gentleman, I'd like you to meet the man you are helping. My good friend Jack Wesley is the real hero of London and if he had been more agreeable, would have been mentioned by the Queen."

Each of the troops stepped forward and shook Jack's hand, giving him kudos for a job well done. As

Carl stood watching his Dad receive the recognition of whatever had happened in London, Carl's mind clicked on the Sir Graham Elphinston story. He had been knighted by the Queen for breaking up a terrorist attack on the Crown which had also targeted the British Prime Minister as well as the German Chancellor. Carl remembered that the French President had been killed during the attack. He had been suspicious that his Dad had been involved and now he was getting confirmation.

Soon the troops were shaking Carl's hand and telling how his Dad saved the day. As things were settling down, Carl heard someone announce the Germans had arrived.

A van pulled up in front of the hangar. The doors flew open and more troops in camouflage stepped out. The back was opened and gear was retrieved. The van soon drove off and the newly arrived personnel entered the hangar. As they set their gear down by a cot, the Australians gathered around and greeted them.

The new arrivals dropped their gear and then headed to the plane sitting outside. Two members went inside while the six others stood outside the door. Soon more gear was being off loaded and carried into the hangar. Carl stared at the automatic weapons. When the Panzerfaust came out, Carl stepped back. The German's had invented the first rocket propelled grenade, or Panzerfaust, in World

War II. Refined and improved since, the shaped charge in the warhead could cut through tank armor.

The hangar became a buzz of activity as the sixteen troops all bent to the task of preparing for their mission. Ed and Mike were busy in one corner making a rudimentary model of their attack. At about midnight it was announced that lights out would happen and everyone needed to get some sleep. Things would happen fast in the morning and everyone needed to be ready.

Carl had a cot by his Dad and he purposely pushed it close. Laying down together side by side, Carl put his arm on his Dad for protection.

"Son, it will work out. And when we're done, Daniel and his crew will never cloud our life again," Jack said.

"Just come back alive, Dad, that's all I care about."

Chapter 16

Yuma, Arizona

Carl was rudely awakened at first light by the roar of a large plane doing a flyby of the open hangar. He pulled on his boots and stood up. He grabbed his fleece for warmth in the cool desert air. While enough light shown for a landing on the runway, the sun had not broken the horizon.

Carl had had trouble falling asleep as he worked through all the things that could go wrong. His Dad was going to be placed in harm's way and that frightened him. If not for his sister needing rescue, Carl knew that the job his Dad was about to do was almost suicidal. But he knew his Dad. There would be nothing that would keep him from saving either Inez or himself if that's what was required.

The others had all risen and had gathered around the small kitchen. Coffee and doughnuts were being eaten as Jack and Graham worked making eggs and ham. Men were lingering in groups as they all talked over their mission. With the roar of the big plane, they all walked out to the front of hangar to see what was arriving.

Carl stepped up and saw a Hercules C-130 transport plane lining up on the runway. The plane slowed and settled onto the pavement. The four engines roared as it slowed and, once stopped, turned around and taxied back to the hangar. It took up a position opposite the other transport plane beside one of the helicopters. It pivoted into place and, before its engines were even shut down, the large rear ramp began to drop.

Carl noticed four men in U.S. Air Force uniforms inside waiting for the ramp to touch the tarmac. Once down, the plane was unloaded. A mechanical mule that had room for one driver atop it pulled a four-wheeled box off the plane. The mule's small size was overshadowed by the size of the box, but it had enough power to pull the unit into the hangar.

The four airmen went to work opening up the panels of the metal box. Soon, displays and keyboards were revealed as two of the men sat down on the consoles on rolling chairs stacked inside the box. Next the mule went back into the C-130 and soon pulled out a wheeled generator. That was maneuvered into position just outside the hangar and a large power cable was snaked up to the console. Attaching the cable, the two operators sat and warmed up the electronics.

There was noise outside and Carl looked out to see a drone fly down the runway and land. Soon after a second drone landed as both taxied by themselves over to the hangar. Carl spotted his uncle talking to Mike and made a quick trip to join them. Jack came up right behind him.

"Jack, our electronic tracking just showed up," Ed said.

"Two Reapers. Next generation of the Predator drone that everyone is familiar with," Mike said.

"How did you ever get them?" Jack asked.

Before anyone could answer, an Air Force captain stepped off the plane. He walked right over and took Mike's hand and introduced himself.

"Well Captain, glad to have you here," Mike said.

"I assume everyone here is cleared for this operation?" the captain asked.

Carl moved slightly behind his Dad as he wasn't sure what his status was. He didn't even know how his Dad was gathering all this war-making personnel and material. But he was determined to be part of it, so kept quiet and unobtrusive.

"We're good, Captain," Mike said. "Ed Wesley, with the U.S. Senate."

The two shook hands. Then Mike turned toward Jack. "And Jack Wesley. It's his daughter that's been kidnapped."

"Sorry to hear that, sir. Major Reiner and I served together in Special Ops when we were at Cannon Air Force base with the 27th Special Operations Wing."

"Well, my daughter and the major were supposed to be enjoying their honeymoon together," Jack said.

The two men looked at each other aware of the couple's plight.

"Don't worry, sir, we'll get them back," the captain said.

"So you are going to be my eyes in the sky to track me, my brother says," Jack said.

"Roger that. Let's get started."

The captain took Jack over to the large box that was now operational, four operators sitting at their consoles. Outside a fuel truck arrived and began fueling the drones. The small transport plane was then fueled followed by the two helicopters.

"Ok sir, we need you wired up, so to speak. Please take off your shoes."

Jack slipped off his shoes and the captain went to work installing a radio direction finder in one of them. An RDF would send a signal up to the drone and Jack's location would be displayed on the console.

With his shoes back on, the captain took out a belt from his kit bag. He handed it to Jack and instructed him to replace his own belt with the new one. It held an RDF device in the buckle. A syringe looking device was retrieved and Carl grew nervous.

"We are going to inject an RDF in your upper arm. We'll place a Band-Aid over it and hopefully they won't notice. Just keep your arms down if you can so they can't see your inner arm," the captain said.

Once the device was inserted, the captain pulled out another small device. He held it up so Jack could see it.

"This is the one you will break when you locate your daughter and Major Reiner. It will sit in your mouth back in a corner. When you find them, crush it with your teeth. If you can, spit it out where it won't be noticed."

"Can I swallow it?" Jack asked.

"Not advised," the captain said. "There is a small lithium battery inside that will erode in your stomach and they can burn in their decaying. With the signal going dead we will know where all three of you are."

"And if they discover all the RDF devices. What then?" Carl asked. He stepped out from around his Dad, but Jack stopped him. His hand on Carl's arm said it all.

The others all looked at the two with the question unanswered. They all knew the chances of Jack surviving if Daniel found all the devices were slim.

At the stress on his nephew's face, Ed spoke up. "We know from DEA surveillance where Daniel's compound is. We assume that Inez and Eric are there. We just don't know which building they will be in."

The Drug Enforcement Agency, or DEA, knew many things in their investigation of all the drug cartels. Daniel's group was small but well known. Nothing had ever been done about them before since most of the operation was conducted in Mexico where the DEA couldn't go legally. And Daniel kept his business in Las Vegas out of the way such that the DEA hadn't gathered the necessary facts to arrest him.

Greg walked over. "We are ready to outline the rescue and then we need to get moving. Things may be tied up at the border so we need plenty of time to cross."

Carl was taken aback by this neighbor talking like he was going with his Dad to Mexico. *I have barely gotten to know him and now he is in a critical spot in this rescue* Carl thought.

Everyone was gathered around a mockup of the compound in Mexico. On the wall was a large map of the San Luis Rio Colorado area. Mike stepped to the opposite side of the model from the others.

"Ok, listen up. We are all here now. Mr. Wesley will leave soon for the border. He will be accompanied by Greg and Karma who will drop him off at the described pick-up spot. I will cross soon after in a separate van with communication gear to coordinate."

He pointed to the map and outlined San Luis Rio Colorado. Then he moved to the small village marked Islita.

"The compound is just southwest of Islita which is nine miles south west of San Luis. Captain, please add your portion."

A captain with the Australian SAS stood up and walked to the map. As a special operations unit modeled after the famous British Special Air Squadron, or SAS, he had been on many missions. He coolly outlined what his part of the rescue involved.

"We will be inserted by one of the Hueys just two kilometers southwest of the compound. We will go in at night, which will be just after our target meets with his kidnapper. We will move to the west side of the compound and await orders to attack."

He then offered his outlook on the model of the compound. Since they didn't knew where the people were to be rescued, they would have to make an attack plan when and if they received that information.

"Good work, Captain. I know we can rely on you and your men."

Then Mike turned to the other group that had arrived by van. "Sergeant, if you please. And I'm glad to have the KSK here with us."

Carl turned to Ed standing next to him. In a low voice he asked what KSK stood for.

"KSK is short for Kommando Spezialkrafte, or the special forces for the German Army. They were training nearby at the John F. Kennedy Special Warfare Center in the free fall school."

The German sergeant then announced that his eight men would parachute to a spot east of the compound from the twin-engine plane outside. They would then make their way to the compound and link up with Mike, Greg, and Karma.

Next, the Air Force captain explained that the Reaper drones would maintain constant coverage over the compound. In addition, each Reaper carried six Griffin guided missiles for attacks on the ground. Smaller than the normal two Hellfire missiles the Reaper carried, the Griffin had a thirteen-pound warhead that would be more than adequate for the buildings in the compound.

"So, any questions?" Mike said as he stepped up again. "If not, everyone double check their gear. Make sure that the comm links work. We don't need any friendly fire accidents."

The group broke up with the troops heading back to their bunks where their weapons waited. The pilots went to check their machines, which left the Wesley family standing together.

"Well, I guess I need to get going," Jack said.

Carl hugged his Dad and held on. His eyes began to water up as Jack reassured him that things would work out fine. Inez and Eric would be back in the U.S. and they could all head back to Montana together.

Greg walked over and stood by quietly. Karma pulled the rental car up out front and waited at the wheel. As a small dark individual, of the three, he looked the most Mexican. They figured that might speed up the process of entering Mexico. Not that Karma knew any Spanish. And they weren't carrying any weapons or other things that would set them apart. They were just three tourists heading across the border for a quick visit.

Jack finally said his goodbyes and walked to the car. He climbed into the front seat as Karma sat in the driver's seat. Greg took up the rear seat. Carl knew they would be at the border within the hour so walked over to the air force console and watched as the first Reaper's engine turned over.

The operator sat and viewed the video display while just outside the rear-engined drone taxied out to the runway. The propeller-driven unmanned plane could linger airborne for 24 hours. At that time the second Reaper would be dispatched to take over surveillance.

Mike made his way to a cargo van parked near the hangar and drove off. With the Reaper airborne, both Jack's location and Mike's van were displayed on the console. Carl stood and prayed that this was all going to work.

Chapter 17

San Luis, Mexico

The drive from Yuma to the border crossing at San Luis had been uneventful except for one thing. Jack noticed Greg laying down on the back seat of the rental car. His eyes were closed the entire time, only sitting up when Karma warned him they were approaching the border.

Jack turned to see Greg struggle to sit upright. He had his left eye closed and the look of pain showed on his face. Greg stared straight ahead with his one open eye without comment. Jack turned as they approached the U.S. side of the border. Karma slowed as the Homeland Security personnel manning the gate looked them over. He waved them through.

The traffic was heavy once in no-man's land between border stations. The crossing at San Luis was not a big one and the early time of day meant more people moving north entering the U.S. The north line congestion contrasted with those heading south and they were soon at the Mexican gate.

"Passports please," the guard asked.

Karma handed over the three passports and waited while the guard looked at each carefully. After Jack's American passport was expected, he slowed on

Greg's British passport and finally stopped on Karma's Nepali passport.

"What is your reason for visiting Mexico?" he asked.

Jack was the one that answered. "Just showing some out-of-town guests a little of your country."

"Open the trunk please, and I need to see the papers on the car."

Jack had anticipated driving the rental car into Mexico and had stated so at the rental agency. Rentals in southern California routinely entered Mexico and the clerk had just added the extra insurance that the Mexican government required. He also added the cost the company charged for the risk to their vehicle that Mexico threatened.

Jack walked back to the rear of the car, papers in hand. He showed them to the official. After a cursory look in the trunk, he slammed the lid down. Then he reviewed the rental agreement.

"This is your rental, yes?"

Jack noted that his name was on the rental contract.

"I don't see any other drivers listed."

"Sorry, I forgot. I'll be driving in Mexico the entire time."

The guard looked at him carefully and then back at the papers.

"OK, you may proceed."

Jack walked up to the driver's door and motioned to Karma that he would be driving. The Gurkha climbed out and walked around the front of the car, sitting down in the passenger seat. Jack climbed into the driver's seat and immediately racked the seat back to fit, the one-foot difference between them noticeable.

"Enjoy your visit," the guard said and handed the papers back to Jack. He stamped each passport and marked the date on each. As the passports were returned, the gate went up, Jack slipped the transmission into gear and drove off.

The GPS unit on the dashboard showed the route to the designated rendezvous spot. Since they were early, once Jack reached San Luis Rio Colorado proper he found a restaurant to stop at. Being an Americanized version of a fast food place, the three ate slowly, waiting out the time.

By the time lunch was completed, Greg was looking a little better. His color was back and the stress of pain on his face had subsided. Karma sat showing no emotion at all to his friend's plight.

"You know, Jack, we could tail you once you get picked up. It's a lot to trust all those little electronic gizmos," Greg said.

"Too much risk of you being spotted. I'll trust the Reaper to track me. You just make sure you meet up with the team when they land."

"No worries on that mate. We have our GPS coordinates locked in if the compound is where your daughter and her husband are being held."

"And if anything goes wrong, I want to thank all of you for sticking your neck out for me and mine," Jack said.

"It's going to go like clockwork Jack, so don't worry."

I wish I could Jack thought.

* * *

Back at Yuma Proving Grounds, Carl was intently following the flight of the Reaper over the Mexican border. The little glowing points represented his father as he sat waiting for his meeting with the drug gang. Mike with the van showed up just entering Mexico at the same crossing. The console operator provided Jack's location to Mike by secure communications link.

Ed Wesley walked over to Carl and put his arm on his shoulder. Carl had always been close to his Dad's one sibling, at least whenever they had gotten together over the years. Ed lived in Wyoming the whole time of Carl growing up. But due to Ed's job in Washington D.C., he only saw him when they did a camping road trip to Jackson Hole.

Those visits had been the exciting part of car trips with the family. Ed led a different lifestyle than his brother and Carl loved the difference. Ed's car collection or his spectacular house overlooking the Teton Mountain range were all impressionable to a young boy. And Ed's job as Chief of Staff to a congressman at that time was exotic compared to his Dad's life as a cop.

"Things are going well," Ed said.

"So far, you mean. Dad hasn't met his captives yet," Carl said.

"At least everyone is safely in Mexico. We just need to get the full team inserted and in position when we know where you sister and Eric are."

"If they are where we think that is. They could be anywhere."

"We have good people who know their work. It will work even if we have to make adjustments."

Carl realized the airmen were listening to their conversation, so Carl took Ed outside by the helicopters. Now alone, he asked, "How does Dad swing all of this? I know you have connections, but the Germans and the Australians? And how did this Greg guy just happen to be living next door to us in Missoula?"

"Carl, slow down," Ed said. "Greg is retired British SAS. The Crown asked him to babysit Jack just for such an occasion as this. It seems he jumped at the chance to live in the American West."

"The Crown, as in the Queen?"

"Your Dad saved her life as well as the Prime Minister's life. While Graham got all the credit, the Crown felt some measure of security for your Dad was called for."

"And Karma?"

"Old friend of Greg's from the SAS days, I guess. And the Aussie SAS troops were the closest British unit to Yuma at the time they were needed. That Graham showed up just sort of lent a stronger connection to them joining us."

"And the Germans?"

"Again, when your Dad saved the Queen, he also saved the German Chancellor," Ed said. "And again, the KSK troops just happened to be training here in Yuma, so they were included."

"And the air force?"

"Well, we didn't want any Americans going over into Mexico and starting something, so the only Americans are sitting by the console monitoring things. And Eric is one of theirs."

"Are they here because of you?" Carl asked.

"Sort of. Mike is the one with the real connections, but you never saw Mike. That's the rule. Mike never exists anywhere."

"I understand, Uncle Ed." Carl was glad that he was getting some inside information and that his uncle trusted him enough to fill him in. He knew that there was more to the story, but he would let the rest come to him if his uncle wanted to elaborate. Like how do drones, planes, and copters cross and recross the border without any red flags going off? Homeland Security would obviously see such things on their radar, so someone had to know what was happening. But if Mike really was who he was, then such flights could be made to disappear.

The day wore on and the time for Jack's rendezvous grew closer. Everyone made their way to the air force operators to watch the pick-up and where it would lead. The troops were ready and would fly off as soon as it was dark. Carl looked at the gear lined up on the hangar floor and imagined it all being used to free his sister and her husband.

As the designated time approached, Jack's indicators started moving as he drove to the drop off. All five RDF devices were live and active. In addition, the transponder the airman had put on the rental car was showing on the screen, as well as Mike's van and its transponder.

Soon the car showed itself moving off from dropping Jack and heading south toward Islita. The car stopped on the outskirts of San Luis Rio Colorado and sat. The van stayed near Jack's RDF lights.

A few minutes later and Jack's lights were moving. Someone had picked him up and were now heading south out of town. The five lights stayed steady as the Reaper circled over the Sonoran Desert high enough not to be noticed.

Once out of town, the lights stopped. When they started moving again, two lights stayed in place while three moved on. The three moving glows on the console passed the rental car transponder and continued toward the compound. Meanwhile, back in the desert the belt and the shoe were sitting by the side of the road.

"OK, we lost two signals on our target, the belt and the shoe," the Air Force captain said. "But we have three still."

The van transponder was moving also as it kept a safe distance behind Jack. The rental car and the van transponders passed each other as one vehicle went by the other.

Carl was imagining what was taking place across the border. His Dad was now in the hands of the gang that wanted revenge for their leader's death. Carl said a quiet prayer that everything would come out safely. And so far, the bad guys were heading right toward the compound as planned.

Chapter 18

Islita, Mexico

Jack lay in the trunk of a car without his shoes and pants. When his ride had arrived, two Mexican nationals had offered him the back seat. As they were in front of a bodega shop and in a very public spot, Jack knew that the drug gang would be careful not to draw attention to themselves. Although in this part of Mexico, Jack was sure the cops were all on the payroll.

It was when they had reached the outskirts of the city that the driver had stopped. The passenger stepped out and opened the back door for Jack to get out. He had a 9mm handgun in his hand to assure compliance. Once standing, the driver popped the latch for the trunk and the other one motioned Jack to the rear of the car.

There Jack was instructed to take off his shoes and pants. He was then motioned into the trunk and the lid slammed shut. He still had three RDF devices on him and he imagined the Reaper tracking his path. He knew there was a very competent cavalry waiting to ride over the hill to rescue him. He just had to locate Inez and Eric before he made that happen.

After some time and many turns as if the driver was making sure they weren't being followed, the car settled into a smooth highway ride. A right turn onto a gravel road and then a stop. That was followed by a short drive forward as if they had entered the compound. Jack knew from the aerial photographs he had studied that the compound was about 200 meters square with ten foot walls all around it. There was one gated entrance large enough for a vehicle. He listened intently and thought he heard the squeak of steel on steel of a gate closing.

The trunk was released and Jack looked up at two people holding AR-15 type rifles on him. At least he assumed they were semi-automatic. With drug money, they could have been fully automatic weapons. He didn't plan on getting close enough to find out.

As he lay in the trunk, a large Mexican walked up and grabbed his arms. A zip tie was produced and Jack's wrists were quickly secured. Then the man yanked Jack out of the trunk and helped him stand up.

The two rifle-totting-guards had backed up as the unarmed man took over. He slammed Jack hard in the stomach with his fist and Jack fell to his knees. Jack received a knee to the side of the head and he fell to the ground. Kicked in the side, Jack pulled himself into a ball for protection.

"Let me introduce myself. I'm Alfonso."

"Where's my daughter, asshole?" Jack asked.

He received another kick to his side in answer.

"You'll see your whore daughter soon enough. But first let me give you something from Ernesto. You remember Ernesto, the guy you burned to death."

Alfonso bent down and swung hard at Jack's face. The fist caught him against his cheekbone and Jack's head slammed into the ground. The taste of blood filled his mouth. Jack set his left hand on the ground for support to raise himself up. Alfonso stomped hard onto the hand. The pain of bones breaking made Jack roll over onto the opposite side. As he clutched his hand to his chest for protection, Alfonso kicked him again in the back.

Blood was filling his mouth and it was all Jack could do to keep the RDF tucked away in the back of his gum. He carefully spit blood out while making sure the RDF stayed in his mouth. Trying to spit while his tongue was occupied meant the blood just splattered out of his mouth.

"Get him out of here. Daniel will be here tomorrow. The real fun begins then, hombre."

Two new guards showed up and grabbed Jack by his two arms. They dragged him toward a small cinder block building. Jack tried to locate himself inside the compound so he could maintain his location. He thought they were taking him to the building in the southeast corner of the compound.

They both dropped him on the ground as one took a key and unlocked the door. Swinging inward, they forced the heavy metal door open.

Grabbing him once again, they stepped into the dark and dropped him. They turned, slammed the door shut and locked it.

Jack felt hands on him in the dark. He let more blood ooze out of his mouth making sure the RDF was safe.

"Dad?" a quiet voice said.

"Inez?" Jack said back.

"Oh Daddy, you came for me."

The two bodies found each other in the dark. The room had no windows or openings. Little light filtered in through the cracks under the eaves where they didn't match up with the tops of the walls. The compound had lights illuminating the entire area outside, and just enough light made it way into the room.

"Daddy, you're hurt," Inez said. She began to run her fingers over Jack to assess the damage. Jack groaned in pain when she hit a more sensitive spot.

"Are you both here? I don't hear Eric," Jack asked.

There was a long pause which Jack knew didn't bode well. He waited, holding his breath.

"Daddy, they killed him. On the boat trip down."

Jack managed to sit up against the wall and did his best to console his daughter. She had been kidnapped and locked up, her new husband killed, and who knows what else. He wanted to hold her and make it all go away.

But it wouldn't all go away. He knew his daughter would be scared. Every father dreads being unable to protect his children, especially daughters. He heard her crying.

He pulled the RDF device out of the side of his gum and positioned it between his front teeth. He bit down as hard as he could. Once he had two pieces of RDF device in his mouth, he maneuvered each piece and bit again. Once he had four pieces, he took all four pieces out of his mouth with his good hand. He stood up, the pain in his kidneys being most noticeable, and turned to the wall.

Jack felt the top of the wall and found what he was looking for. The cinder block building did not have a plate along the top. The rafters had just been tied to some re-bar imbedded in the blocks. In between the rafters the blocks were open all the way down to the footing. He dropped the RDF into a void and checked that they didn't land on the top of the block.

Sitting down again, he spit out more blood and it ran down the front of his shirt. He had completed his mission, and now it was up to others to finish things.

* * *

"We have confirmation of the location," the air force captain said over the radio. "Southeast corner building. The mouth RDF went dead five minutes ago. Arm and crotch RDF still functioning."

"Roger that. Building in the south east corner," Mike replied over the radio. Greg and Karma were sitting in the back of the van with him. The three had met up when it was determined that the compound was indeed the location.

The van held ladders on top with a painting company name on the side for a disguise. Antennas for communicating sat hidden among the ladders on the roof rack. Parked on a side road away from the compound made sure it didn't attract attention. The rental car was nearby.

This part of the Sonoran Desert held irrigated fields. Along the road were small dwellings spaced out over the land. It was a rural setting and any vehicle would stand out if not related to farming. But since it was night and they would be gone by morning they were confident no one would pay them much attention.

The three knew that the troops would be loading up for their trip to Mexico. The eight KSK special forces would be in their parachutes, their gear bags hooked onto their harness. They would load up into the twin-engine Aviocar transport for the trip south. The German pilots who had been assigned for their jump would fly them and drop them.

Next to the German team, the Aussie SAS special forces team would load up one of the UH-1 Iroquois. The Australian pilot for the Huey would take off with night goggles on and insert his team at the designated spot.

Greg sat in the van waiting. He was anxious for the KSK team to drop on their location. He and Karma had left their gear bag with them to be brought over the border - things that they would need but wouldn't pass Customs inspection.

As they received the signal that the KSK troops had jumped, they knew they had the van's transponder for a target. Greg stepped out of the van and walked to the rear doors. He looked up into the night sky to see if he could see anything, the stars of a clear night the only things visible. The dark desert held no man-made light and with no moon, the night was total.

Whisking sound was the only indication of the troops' arrival. Thumps of parachuters hitting the ground soon were evident around him as Greg waited. Karma joined him as they stared out into the bleak nighttime scene at nothing. Suddenly a soldier loomed up out of the dark and walked to them. He had his monocular nighttime scope down with his Heckler and Koch HK416 assault rifle ready.

"Colonel Roberts, off to your left," Karma said.

Greg turned to see all seven KSK troops lined up. The German sergeant in front of them reported in.

"We have your bag sir."

Greg and Karma zipped open the bag and pulled out their equipment. They climbed into the body armor first and then swung their combat webbing kit on. Attached were extra magazines for their M4A1 assault rifles. Different from the H&K that the German's used, the British used the American version assault rifle.

They both clipped their assault rifles onto their webbing and then shoved pistols into the pouch on the vest. Communication gear was placed on their heads as they checked for its operation. Satisfied they were tied into the net, they changed pants and boots from civilian clothes. Karma slid his kukri knife into its sheath while Greg added a standard combat blade. They were ready.

"Sergeant, have one of your men set the rental car," Greg ordered.

One of the troops took the rental car to the main highway close by and parked it on the side of the road. He soon returned and handed a detonator to Greg who passed it on to Mike in the van.

"OK, we know where they are being held. As we outlined in our plan, we will attempt to close on the compound and if we can reach it undetected, we will pass that on to you. You have your entrance device?" Greg asked.

"Yes sir. I have one of my men ready for breaching. Just tell us when," the German sergeant said.

"Ok Karma, ready?"

The Gurkha needed no invitation and moved out. Greg fell in behind as they quickly marched toward the compound. Greg had spotted a drainage ditch coming out of the compound toward the highway. If they could crawl up the ditch they might make the compound walls unnoticed. He did not know if the drug gang had night vision, but assumed they had the money to afford it. Whether they felt threatened in this part of Mexico and would be that careful was another question.

Karma slipped down into a ditch that led toward the compound. The lights inside the compound shown over the walls and made locating the site easy. It would also make night vision difficult to use for anyone inside the compound. The compound had a tower in the center that offered a clear view in all directions. But at night, the lights would interfere with seeing out past the walls.

The two men low-walked as they crouched forward, avoiding going to their hands and knees. Greg felt the burn in his legs from the cramped walking along with the extra weight of weapons and gear. While he had always been a hard-ass when he was active duty, the retired life had changed his conditioning.

But the little Nepali didn't seem to mind any of it. And from his experience with Gurkhas, they would never show weakness. Halfway to the compound, Greg had to stop. The pain in his head was excruciating. He pulled a pill bottle from one of his pockets and threw two more pills down his throat. He knew he was risking much fighting in his condition, but Greg didn't care.

Once hidden from view by the walls, they quickly moved up. Looking up, Greg considered shoving Karma up the wall and then having the Gurkha pull him up. They had done similar wall climbs in many years of training. The risk lay in being spotted by the guard in the tower.

A tug on his pant leg got Greg's attention. He dropped down to where Karma was lying in the ditch looking under the wall, the drainage ditch continuing into the compound. Used when heavy rains hit the area, the now dry ditch was a direct line inside. Except that when the wall was built, someone had placed lengths of re-bar across the opening to block access.

"We didn't bring anything to cut it," Greg whispered into his comm set.

"Very rusty. I'll check."

Karma turned around and slid forward feet first. He kicked hard at the re-bar. Greg bent down to see if there was any movement. Karma kicked again and his boot went through one bar. He lowered his boot and kicked at the lowest blockage. Three kicks and it let go. He moved up and kicked but nothing moved. He climbed out and took a strap off his webbing. Using the sheath with Greg's knife in it as a tourniquet, Karma wound the webbing around the two bars above the two broken ones.

The tightening webbing pulled the two bars together as Karma twisted. Reaching for the two broken bars, he pulled them toward him and bent them out of the way. He turned over on his back and moved his head under the bent bar. Then, shimmying and kicking with his feet, his body slipped under the re-bar. He moved out of the way inside the compound while remaining in the ditch.

Greg had watched the smaller man just fit through the opening. He took off his web kit and shoved it inside the walls. Then he took off his body armor and placed that inside. He flopped onto his back and moved his head under the re-bar. As his chest reached the bent bar he pushed up in the bar while exhaling and just made it under the bar. His hips and legs followed and he was now inside the compound. He threw his gear back on and retrieved his knife.

Joining Karma in the ditch, they surveyed their location. With their rifles trained on the tower about 100 meters away, they located the building holding Jack in the southeast corner. Located 100 meters to their left, two guards stood outside holding rifles, open ground between the ditch and the guards.

Greg slid down into the ditch so he was out of sight. He needed to contact the outside world.

"We are inside the compound and have located the building. Have everyone move up to point Tango and be ready. Initiate Griffon strike in fifteen minutes by my mark," Greg said.

One after another the KSK sergeant confirmed the orders followed by the SAS captain and finally the Air Force captain confirmed the time to start. Greg pulled Karma back into the ditch and got ready. *All hell is about to break loose and we need to be hunkered down as much as possible* Greg thought.

Greg motioned to Karma which guard each would take out when the excitement started. Karma acknowledged his target. They were ready.

Chapter 19

San Diego, California

Twenty-four hours prior to Greg and Karma crawling through the ditch into the compound, a young couple strolled along Black's Beach in San Diego. And in keeping with the tradition, they were naked. Black's Beach was world famous for being clothing optional. Sitting just below the University of California at San Diego campus, new students to both UCSD and college life would experiment with new things. And swimming nude in the Pacific Ocean late at night had appealed to both of them. It would be a Saturday evening break from studying.

The term was young and life was free for these two freshmen, and the reputation of Black's Beach had preceded them. Parking in Torrey Pines State Park, they had hiked the two miles to where the nudist portion started. Taking off their clothes, they had shoved them into a day pack. Leaving the pack in the dry sand, they had run into the water. The warm ocean felt marvelous on their bodies and they moved closer and embraced. Soon they were overcome with desire as the waves knocked them about.

Struggling to find their footing, the woman had climbed into the man's arms and wrapped her legs around him. She was inviting him to take more when something had bumped her in the back. She had turned but in the dark couldn't see anything. Another bump and she had reached behind her and felt a head. Screaming, she had kicked her male partner as she ran from the water.

"My God, it's a body," she had screamed.

"Oh shit, where?" her male friend had asked. He stood in the water where they had been standing. A new wave rolled in and he had screamed, running out of the water.

"Did you see it?" she had asked.

"Shit yeah. Jesus, what do we do?"

"Get dressed. We need to get out of here," she had answered.

The young man took his clothes and handed the woman hers. They had quickly dressed but as the young woman had started north back to their car, the young man had stopped her.

"No, this isn't right. The body may float off. We need to contact the authorities and stay with the body until they come," he had said.

"I'm not staying, so let's go. Right now." She had said with as much threat as she could muster.

"You can go if you want, but I'm staying."

The young man walked over to where the body was rolling slowly up the beach as each wave hit it. While it appeared to be headed to a firm place on drier sand, the young man knew that was not a certainty. He sat down in the dry sand.

"Are you kidding me?" the young woman said. "I don't believe this."

"Do you have your cell phone?" the man had asked.

"Use your own damn phone."

"It didn't have any power so it's back in the dorm charging. Just give me your phone."

The woman had stomped over to where the man sat and held it out to him. She had as much of a scowl on her face as she could make, but in the dark the man didn't really see it. He had taken the phone and dialed 911. Soon he was talking to emergency dispatch personnel explaining the situation. He had clicked off and handed the phone back to the woman.

"Thank you. They are sending the fire rescue boat out."

She plopped down in the sand next to him. "And we wait until they show?"

"Yes," was all he had said.

The two sat silent as the body continued its slow roll up the wet sand. Soon only the bigger waves moved it as the surf continued to roll in. Since the swells were not large the rescue boat would be able to beach itself without risk. The dispatcher had explained that Black's Beach was inaccessible by land at high tide as the points of land jutting out on both ends blocked passage.

The man had discovered that they would not be getting off the beach until low tide or daylight. There was a trail down the cliff from directly above but he had heard you should only use it in daylight. There was too much risk in the dark.

As the slow steam of an unhappy female had shrouded any conversation, the young man sat watching the body. Seeing the lights of the fire rescue boat come around the headland, he raised the flashlight he had brought for their hike and turned it on. He stood and made a sweeping motion with the light so it would be recognized out on the water.

The boat was soon just offshore where it turned inland. Bright lights on the boat lit up the area in front of them so the operator could judge the waves. It was soon scraping onto the beach a short distance to the couple's right. A fireman stepped off the boat with an anchor, walked a short distance up the beach and had dropped it in the sand.

As the operator raised the twin outboards, the other two crew had walked over to where the couple now stood. One of the crew went to check the body while the other approached the couple. Being a long time resident of San Diego, the fireman had known what the couple had been up to on the beach, so skipped that question.

"How long ago did you discover the body?" the fireman had asked.

"About ten minutes before we called," the man answered.

"Ok. We'll load up the body now but I'd like to give you a ride back where you can answer some more questions."

The woman had spoken first, "Do we have to? We called it in. Isn't that good enough? We didn't put the thing here."

"You're welcome to stay. I'll just need one of your names and addresses in case the police need to speak to you."

"The police. We haven't done anything wrong," the woman said.

"Didn't say you did. Just normal procedures with a thing like this."

The young man spoke up. "It isn't a problem. I'll provide you with what you need."

The fireman had thanked the young man before he enquired on the ride out, "If you skip the ride you'll be here till morning when low tide opens up the access."

The young woman stomped toward the boat in frustration. The young man had shrugged in response and the fireman had accepted the man's response as if to say he had seen it all in his career.

As the woman climbed into the boat, the dead body lay in the bow, its foot hanging over the gunwale. "I have to ride with that?" she exclaimed as she pointed to the body.

The firemen had shook their heads in response as the two crew shoved the boat out into deeper water. The twin outboards were lowered into the water and started. When the two crew clambered aboard, the operator hit the throttle. The boat swung into the waves and climbed each one until it reached deeper water. Swinging south toward San Diego Bay, the boat ran through the night with its six people on board, five holding on tight.

By ten in the morning the coroner had the body in the morgue and an attendant was examining the body. The young man who had called the body in had answered as many questions as needed and had headed home alone. The woman had disappeared as soon as they had docked.

The dead body had been in the ocean for some time and the normal abuses the sea plays on human flesh had taken place. The face had been eaten away as well as other small parts of the body. The gas that had formed allowed the body to rise to the surface and float ashore and had stretched the body in a bloated fashion. As the attendant slowly moved over the body, the county coroner walked in to perform an autopsy.

"Is the body all ready?" the doctor had asked.

"Just looking for any obvious markings. I think I have one here."

"Where?" the doctor asked and moved around the table to where the attendant stood. Pointing out a tattoo still visible on the dead body's upper arm, the doctor moved in close to examine the markings, turning his head to take in the shapes better. After running his gloved fingers over the skin, he had stopped. He had stood up and looked at the attendant. "Put him in a locker. I need to make a call."

As the doctor pulled off his latex gloves and turned to leave, the attendant grabbed a gurney to load the body onto so he could move it into a refrigerated storage chamber. It would be kept cool until the doctor needed it for an examination.

The doctor had recognized the tattoo from his time in the service. He worked part time for the county but was a full time doctor at the U. S. Navy Medical Center at Coronado. He knew the tattoos of the warriors that came through injured and this one was recognized. He placed his call and was soon transferred many times until he contacted the right unit.

* * *

At Yuma Training grounds the Reaper drone crew continued to monitor the compound from high above Mexico. The four operators had taken turns as the Reaper patrolled continuously over the operation to free the hostages.

With twenty-four hours endurance, the second Reaper sat on the tarmac outside the hangar where the crew sat at their consoles. The U. S. Air Force Captain in charge of the Reaper team stood behind his men and watched the computer screens. He was focused on the task at hand as everyone waited for events on the ground to take place.

The message was received that all units were in position, which meant that the Reaper would initiate the action. A clock had been initiated on the computer screen as the main operator maneuvered the Reaper into position. Their job was to unleash a Griffin air-to-surface missile and take out the guard tower in the center of the compound.

The captain watched intently as his airman lined up the sights on the tower. Everything was as it should be and the captain knew his part of the operation was going as planned. A cell phone buzzed in his pocket and he stepped back to answer. Far enough from his operator to not distract him, the captain accepted the call. The indicator showed the call coming from headquarters.

As he answered, his voice went silent. He grunted a few times as he mainly listened to the other person on the line. Confirming orders, he clicked off. He walked back over to the console trying to hold his composure in front of his men. It would be bad to interrupt them as they concentrated on hitting the target at the time designated by the field operatives.

Chapter 20

Islita, Mexico

Jack Wesley lay motionless on the concrete slab. The single room building he was trapped inside smelled badly, but that wasn't his chief concern. His major concern was getting his daughter Inez safely out of the trap they were in. As he was powerless to save her, he was praying that the team that had been assembled outside was doing their job. *And if they are really outside* Jack thought. *My life and that of Inez's depend on it.*

His body screamed from where he had been beaten. But he shoved all of that aside as he concentrated on how to save his daughter. They needed to be ready when the rescue came and he knew from experience that rescues came heavy, where heavy meant much gunfire and explosions.

In any hostage rescue event, the hostages needed to be as low and unobtrusive as possible. Anyone standing and moving tended to get shot. Although the cold concrete floor was uncomfortable, he had his daughter lying beside him in the middle of the building. When he had discovered another woman in the building with his daughter, he had tried to communicate her need to lay on the floor with them.

But between the language difference and her complaints of the floor being too cold, Carmen now sat on the floor, leaning against the wall opposite the door. Her feet stuck out to where Jack and Inez lay.

A terrible explosion rocked the building as the flash of a detonation lit the room. Jack moved his hands behind his head so as to lay face down. Inez followed his movement, their arms protecting their face and head. Carmen screamed and leapt to her feet at the noise of the explosion.

Jack heard two rifle pops, and assumed any guards outside their door had just been dispatched. Then two more explosions shook them as Carmen continued her screaming. Jack moved his arm over Inez to comfort her and to hold her in place. He felt her trembling as the entire compound seemed to be exploding around them. He pressed down on her body to give her the strength to weather what was coming.

Jack knew the order of things if everything went as planned. From the three explosions things seemed to be on target. The noise of the lock being removed on their metal door announced the next part of the plan. As the door swung open, the plan suddenly changed.

A loud crashing noise hit them as well as chunks of cinder block as a part of building's west wall disintegrated. Pieces of block splattered against them as a hole in the east wall announced where a heavy caliber bullet had exited the building. Two men collapsed onto Jack and Inez.

"Bloody hell, what the hell was that?" Jack heard Greg ask.

Before anyone could answer, another round hit the west wall and another huge hole blasted out chunks of cinder block leaving a second exit hole in the east wall. Jack heard automatic fire in the distance and assumed that was the Aussies and the Germans entering the compound. Jack rolled over to look at the two gaping holes in the west wall and into Greg's startled eyes.

"They must have a fifty cal," Greg said.

A fifty cal referred to the large caliber sniper rifle that had become famous recently. Often bought by gun enthusiasts, the fifty caliber round was large enough to tear through cinder block walls.

A third round answered both questions as it hit about three feet off the floor. Carmen had retreated in terror to one corner as the large bullet found her. After knocking a hole in the west wall it tore through her chest before exiting the east wall. Her body slumped onto the floor with blood and human body parts leaving a trail down the wall.

Inez screamed at the hideous mess her cell mate had become and Jack grabbed her tight to keep her on the floor. The shooter had consistently put three bullets through at about the three foot mark. If they stayed low they were out of the path and only had to contend with flying chunks of concrete.

A fourth round struck near the door and another shower of concrete and dust filled the room. Greg swiveled around to face out the door. Firing from a prone position on the ground, he shot drug cartel members as they rushed out of their lairs. Karma crawled up beside his friend and added supporting fire. A fifth round hit the west wall but this time struck the metal door propped open inside the room.

The bullet hit the heavy steel reinforcing strap that had been welded to support the weight of the door. In its work to keep the door from sagging when it opened, it also worked as a strong metal target. While it wasn't strong enough to stop the bullet, it was strong enough to deflect it. The large caliber bullet, now deformed by the metal bar, slammed into Greg lying beside the door.

Greg slumped, dropping his rifle. Jack, seeing the hit, crawled forward just as Karma turned to his friend. As Jack reached both of them it was obvious that Greg was dead. The bullet had torn into Greg's head, tearing the back of his skull off. Red and grey matter oozed from the gaping hole.

Karma, recognizing his friend was dead, dropped his rifle and took out his Kukri knife. He slithered off heading west. Jack picked up Karma's gun and took aim at any enemy within sight. He had to be careful, as he knew there were Germans and Aussies within the compound. His job was to protect his daughter as he lay in the door jamb next to Greg's body.

A seventh round crashed into the building and immediately Jack felt pain in his left leg. He turned and felt a wet spot on his leg as he stuck his finger into the hole that had been punched into him. Inez crawled up next to Jack and took up Greg's rifle.

"You know how to shoot that?" Jack asked. He moved his good hand back to the trigger as his crushed left hand made an attempt to hold the barrel.

"Pull the trigger, right?"

"One shot for each trigger pull. It's on semi mode, not full auto."

"Where did that other guy go?" Inez asked about Karma.

"I think he went to silence the fifty cal," Jack answered.

The compound grew quiet as the gunfire slowed down. The big sniper rifle had not hit the building since Jack caught the ricochet in his leg. He twisted around and crawled back to where Carmen's body lay. He ripped off her blouse and tied it around his leg. The bleeding in the dim light slowed as he found Greg's knife to use as a stick for a tourniquet.

Applying pressure, he tightened the tourniquet and his leg wound stopped bleeding. As he moved back into firing position, shots came his way from a building across the compound. He shoved Inez back into the building and returned fire. Not sure who was shooting at him, Jack knew that his team would know where he was located and would not be firing at their building.

A round struck Jack in the left shoulder, forcing him to roll to his right. His lower body, now exposed was hit by a second round in the left thigh. Jack looked out the door and saw someone rushing toward them. The man held a submachine gun on full auto. He tried to raise his rifle but his shoulder wouldn't work. His left hand was useless and he couldn't swing his rifle with just his right hand. As he struggled to take down the charging shooter, a round slammed him in the head. Jack's world went black.

* * *

The captain of the Australia SAS Special Forces raced around the corner to see the Mexican drug cartel member running for the hostages. He opened up with his M4 Carbine and the thug collapsed in the dirt. Two of his men moved up beside him in support.

The SAS had waited outside the compound walls for the Reaper drone to hit first. Once the explosion of the guard tower announced hostile intent, the borrowed Panzerfaust had blasted a hole in the west wall. He had heard a similar explosion from the east where the KSK German Special Forces had used their Panzerfaust to gain entry through the wall.

Since then, the seven SAS troops had methodically cleared each building of hostiles on the west side. Most had shot back and they had died for their effort. The captain had been very careful moving forward, as he knew the KSK would be clearing the compound from the east. And it was their job to support the main effort to rescue the hostages.

As he crouched against a wall, one of his men motioned that someone was approaching from the south. A password was spoken and the man approached. Karma walked up carrying a large caliber sniper rifle. He threw it down at the captain's feet and in his other hand he held a bloody knife. The captain understood the message being sent. The captain had worked with the Gurkhas before and knew their ability. That Karma went after the sniper with just his Kukri and had prevailed didn't surprise him. He was just glad the Gurkhas were allies and not enemies.

"We have casualties and need an evac right away," a voice come over the communication. "All clear on the east side."

The SAS captain knew that would be his German counterpart, but didn't know what casualties they had sustained. He knew all of his men were fine.

"Red team approaching hostage location," the captain announced as he instructed two of his men to move out. Soon the red team and the blue team were united. Two German special operations troops stood guard over ten captured individuals. They were against the wall where the German's had blasted a hole to enter.

The captain walked quickly to where the hostages had been held and stopped at the sight. A KSK medic was working on Jack while Colonel Roberts was obviously dead. Two of the Aussie SAS troops walked up to announce the compound was clear. Acknowledging the report, the captain turned to his counterpart in the KSK.

"What happened Sergeant?" the SAS captain asked.

"As we came through the wall we were met with heavy fire. It held us back before another Panzerfaust took out their building."

The captan looked toward the northeast corner of the compound and could make out a crumpled cinder block building. The Germans, meeting more resistance than the Aussies, had been held up on the initial entrance and, the hostages and the Colonel had suffered.

"Incoming chopper," the radio squawked. "Second heavy on its way."

The plan called for two helicopters to extract the team once the hostages had been rescued. Now with causalities, they needed to move fast.

"Sergeant, how many captures do you have?" the SAS captain asked.

"Ten sir, two women, one child and seven men."

A voice that had been listening to the exchange popped into the conversation.

"This is green team. You need to place the men in the building that had held the hostages."

Green team was the Reaper captain and his crew operating the drone. That he was injecting orders to the field commander was unusual.

"Come again, green team? This is red team commander," the SAS captain said.

"I repeat. Orders are to place captured hostiles in building previously holding hostages."

"Copy that, green team. That is not the plan."

"This is white team. Please follow new orders as per green team."

White team was the overall commander of the operation. Mike worked for the company that went unmentioned, but everyone on the operation knew where the authority was coming from.

"Yes sir," the SAS captain responded. "Any new orders on non-combat captures?" He was referring to the two women and the child.

"Follow original plan on them," came the response over the net.

The German medic had inserted an IV into Jack and had triaged his wounds as best he could. He gave a sign to his sergeant, who spoke up.

"We need to move our wounded now."

The noise outside the walls announced the arrival of the first evac helicopter. Four KSK troops lifted Jack and carried him toward the Huey. Another held Inez and helped her exit the compound over the debris and onto the helicopter.

Four more troops lifted Greg's body and moved it for evacuation. Karma climbed in beside his friend's body, buckling the seatbelt. The seven Aussie SAS troops plus their captain climbed on board the copter. As the KSK medic continued to monitor Jack, the pilot increased power and the Huey went airborne.

The original plan called for the helicopters to cross the Mexican-American border in a designated alley. Homeland Security had been informed of two planes that would be crossing and to not log them into any official report. With other clandestine operations against the drug cartels happening frequently, two more would not raise concern.

The captain rode in silence as the Huey shook its way north. In the dark he could only make out where cities lay from the air, but in one spot he saw the obvious line where Mexico moved right up to the border in lights and the American side was dark.

As the helicopter swung in to land at the army airbase, the pilot using night vision checked that the runway was clear. The light from the open hanger made landing easy, and Jack was quickly unloaded.

The C-212 Aviocar engines were already turning and the SAS moved Jack immediately onto the transport plane. Carl and Ed Wesley met Inez at the helicopter door and escorted her onto the transport plane. Moving Greg's body onto the plane, Karma climbed on board continuing his vigilance of his dead friend. The German medic joined them as the order to take off was yelled to the pilot. With one space available, Ed yelled at Graham to climb aboard. Using the training of special operations that the pilots had received in the use of night vision, the plane taxied into position on the unlit runway. The engines increased power and the brakes released. The Aviocar leapt down the runway and was soon airborne.

Chapter 21

Islita, Mexico

The remaining German special forces moved the men they had captured into the building that Jack and Inez had been held in. As the door was locked behind them, the drug cartel members instinctively moved to the opposite side of the room from the mutilated corpse that had been Carmen. The few remaining lights in the compound added to the light that filtered in through the bullet holes that had been punched into the west wall. While the east wall had smaller holes from those same bullets, it was the west holes that intrigued the captives.

The cinder blocks had been smashed and now, with effort, could be preyed loose. The seven men trapped inside the building immediately recognized their escape option and grabbed chunks of block to smash the holes bigger. While it caused fingers and hands to be bloodied, the effort seemed to be paying off as small bits of wall were knocked loose. All seven took turns working hard to gain a hole large enough to escape.

Outside, the German troops gathered the two women and the one child and stepped outside to await their helicopter. Now only speaking German as had been planned, they watched the inside of the compound for anyone who had been missed.

Soon a second helicopter flew over the compound and circled around to land. Just as it touched down, a large explosion off to the northeast lit the sky. The men moved the captives aboard and, once all the KSK troops were buckled in, the pilot lifted off.

The pilot announced the extraction as the chopper moved west from the compound. Hearing the acknowledgement of the helicopter's location, the KSK sergeant witnessed a missile strike followed by a fire ball from an explosion in the compound. He looked to see the building that held the drug cartel men reduced to rubble along with everyone inside. As the copter flew west, four more fireballs erupted from the compound as the Reaper drone unloaded its four remaining Griffin air-to-surface missiles. The KSK troops watched in silence as flames consumed the compound.

Unlike the first helicopter, this one flew west before it landed beside a lonely stretch of Mexican highway. A bark in German and the three captives were rudely shoved off the Huey. Once they had moved away from the copter, the pilot lifted off again. Now unburdened, the pilot returned to the correct course and crossed into the United States where Homeland Security waited for a second clandestine crossing.

As the helicopter landed next to the first Huey, the U.S. Air Force captain stood in the doorway of the hangar. His expression spoke volumes to the Germans as they unloaded. They walked by him as he continued to stare out towards the runway. Soon the quiet engine of a Reaper drone was heard as it settled down onto the runway before it taxied to the hangar. The captain turned, an expression of satisfaction on his face.

* * *

When word of Jack's injuries had been communicated, his brother Ed made the quick decision to transfer Jack to the Medical Center at Naval Base San Diego. It was a judgement call as to where the quickest and best treatment for Jack could be found. Yuma had a hospital, but from the news of Jack's wounds, a military facility was needed.

The Bob Wilson Naval Hospital had been treating combat injuries for years and had one of the best records for keeping wounded warriors alive in the country. But it was a tense flight as the Aviocar flew through the night to Coronado Naval Air Station where an ambulance waited.

Moved quickly from the transport plane to the ambulance, Jack rode the short distance to the hospital. A team of physicians were waiting as he was wheeled into surgery. They had been apprised of his injuries in flight by the KSK medic with the treatments he had already received. The medic had worked hard to keep Jack alive.

Seeing the amount of liquids intravenously pumped into her father, Inez had grown nervous during the flight. Upon arrival, Carl and Ed Wesley took Inez to the waiting room. She broke down crying as the three sat down.

Ed sat stunned by the condition of his niece. Covered in cinder block dust, she had blood on her from helping Jack. Ed offered to find a nurse so she could get checked out and cleaned up, but Inez refused. She would remain until news of her Dad arrived. She didn't realize how long a wait she would have. Carl joined her as they awaited news of their Dad.

* * *

Carl's wife Stacey had remained in Missoula with the two children. Carl kept her informed all along without mentioning the operation that would rescue Inez. She knew enough to not ask any questions and left it to her husband to tell her what he could.

But things had grown quiet for the past eight hours and she was beginning to worry. As she got breakfast for the children she knew that Carl should be calling soon with news. And if there was no news that meant that things had not gone well. She didn't know how badly things could go, but she knew who they were dealing with.

Violence was second nature to the drug cartels. That Jack had dared attack one member of the cartel only meant that violence was now part of her family. She worried about her children if things didn't go right in Mexico. If Inez wasn't rescued and if something happened to Jack, then the entire Wesley family would be threatened. As she looked out the window of her kitchen at the snow falling, a shiver went up her spine. Not from the cold weather outside but from the threat that hung over their lives.

As she turned to check her two sons, one in a high chair eating, the other on a booster seat at the table, a shadow moved past her back door. She froze in terror and started to reach for the handgun she kept in an upper cabinet. Carl had shown her how to use it after she insisted on her own personal protection.

As she opened the upper cabinet over the refrigerator to reach for the revolver she saw a face move up to her back door. A gentle knock followed by an accented call for her name relaxed her. She closed the cabinet door and unlocked the back door. Her neighbor from across the street stood there.

"Miguel, you startled me," Stacey said.

"Sorry, Miss Stacey. I just wanted to tell you I shoveled the front walk and now I'll get your back walk."

"Oh thank you, Miguel, but I told you the front was adequate."

"On no ma'am. I get the back walk too. Until Sir Carl gets back. How is he doing?"

"Still in Arizona, I'm afraid. But I hope he's home soon," Stacey said.

"Well, you are good until he returns. How are you for firewood? I can bring some in for you."

Carl and Stacey had a wood stove that they used for the really cold Montana nights. But while Carl was gone, Stacey relied on the natural gas furnace. *Less work than lugging in firewood* she thought.

"Firewood is fine. Again Miguel, thanks for all your help."

He waved as he retuned to shoveling her back walk. Stacey shut the door and locked it, keeping the warm air inside and the cold out. Miguel and his family of six had been a Godsend with Carl gone. They had always been good neighbors but lately they had been extra helpful. Stacey was glad she and Carl had settled in Montana where neighbors took care of each other.

* * *

Ed Wesley sat in the waiting area with his niece. Inez had finally been persuaded to have a doctor look her over as the vigil of Jack's surgery continued. Now cleaned up with some hospital clothes on, she sat with the others.

Carl continued to pace the room as his nervous energy kept him from sitting down. Graham Elphinston sat quietly by himself. At the seven-hour mark a doctor in blue surgical scrubs walked out from the restricted area. Ed stood and greeted him. Carl and Inez moved in closer to hear the news.

"Mr. Wesley is in critical condition. We have finished working on him but the news is not good."

At the news, Inez staggered. Carl grabbed her in support. Ed suggested that Carl help his sister sit down while he spoke with the surgeon. The tone tried to convey that Inez wasn't strong enough right now to be part of the conversation. Carl took the hint and moved her away.

"Go ahead doctor, you were saying?" Ed said.

"Yes, your brother is lucky to be alive," the doctor said. "Four bullet wounds would kill most men. Luckily they were 9mm bullets and not rifle rounds. And the hunk of metal we took out of his left leg wasn't a bullet at all but some sort of rusty iron that a bullet must have hit and torn a chunk off."

Ed looked over to make sure Inez was not hearing the details. She was sobbing in Carl's arms.

"What's his prognosis then?" Ed asked. He held his breath for the answer.

"The head wound did not penetrate the skull. It hit him in the forehead, traveled around the skull under the skin and exited the back of his head. What trauma it caused inside on his brain we will have to wait to see."

"And the other wounds?" Ed asked.

"Actually the round he took in his shoulder is the most troubling. He must have been laying down as the bullet went between the clavicle and the scapula, or the collarbone and the shoulder blade. The path took it straight down into his chest cavity where it punctured his right lung. It stopped very close to his heart."

"Were you able to remove it?" Ed asked.

"Yes, but the damage it caused along with the beating he took makes us very concerned about his pulmonary function, and infection."

Ed looked at the doctor with a look of a brother wanting a final answer. He needed to know if Jack would live.

"The best I can say is the next 72 hours should tell us something. Until then, I'm afraid we are only guessing," the doctor said. He shook Ed's hand and promised to return with any updates.

Ed sat down and Graham moved over to join him. The two talked over what should be done next and Ed reached a decision. He would talk it over with Carl, but not until Inez had been dealt with properly. She had been traumatized badly and needed help.

Ed found the medical director and asked that his niece be properly evaluated. There was some hesitancy on treating a civilian in a naval hospital until Ed reminded the doctor that Inez was now a widow of an Air Force Officer and that Ed's Senator sat on the Armed Services Committee in the U. S. Senate. Ed didn't really care which lever worked but, Inez was soon being treated.

As Ed was about to discuss Jack's injuries with Carl, a familiar face walked in. Mike had somehow gotten out of Mexico and found his way to San Diego.

Chapter 22

San Diego, California

The Bob Wilson Naval Hospital sat in the middle of Balboa Park in San Diego where it overlooked Coronado Bay. The view from the helicopter landing pad atop the hospital afforded a vista of the city out to the Pacific Ocean. And when no helicopter was landing or taking off, it was a place of solitude.

Although a restricted area, access was gained by two government officials who needed a place where no one would overhear what needed to be discussed.

Ed explained Jack's injuries to his friend Mike. As the person responsible for the mission to rescue Ed's niece from the drug cartel, Mike expressed his feelings. The rescue mission had gotten one of the men killed and another one clinging to life.

"What went wrong?" Ed asked.

"Just luck of the draw," Mike said. "The KSK team breached the compound's wall right where Daniel's gang had most of their men. It took them longer than anticipated to get to where the hostages were locked up."

"But Inez said that they were taking hits from a big gun on their other side," Ed said.

"I debriefed the Australians before I got here and one of the cartel members had a .50 caliber sniper rifle. That's what was bunching big holes in their building in an attempt to kill the hostages."

"So that was what hit Jack in the left leg. It must have hit the metal door and torn out a chunk that ricocheted into Jack."

Ed asked Mike how he got back to Yuma so fast to be in San Diego within twelve hours of leaving the scene.

"We work with the DEA all the time down in Mexico. They have agents living and working down there that feed information back to the States. Crossing the border either way is very routine."

"So the local police didn't bother you?" Ed asked.

"Well, Jack's rental car hopefully had full coverage because it won't be returning to the company," Mike said. "One of the KSK troops put a satchel charge in the car parked on the side of the road. I parked my van between it and the compound. When I saw the local police approaching, I hit the detonator. They had the remains on the roadway to deal with which left me plenty of time to exit south."

"So no problems?"

"No, I swung around to the south before doubling back to the border. I crossed west of where we entered. I heard on the radio net where you were headed so I drove through the night to get here."

"One more question, my friend," Ed said. "The German sergeant raised a question on the Reaper flattening the compound. That hadn't been in the original plan, and I think he was a little pissed off about it."

"I gave the go ahead. I'll talk to him when I catch up with him," Mike said. "Did you have a problem with it?"

"No, not at all," Ed said. "The Air Force captain spoke to me about his phone call from headquarters. They had received a call from the coroner who identified Major Reiner's body."

"Yeah, I figured it was payback time from the Air Force, so I agreed to the change in plan."

While the sun settled toward the Pacific Ocean, the two men enjoyed the breeze coming in off the ocean. The scene around them was of a beautiful evening in a coastal American city while the conversation consisted of death and destruction. The contrast hit both of them. Mike's phone broke any solitude the roof offered. After listening without much speaking, he hung up.

"That was my source inside the DEA," Mike said. Word has it that everyone at the compound in Islita was killed. The only surviving members of Daniel's gang are in Las Vegas."

"So I guess we shift our focus to Nevada," Ed said.

The look Mike gave his friend spoke volumes. There was no need of more discussion, only action. They stood at the safety rail and stared at the setting sun. One more mission needed to be completed. One more team needed to be sent out.

* * *

LaMarcus Lewis sat waiting at Los Angeles International Airport. His short flight to San Diego had been delayed for some reason, so he studied the crowd in the gate area. He had been flying now for eighteen hours and was ready for a hot shower, some food, and sleep.

His flight out of southern Thailand on a local prop plane to Bangkok had been the hardest. With only one flight a day and him with short notice, he had arrived at the local airport with no confirmed reservation. Just a hope that he could get a standby seat. Luckily, one did open and the rest was academic.

Once in Bangkok, he grabbed the first non-stop flight to Los Angeles. While he waited in the airport for his fourteen-hour flight, he got on the internet and booked his onward flight to San Diego. Now he was hung-up at LAX. LaMarcus thoughts of food were interrupted by thoughts of what lay at the end of his journey.

Jack Wesley and LaMarcus went way back to their time serving in the Marine Corps together. Initially not friends, a stint together as a sniper team forced them to work out their differences. They had been lifelong friends ever since. Often joining up together, they had experienced many battles, but now LaMarcus sat worried that he was flying to his friend's funeral. While the hunger grew, he knew he couldn't leave his gate in case they finally called for boarding.

The entire time since getting an email from Jack's son Carl, LaMarcus had been fixated on what had happened to his friend. Carl had not elaborated but had said enough to get LaMarcus to leave his retirement resort on the ocean and fly half way around the world. There was unfinished business, and LaMarcus thought he knew what it entailed.

After an hour delay the gate attendant finally called for boarding. LaMarcus gathered his six-foot-two-inch frame and moved to get in line. He could endure the twenty minute flight in the tight seats once more. He owed it to his friend to be there.

Carl was waiting at the bottom of the escalator when LaMarcus exited the secure area of the airport. He held a sign with Lewis printed on it just in case LaMarcus didn't recognize him. But LaMarcus picked out Carl right away, the resemblance to his dad obvious in his build and facial features.

"Carl, you look just like your Dad," LaMarcus said.

"LaMarcus, thanks for coming. I know it was a long flight for you," Carl said.

As they stood and waited for LaMarcus's checked bag, they kept the conversation light due to their fellow passengers standing nearby. Once he had his bag, the two headed to the parking garage and Carl's rented car. Once alone inside the car, they could finally talk.

"So tell me, how bad is your Dad?"

"He's been in the hospital now for three days. He took three bullets, one in the leg, one in the shoulder and one in the head. Also, he got some kind of wound in one leg from shrapnel of some kind. Plus he took a beating by the cartel thugs before they locked him up. Some broken ribs and a broken hand."

LaMarcus cringed at the extent of Jack's injuries. *And a head wound*, he thought.

"My sister finally broke down completely and they have her sedated in the hospital. She lost her husband in all of this and now feels that Dad is going to die because of her."

LaMarcus grimaced at the news. "Nobody's fault but some damn drug dealers."

And LaMarcus knew exactly who to blame. He and Jack had been present when the initial trouble with the drug cartel had started. Many people had died already as the feud between the Wesley family and Daniel's family continued.

Reaching the hospital, Carl led LaMarcus to Jack's room. Still in intensive care, LaMarcus could only look through the glass wall that separated him from his friend. Sitting outside the access door were two very stern looking guards. While dressed in civilian clothes, the short haircuts combined with the bulging clothes made their presence known.

LaMarcus turned away to talk to Carl. "So who are Laurel and Hardy over there?"

Carl turned to where LaMarcus was staring and turned back. "Security."

"Jesus, is Jack still in danger?"

"We all are, according to my uncle," Carl said. "His friend Mike has passed on that the cartel is still active even though their numbers were severely reduced in Mexico."

LaMarcus knew the uncle's connection to the Federal government and the resources for information that would be available to him.

"Carl, where is your uncle?"

Carl took LaMarcus to the nearby waiting area where he was introduced to Jack's brother. Another man appeared when LaMarcus asked for a spot to chat privately. As they headed to the roof and the helicopter landing pad, LaMarcus asked that Carl go check on his Dad.

Alone on the roof, LaMarcus had a formal introduction to Mike. The name and his company connected immediately with LaMarcus. Jack had spoken of the mysterious friend of his uncle that could fix things permanently. And a man who had the weapons to accomplish any task.

"So I understand that Jack isn't safe yet," LaMarcus said.

"You're not safe," Mike said. "Our sources say that Jack's big black buddy is also targeted."

"I guess that would be me," LaMarcus said. "Don't think Jack has too many brothers he hangs out with. So what do we do?"

Ed spoke up. "I know what you and Jack did to Ernesto and why you are in the crosshairs."

"You do? I figured that was just between Jack and me."

"You forget who else was there. Jack passed on the information to me when you two big brave warriors lit out for parts unknown. There was a third person involved, you remember? I was asked to make sure they were safe."

"Oh yeah," LaMarcus said. "I kind of forgot."

"Well she is safe," Ed said. "But to make sure, I've maintained close tabs on your friends."

"Thanks."

"So are you ready to clean up yours and Jack's mess for good?" Ed said.

"Tell me where I have to go and consider it done. But flying international didn't allow anything like what I need in my luggage."

"Let us worry about that," Mike said. "For right now go and rent a motorhome. Here's the address. Use your credit card but only pay cash for fuel so there's no track on where you've been."

Mike handed LaMarcus a throwaway cell phone and told him to only use it to call him twice. Once when he was ready for his gear and once when he needed to dispose of it. The three men shook hands and headed down to the lobby. LaMarcus grabbed a cab to the motorhome rental agency, Ed returned to Jack's bedside, and Mike disappeared to await LaMarcus's call.

Chapter 23

San Diego, California

For over eighty years the naval hospital had been part of San Diego. And over all those years, like other hospitals the world over, it had been added onto on a regular basis. Now a sprawling medical center that took up a large chunk of Balboa Park, the hospital had made sure that one thing was preserved.

Located just to the north of the main hospital entrance was a children's park. Here the young children of patients could play and expend energy. Restricted from entering the hospital, the younger children needed a park close by to await their parent's absence as they were tended to by friends or family.

The vigil for Jack Wesley continued with no change in his condition. Unconscious since being shot multiple times, Jack clung to life with the help of modern medicine's numerous machines. One after another complication had been dealt with as his body fought the damage inflicted during Inez's rescue.

Outside in the park, two women sat and watched two young children play in the sand box. A lid that kept animals out of the sand had been removed and placed nearby. Small plastic shovels and pails were provided as one of the little boys piled sand into his pail and then tipped it over. One of the women rose and walked the short distance to the boy and sat on the edge of the board that held in the sand.

Taking her own shovel and pail, she filled hers and packed it tight. Then she quickly tipped the pail over and shook it slightly. A neat mound of sand shaped as an inverted pail sat on the sand. She repeated the maneuver numerous times until she had a small castle-like structure. The small boy tried to mimic the woman but wasn't coordinated enough to get the pail inverted and the sand set.

His frustration grew at his inability to match the woman's clever work. He stood and walked purposely into the woman's sand castle and stomped it to pieces. He then finished his destruction with a purposeful kicking of sand everywhere.

"Giovanni, smettila," the woman said.

"Momma," he said in return and went back to sitting and playing in the sand. The young woman stood up and returnied to sitting on the park bench. The curls on her head bounced as she moved, matching the dark curls of the little boy.

The woman knew that she would pay a price later for the fun in the sand in their hotel room as she washed his hair. Hair that was a nightmare to comb and certainly would resist the sand that he now dumped onto his head. She sat back and let him have fun playing in the sand. She wasn't dwelling on the state of the boy's hair. She had more serious concerns and had flown a long distance to be near them.

* * *

A second woman sitting on a separate bench nearby looked up and saw two older boys playing on a play structure. One appeared to be five years old, the other probably about three. The two looked to be brothers from their similar appearance as they ran hard through the wooden structure, the younger one attempting to keep up with his older brother.

Suddenly a cry went up from the sand box and the woman quickly focused at the commotion. One two-year-old was throwing sand at a second two-year-old. That action forced a return attack of sand as the two boys were soon engulfed in a sand war.

"Stop that, John," the woman yelled as she moved to separate the two boys. Receiving a spray of sand as she grew close, the second woman moved in and grabbed her son.

"Giovanni, basta fermata," the second woman shouted and then followed with a tirade in a strange language.

As John's mother wiped sand from her face, she turned to the other woman. "I'm so sorry. He knows better."

"Ve bene. It's OK," the second woman said. "Mi scusi. I need to speak in English. My name is Valentina and this is my son, Giovanni."

The two boys had settled down and after promising to behave, were placed by their mothers back in the sand pit. They were soon working together building sand castles as best they could.

"That's better. Two-year-olds switch moods quicker than us adults."

"Si, they are happy now," Valentina said.

"My name is Kotone, and that is my son John. We are glad to meet you."

Kotone noticed Valentina study the two boys playing. There was a look on her face of recognition. "Giovanni is Italian for John, isn't it?"

"Si, he was named for his father," Valentina said.

The two women sat down together on the park bench as they continued to watch two happy boys playing. One seemed to help the other if one of them knew a sand building technique that the other lacked. Kotone marveled as the two worked together. *They could be brothers* she thought. Then it hit her. She stared more intently at each boy and the similarities between them.

With the exception of the curly hair and darker complexion, Giovanni looked remarkably like her son, John. Or was it just a coincidence? Two little boys playing, many would look alike she thought. But Kotone's inquisitiveness grew.

"Are you here for someone in the hospital? she asked.

"Yes, I am. I flew in from Rome yesterday to be here. He is very badly injured and remains in critical condition," Valentina said, "My husband is at the hotel resting as he flew separately and just arrived."

Kotone relaxed slightly at the news of Valentina's husband being at the hotel. Kotone had a woman's intuition moment and wanted more details about why Valentina was in San Diego.

"So it's not your husband that is in the hospital," Kotone said. "I'm glad to hear that."

"No, it is a very good friend that I await news on. And you?"

"My husband I'm afraid. He is also in critical condition with multiple gun-shot wounds," Kotone said.

"Oh, so he is in the army? You Americans have too many young men being injured in all the wars your government gets involved in. Not like Italy."

"No he was in the Marines, but that was many years ago. He was attacked in Mexico by a drug cartel," Kotone said.

But as she said it there was a look of recognition in the other woman. It startled Kotone, the intensity of it.

Valentina turned from watching the boys and stared intently at Kotone. Kotone shifted slightly, uncomfortable.

"What is your husband's name?" Valentina asked.

"I'm Kotone Wesley. His name is Jack Wesley. Why do you ask?"

"Madre di dio," Valentina said. It was followed by a long string of Italian spoken quickly to her son. She stood up and walked over to her son, standing him up. She brushed off as much sand as possible and then announced that they needed to return to the hotel to check on pappa.

Valentina turned to Kotone. "It was nice to meet you Kotone. We need to go check on Giovanni's pappa. I hope your husband recovers from his injures."

Kotone stood, a little shaken by the quick change. Her intuition continued and she wanted one piece of information before this woman left. "If I might ask, what is your husband's name?"

"Nuncio Tosi. I'm Valentina Tosi." Valentina had a crying two-year-old to deal with and she moved quickly to remove him. Now the second two-year-old began crying as his new friend left. Kotone picked John up and soon regretted the move from the sand she received.

"Goodbye, Valentina. Maybe we'll see Giovanni again here to play with," Kotone called.

"Ciao," was all the response Kotone received in return.

John was soon distracted from his friend leaving as two older boys moved in on the sand pit. They picked up the sand toys and began building a small city of sand. Forgetting his lost friend, John struggled to be put down so he could join the new arrivals.

Kotone placed him by the sand pit and retreated to her park bench. She watched to see how her son would interact with the older boys and even more she wanted to see if the older boys would interact with her two-year-old. An older woman walked over from where she had been watching the older boys.

The two women smiled at each other and then focused on the three in the sand pit. The oldest boy had offered a pail and shovel to John, who accepted the offer and dove in digging. All three boys worked together as their city grew and Kotone sat mesmerized at how John deferred to the oldest boy in what he should be working on.

Each assignment was handed out gently and with careful instruction to John. He accepted the guidance and worked feverishly to accomplish his tasks. The three-year-old was more of a problem, Kotone noticed. He was now the middle child and showed some jealousy as his older brother worked with the younger boy.

Soon the three-year-old had had enough of his big brother's attention being elsewhere and kicked the younger child. John fell backwards and hit his head on the plastic tub that held the sand. As he started crying, both women raced to take control.

"CJ, stop that right now," the older woman said. "Is your boy OK?" she asked as she took CJ out of the sand pit by the hand.

Kotone picked up John and checked the back of his head. John struggled to get down and return to sand digging. His antagonist had been removed and it was his chance to work with the older boy alone. Kotone placed him back in the sand pit and both boys returned to building.

"That's a timeout CJ," the woman said as she led him back to the park bench and forced him to sit. She walked backed to Kotone. "Your son?"

"Yes, and he's fine. Happy as he can be already," Kotone said.

"Grandma, can I go back to playing?" CJ asked from his bench seat exile.

"You just sit there until I say it's OK."

There was something familiar about this woman and these children, at least the older one. Kotone had met this woman briefly before and wracked her brain to remember.

"You're Kotone, aren't you?" the older woman asked. "You were maid of honor at Stacey's wedding."

"Of course, Mrs. Paquette isn't it?" Kotone asked. "I missed the rehearsal and things were so busy at the wedding that I barely got to meet any of Stacey's family."

"I am so sorry about your husband," Mrs. Paquette said. "Stacey asked me to fly in from Denver to watch the children while she and Carl visited the hospital."

"I thought this was JJ," Kotone said "He has grown so much since the wedding. And this is Stacey's second. She was pregnant with him at the wedding. They named him CJ, huh? JJ and CJ."

"Short for Carl Junior."

"Grandma please. I'll behave," came the call from behind.

Mrs. Paquette turned to her grandson. "First you apologize to . . . I'm sorry, I don't know his name. Stacey hasn't mentioned you of late."

"His name is John."

Kotone understood why Stacey had not mentioned her to her mother. Kotone's life was turmoil. But luckily Stacey had stayed in contact over the past three years. They exchanged emails occasionally, which let Stacey know how to contact Kotone when Jack got shot.

Before the conversation got any more revealing between the two women, a familiar voice caught the two older boys' attention. They were gone in a shot running hard across the grass toward a woman.

"Momma, how is granddad doing? Can we see him yet?" they called out in unison.

Kotone picked up a lonely two-year-old who suddenly was missing his playmates. She brushed more sand off John and waited for Stacey. Giving her two sons hugs, they raced back toward the play area. John fought his mother's grip to get down and join the other boys. As she placed her son in the sandbox, Stacey walked up and the two friends embraced.

"Kotone, I'm so glad you could make the trip," Stacey said. "Is this John?" She bent down to give John a kiss on the top of the head. The boy naturally shook his head in an attempt to remove any female attention. He had older boys to impress and such action would not do. Stacey stood and smiled at his reaction.

"Thank you for sending me an email so I knew what had happened," Kotone said. "How is Jack doing?"

Stacey continued to look down at John furiously building sand structures as the two older boys climbed the nearby play structure. Kotone's question hung in the air.

"Hey boys, come over here and play with John," Stacey said, attempting to stall on answering.

"Oh Mom, do we have to?" a unison answer came back.

"Right now," Stacey said.

The two older boys flew down the plastic slide and jumped into the sand pit, ruining the structure John had been working on. Before Stacey could even react JJ proposed building a wicked big sand structure that took John's mind off what had just been destroyed. All three boys feverishly went to work pushing sand into the middle of the sand box.

"Stacey, how is Jack?" Kotone asked.

"Not good, I'm afraid. He's developed an infection where the bullet tore a hole in his shoulder and settled by his heart. They retrieved the bullet but Jack had gotten broken ribs during the beating they gave him. With one lung perforated by the bullet and the broken ribs aggravating his injures, he's in a bad way."

Kotone stood silent as she absorbed what Stacey had told her. She had made the decision to fly to San Diego to see if her marriage still had some life to it. She hadn't flown down to discover she was a widow.

"What do the doctor's say?" Kotone finally asked.

"Wait and see. They keep giving him these seventy-two hour periods. He's on his second one and continues to go downhill."

Kotone staggered as she stood and Stacey caught her. She led Kotone over to the nearby bench and sat her down. Placing her arm around Kotone,

Stacey tried to console her. Kotone bent over and began to sob. Her action caught John's attention and he stood up and walked to his mother. He placed his sandy hands on her knees.

"Don't cry mommy," said John.

The action just opened up Kotone's sobbing as she began to shake. Stacey's two boys came over from their playing and stood by their mother, each placing a hand on Stacey's knees.

"Is she sad about grandpa?" CJ asked.

"Yes dear. She is very sad."

Chapter 24

Barstow, California

By the time he reached Barstow, LaMarcus was regretting his decision. The decision to head to Las Vegas and put a final end to the drug cartel war against the Wesley family did not bother him. It was the two strangers that were foisted on him as he got ready to leave.

Graham Elphinston, or Sir Graham as everyone insisted on calling him, sat in the passenger seat of the Class C motorhome LaMarcus had rented in San Diego. The Ford F-350 chassis the motorhome sat on took on Interstate I-15 just fine as they headed north out of Los Angeles. Soon the freeway would swing around to the northwest toward Las Vegas.

LaMarcus knew the history of Jack and Graham going to war against the Cypriot terrorist attack in London and the subsequent recognition of Graham as the hero of the day. Jack had related the story to LaMarcus during their stay in Thailand over many months. It made it a little better knowing Graham's history and his ability to keep his mouth shut. Jack had never been tied to London and LaMarcus wanted no part of their mission being tied to him.

But it was the little guy sitting behind him that bothered LaMarcus. He knew of the reputation of the Gurkha soldiers in the British Army. Any warrior knew. His time in the Marines had exposed him to many of the soldiers from around the world, but he had never personally met a Gurkha before. *And this guy Karma, whatever his name is, didn't evoke much confidence* LaMarcus thought. *He is definitely over the hill and ready for retirement.*

It had been Mike who had insisted that Karma tag along. LaMarcus didn't know exactly who Mike was, but by his demeanor and the bag of weapons that he handed LaMarcus he wasn't about to ask. *Jack's brother Ed had vouched for the guy, so he must be connected to the Feds somehow* LaMarcus thought. So LaMarcus had two passengers on his mission. He thought about how he could ditch them once he hit Las Vegas and pick them back up after he was done.

"Can we stop here, LaMarcus?" Graham asked. "I need a bathroom break."

It had been a little over four hours since they had left San Diego and the traffic between Ontario and Victorville had slowed them down some. LaMarcus looked over at his passenger. "We do have a head on board you know." The look he got in return alerted him to the cultural difference. "Sorry, we have a loo back there." LaMarcus stabbed a thumb rearward toward the onboard bathroom.

"Yes I know," Graham said. "Then I'll change my request. Can we stop for a bite to eat? I just need to get out of this thing and stretch my legs."

LaMarcus hit the turn signal and checked his right side mirror. Seeing an opening in the right lane he shifted lanes of traffic and checked the next exit. It appeared to be the main business exit for Barstow and the highway information sign indicated a number of national restaurant chains.

"See anything there that looks good?" he asked as he pointed to the highway information sign for Graham's sake. He hit the indicator again and took the exit before Graham could respond.

"I'm not familiar with all your Yank restaurants so you pick one please. Doesn't really matter to me. How about you Karma?"

Nothing came back from the small brown man behind him as LaMarcus slowed down approaching a stop light. The sign indicated that most of the restaurants were to his left so he moved to the left lane and hit his turn signal once more. Karma had yet to utter a sound the entire trip and LaMarcus wondered if his English language skills were adequate. The light changed and the camper turned, passing under the freeway. On the other side, the evening sky lit the stretch of commercial enterprises. Food, gas, and motels lined the service road.

LaMarcus chose a middle of the road national restaurant and pulled in. He switched off the engine after finding an area that had been set aside for large vehicles. The lineup of trucks and RV's announced that he had probably made a decent choice for eating.

The three men stepped out of the camper and LaMarcus locked the door. Once inside the restaurant, LaMarcus maneuvered the hostess to a booth that overlooked the camper. With what was sitting inside, he wanted to make sure things remained safe while they ate.

Service was quick and soon they had their meals. LaMarcus was amazed at the mountain of rice the Nepali ate along with his roasted chicken. Since his time in Thailand, LaMarcus knew the rice routine. Thankfully pork was plentiful there and LaMarcus had eaten his share of pig over the last year. He ordered meat loaf and mashed potatoes

Having turned sixty while living in the tropics, he had come to love the dietary regime. Heavy in fruits and vegetables, he had lost over thirty pounds and loved his new figure. He just had to make sure to get back to Thailand before American eating habits put the weight back on. And he knew his visit would be short; take care of the cartel and make sure his friend would survive his wounds.

Accomplishing those two tasks, he would head home, which is what he now called Thailand. *Not that I have much say in my friend's survival* he thought. *Just eliminate the bad guys so he has a chance at survival.* Once back in the camper heading east on the freeway, Graham finally broached the subject.

"Might I ask how you plan on eliminating the cartel problem?"

"Daniel is the head of his little group. The majority of his gang were killed down in Mexico according to Jack's brother. Daniel and the rest are holed up in their house in Las Vegas."

"And you have the location?"

"Yes, and I've reconnoitered on the internet and I can get a clear line of sight to his house," LaMarcus said.

"And you intend to shoot them all?"

"I was on a sniper team. We shot people. I know how it's done."

LaMarcus' attitude showed and Graham didn't raise any more issues. Karma sat at the dinette table staring straight ahead offering nothing to the conversation. The camper moved away from the setting sun as the road ahead grew dark. The small group remained quiet the remainder of the trip, which suited LaMarcus fine.

The GPS unit on the camper's dashboard announced the first turn as they reached the south side of Las Vegas. LaMarcus maneuvered the Ford onto Highway 215 heading west. He had entered the address that Mike had provided and the route continued as the highway swung to the north. Soon the Summerlin Parkway showed on the GPS unit and the camper dutifully followed instructions as it now headed east. The Rampart Boulevard Exit took the camper down onto the side streets. A right turn followed by another right turn brought them to Mira Villa, the location of Daniel's house.

Being close to midnight when they turned onto Los Cabos Drive, the neighborhood of expensive homes sat quiet. LaMarcus drove slowly and swung onto Las Manaitas Avenue, locating the house they needed. He pointed it out to the others but crept past. From the street the house was dark, the street lights illuminating the front.

Returning to Rampart, LaMarcus turned south and passed a park-like area. Even in the low light, the golf course on both sides of the road was evident. Returning to a commercial area, the camper turned at the large casino sign. An expansive parking lot lay in front of a high-rise hotel, the casino out front. LaMarcus ignored the bright lights and drove around to the service road that lay to the north, a cinderblock wall on the north side of the road separating the golf course from the casino. The camper pulled over and parked.

"We should be able to see our target from here," LaMarcus said. He moved into the rear of the camper where he had thrown the gear bag Mike had given him. He returned with a spotting scope and two sets of binoculars. He handed the binoculars to the others and then set up the spotting scope.

The camper was just high enough to see over the cinder block wall, and LaMarcus placed a box on the dinette to raise the spotting scope's legs. Now elevated sufficiently, he counted the houses from the end of the housing development to locate Daniel's place. Mira Villa had not been completed, so LaMarcus easily counted five houses in from the unfinished blank land.

Daniel's house from this side was of a three-story Mexican style. Since the house was two-story on the front, a daylight basement had been dug into the hill leading down to the park and the golf course. An extensive deck had been added to the main floor, jutting out over the arroyo below. All the houses edging the park had similar attributes of varying styles. LaMarcus didn't care about the others, as he focused on one in particular.

"I see three people out sitting on the deck," Graham said as he sat in the passenger seat holding his binoculars braced against his raised knee. Karma stood next to LaMarcus with his gaze aimed in the same direction.

"I see them. Let me zoom in closer." LaMarcus adjusted the spotting scope which offered more magnifying power than the binoculars. "OK, I have Daniel. There's a woman sitting beside him and a Hispanic male beside her."

LaMarcus pulled out an 8x10 color photo that had been placed in his gear bag. Making sure the blinds were all lowered on the casino side of the motorhome, he flicked on a small spot light. He examined the photo and then checked the spotting scope.

"Here, I have a picture of Daniel. Both of you look and confirm I have him in my scope."

First Graham and then Karma both moved to double-check LaMarcus' view. Both confirmed that they had the leader of the drug gang identified. For LaMarcus, it took him back to when the war had started. Daniel's father Ernesto had tried to pick up a female friend of Jack's at a nightclub in Las Vegas. Jack had defended his friend, breaking Ernesto's nose in the process.

LaMarcus remembered his rushing to his friend's assistance when Ernesto's body guards moved in. He had broken the wrist of one of the guards being arrested and was convicted of assault for his troubles.

But it was after they had left Las Vegas when the real trouble began. They had received word that an old friend of LaMarcus who lived in Las Vegas had been murdered for befriending Jack. The subsequent burning of the friend's home with the body inside had really started the war. And now LaMarcus was determined that the enemy be eliminated forever. *The war would end now* he thought.

"So, do do we shoot him now?" Graham asked.

"I like your style, but I think we might observe the house for a while. I want to make sure we get the rest of the cartel members. I don't want it to spring up afterward."

"But how long do you think we can park here and not attract attention?"

LaMarcus knew the longer the motorhome sat on the service road the more likely someone would take exception of its presence. The police would be called and they would be identified. And being identified was not an option.

"Ho, hold on. Looks like something is happening," Graham said.

LaMarcus returned to the spotting scope and backed out his magnification. Now seeing the entire back of the house, two men in suits stepped out of the house. A discussion seemed to be taking place. Soon all five people stood up and walked into the house. The sliding door was shut and the lights in the living room extinguished.

Soon lights appeared in the upstairs rooms as well as the downstairs rooms. LaMarcus zoomed in on the upstairs window and found Daniel undressing. The woman emerged from what he assumed was the bathroom. She had a negligee on and climbed into the bed. Daniel soon returned from the bathroom with just pajama bottoms on and he crawled in beside the woman. The lights went out in the bedroom.

Slowly all the lights in the house went out as LaMarcus assumed everyone was turning in. He jumped as Karma moved suddenly. Placing his binoculars down on the dinette table, Karma disappeared into the rear bedroom of the camper and shut the door.

"Sir Graham, what's going on?" LaMarcus asked.

"I think we have a change of plans."

"How so? I thought we were here to kill Daniel and his cartel."

"Oh, we are. But we aren't gong to shoot them. Much too noisy."

"What is our Gurkha friend planning?" LaMarcus asked.

"No worries mate. Let me tell you a story. Many years ago Malaya was part of the British Empire. In the 1950's some Malay nationals thought that independence from the Crown was a grand idea. And to entice the masses to support their effort, they chose to promote Communism."

"I've read the history books. Communists insurgents were all the rage back then," LaMarcus said.

"Oh quite right," Graham continued. "Except in Malaya, the British did something no one else tried. They lined up their Gurkha forces and told them to go into the jungle and kill all the Communists. The British would drop them supplies as needed, but otherwise they would be on their own. And oh, by the way, don't come out until the job is done."

"And . . ."

"Well, miracle of miracles, sometime later the Gurkhas walked out of the jungle to announce they were finished."

"And were all the Communists dead?" LaMarcus asked.

"No one ever knew. But the Communist insurgents were never heard from again. Those that weren't killed knew enough to go back to their villages and shut the hell up. No one wanted a Gurkha slinking through the night with their Kukri slicing their head off. Very effective."

"And Karma is going into the house over there and slice their heads off?" LaMarcus said. "He knows how to disarm alarm systems? That's not exactly jungle skills."

The door opened and a dressed-down Gurkha emerged. He had his black clothes on, and a black balaclava hid most of his head with just his eyes showing. His combat boots were secured by his combat pants which held a K-Bar knife in a sheath. Across his stomach the traditional combat knife of the Gurkha, the Kukri sat, the heavy curved blade ensconced in a protective holder.

"Mr. Lewis, Karma has been trained by the finest fighting force in the world, the British SAS.

Combined with his Gurkha warrior heritage, he will know how to deal with his enemy."

"But this is about the Wesley family and the cartel."

"No, Sahib," Karma spoke finally. "You wrong. They kill my friend, Colonel Roberts. This is my fight now. You wait here, please."

Before LaMarcus could utter a comment on who the fight belonged to, Karma slung a black bag over his shoulder and snapped a strap across his chest. He tested that the bag was secure and would not move from his back. He flicked off the small spot light. Karma bowed to both men with his hands pressed together in front of his face, opened the camper's door and was gone.

Chapter 25

Las Vegas, Nevada

Karma Somda was on one last mission for God and Queen. And for Gurkha pride. But actually this mission was for his good friend, Colonel Gregory Roberts. He would avenge his death at the hands of the drug cartel, even though Karma knew he really didn't have to.

Colonel Roberts had wanted to go out of the world as a warrior. The last thing the colonel wanted was a long life as a pensioner. As a devout Buddhist, Karma knew what karma meant. He had been named Karma for a reason, and the Gurkha carried his station in life with him.

It was his job to serve. And after thirty plus years of service to the British Crown, he was almost ready to go home to Nepal and the life that retired Gurkha soldiers all earned. But that would have to wait.

He focused on his task as he climbed the cinder block wall separating the service road from the golf course. Making his way in the dark across the park which held the golf course was basic for him. He had trained in the jungles of Asia for many years and knew how to find his route in more hazardous conditions than this American park.

But he made sure no one would ever see him. More of a shadow than a human, he moved with stealth until he reached the block wall separating his target from the park. On this side, the wall was more a retaining wall of average height. For a small man of his build he still climbed it easily. The house remained darkened as the inhabitants slept their last night.

Looking carefully, Karma noticed the motion sensors by the lower patio area. They would trigger lights or even emit a warning inside the house if activated. Karma would avoid either warning in his attack. Determining the dead zones where the motion detectors didn't reach, Karma moved to his right and crawled through the small plants that sat above the retaining wall.

Gaining the side of the patio, he scaled a larger retaining wall that held the earth back from the daylight basement. He moved so slow that even if he was within range of a sensor, his barely perceptible movement would not trigger the warning. Once atop the retaining wall, he stepped easily to the elevated deck off the main floor.

Since most people would not be able to reach this space, Karma noticed no additional sensor had been installed. He bent down and removed the gear bag on his back. Laying on the wooden deck, he retrieved a small glass cutter after placing the night vision monocular on his head. The tunnel like vision in his right eye aided his sight of his surroundings but killed his peripheral vision.

Taking the glass cutter, he licked the suction cup and squeezed it on the living room glass window. He gripped the cutter and made circular motions several times until he felt the cutter loosen the small piece of glass. The glass was removed leaving a one inch hole in the window. He reattached the cutter and proceeded to cut the inside pane of glass in the thermopane window.

The cutter was placed aside and a pressurized tank removed from the bag. An attached hose was slipped into the house. Karma squeezed a soft plastic substance into the hole, sealing it. Once the hose was attached to the tank, Karma turned the valve. He would let the central air conditioning do his work for him.

As instructed by Mike, he set his stopwatch running and waited for the gas to work. Connected to the CIA, Mike had access to things that killed people. The pressurized tank had been provided and Karma trained in its use. Mike had decided that this method of eliminating Jack's enemies would be quieter and more successful than using a gun. With so many targets to hit, it would take even an expert marksman too long a time to kill everyone. And the risk of discovery was much higher with a gun.

The gas had been developed by the Russians after the Beslan School massacre in Beslan, North

Ossetia, when Chechen terrorists took over 1,100 people hostage. The ensuing explosions and fire during the rescue attempt left over 300 people dead, mostly children.

The Russians had always been big on poison and developed a poison gas to inject into any building to kill everyone. A different version had been developed to incapacitate so that hostages might survive any rescue. The CIA had worked on the same issue and Karma had the results.

He checked his watch and noted it was time. He withdrew the hose and placed the tank in his gear bag. Retrieving a large machete from the bag, he now had to complete part two. While he much preferred to use his Kukri, he understood the need of the machete. Retrieving his glass cutter, he cut a hole in the patio glass door near the lock. With one finger, he reached in and unlocked the door.

Pulling out a self-contained breathing device, Karma slipped his night vision off and pulled on the face mask. He tested that he could breathe properly and then put the night vision back on. With the self-contained oxygen, he had ten minutes of air to work in the deadly poison gas.

Karma steadied himself. He had to move fast now to complete his mission. Gripping the machete in his right hand, he grabbed the handle with his left and flung the door back. He ran into the house making for the stairs. He knew he had twenty seconds to enter the code to disable the alarm that had picked up his motion once inside the living room. Since he had no code, he had twenty seconds before the police were notified. Then he had the additional time it took them to respond to the house.

He reached the door at the top of the stairs and opened it. In the night vision he saw two people lying in bed motionless. While they should be dead from the gas, he was there to both make sure and send a message. He leaned across the bed as he swung the machete. The man received the same stroke. Before leaving, he opened the sliding door to the outside deck.

In the next two upstairs bedrooms, each occupant's head was separated from the body with a single machete swing. The lights came on as the alarm recognized that no one had entered a code. Karma knew the police were now getting a report of a break in. He flipped the night vision out of the way as he breathed heavy racing down the stairs.

Reaching the basement, he opened one bedroom door and swung his machete. The second bedroom occupant received the same stroke. Karma turned and ran for the basement patio doors to the outside. Pulling open the sliding glass door, he dropped his machete as he left the house. Bounding over the retaining wall into the park, he pulled off his face mask as he ran and stuffed it into his gear bag.

The house behind him was ablaze with light, but out in the park the night took over. As he looked left he saw flashing lights as a patrol car raced to the scene. Reaching the paved walking path, he turned left and ran into the dark. His night vision back in place let him move off the paved trail into the small trees and plants along the golf course. He doubled backed to the place he needed on the south side of the golf course.

Karma reached his spot and climbed the cinder block wall, the camper on the other side. The motor was running as LaMarcus sat in the driver's seat. He grabbed the door handle and climbed on board. The camper was moving before Karma had fully shut the door.

LaMarcus swung the motor home onto the side street and headed to the south of the casino resort. Turning right on Rampart Blvd., then left onto W. Charleston, they headed east into Las Vegas. Another squad car flew past them in the mirror heading north on Rampart.

Karma slowly removed his leather gloves and placed his gear bag under the dinette. While Graham sat in the passenger seat, the three carefully drove until they met Interstate 15 heading back to Los Angles. LaMarcus swung up onto the freeway and settled in for a long nighttime drive back to San Diego. Karma would not make it to San Diego.

As LaMarcus neared Los Angeles, Karma requested a detour to Los Angeles International Airport. The GPS coordinates combined with the early morning hour made crossing the city a quick trip. Karma left his gear bag in the camper but grabbed a personal bag he had left Missoula with. He had changed into more traditional street clothes from his black outfit and looked presentable as he stepped out of the camper.

He announced that he would buy a suitcase in the airport and fill it up with various gifts for his family in order to look like a normal traveler. LaMarcus and Graham wished him well and drove off into morning rush hour. It would be four hours before they reached San Diego.

As they approached San Diego, LaMarcus placed his second call on his throw away phone to tell Mike they would meet him at the designated spot. He swung the camper off the freeway and into an industrial zone. Two more turns took him to a lonely spot under the freeway where he switched off the engine.

Climbing into the back of the camper, LaMarcus grabbed the gear bag and inventoried its contents. He reached under the dinette and grabbed Karma's bag from the night before and placed it with the other gear. As he zipped up the bag, Graham announced Mike's arrival.

No words were exchanged as Mike stepped into the camper. He grabbed the gear bag and turned to leave. Stopping in the doorway, he turned back to LaMarcus.

"Cell phone?" Mike said.

"Oh yeah, almost forgot." LaMarcus handed the burner phone to Mike.

"Word is you completed your mission."

LaMarcus half smiled at the news that the drug cartel would not be bothering him or Jack ever again. Graham sat in the passenger seat and watched the exchange but said nothing. Mike turned without adding a word and stepped out of the camper. He walked over to his car, popped the truck and threw the bag in. He drove off.

"Nasty work," Graham finally said.

"Yeah," LaMarcus said.

Chapter 26

Bob Wilson Medical Center, San Diego, California

Jack Wesley had made it past the 72-hour window the doctors had initially given him in their estimate as to his chances on survival. Jack had even made it past his second 72-hour wait-and-see-period. But he had made it by not a lot, at least according to his chief doctor. Because of the damage to his lungs from both the bullet wound and the broken ribs, Jack had developed an infection. Now the worry switched to pneumonia, a certain killer if not controlled.

As Carl sat with his Dad, his brother Ed stood just outside in the main intensive care room that held Jack. The doctor had just given Ed the latest update and it didn't sound good. Jack had been given a third 72-hour period in which the infection needed to be brought under control. After that, an uncontrolled infection would so wrack his immune system that death would be certain.

Carl looked up and saw his uncle through the window. Carl knew from Ed's expression that the news had not been good. He had deferred to his uncle the role of family representative to the hospital so he could focus on his Dad and sister.

Inez had improved enough to be moved to a residence that the hospital maintained for visiting family. Carl and his family joined her, which offered a diversion for Inez. With two small children to care for, along with Stacey's mom, Inez had something that would keep her away from the hospital until more encouraging news was available. She seemed to accept her banishment from Jack's room as if to avoid what had happened.

Stacey stuck her head into Jack's room and caught Carl's gaze. He motioned her in as she sat down beside her husband and took his hand in comfort. Carl continued to hold his Dad's uninjured hand as much as he could in spite of the tubes and wires that monitored his condition.

The two sat quiet as they prayed for Jack's recovery, Ed maintaining his station as protector outside the room looking in. As Stacey noticed tears running down her husband's cheek, she leaned closer and placed her arm around his shoulders. Tear drops fell off his face and hit her hand clasped with his in his lap. A quiet knock on the door got Stacey's attention. She stood and walked over to open it.

"Mr. Wesley?" a woman in a pantsuit asked. On her identification name tag her position said 'Family Affairs'.

Ed immediately stepped over. "Yes, what is it?"

"I'm sorry to disturb you, but Mr. Carl Wesley?"

Before Stacey could inform the nurse that she was Carl's wife, Ed spoke. "That's my nephew. What do you need with Carl?" His voice carried a bit of annoyance at the intrusion.

"I'm with the hospital Family Affairs Office. We offer counseling services to our family members."

Ed continued his sour stare. "Yes?"

"We have someone claiming to be Mrs. Jack Wesley in our office. She has asked permission to see her husband."

"You have our list of those family members that may be admitted to my brother's room," Ed spoke tersely.

"Hold on Uncle Ed. I notified Kotone about Jack," Stacey said.

As the group continued its little meeting at the door, it soon got the attention of Carl. He walked over to Stacey wiping the moisture from his eyes. He purposely moved everyone outside the room so the door could close.

"What's going on?" Carl asked. He looked at his uncle as Ed had been the central figure since this had all started.

"Don't look at me, ask your wife."

"Carl, I emailed Kotone," Stacey said. "I thought she should know about Jack. The hospital says she's asking to see her husband."

"She's here? Now?" Carl exclaimed "Shit."

Ed spoke up, "As the oldest child, it's your call, Carl."

Carl stared straight ahead at nothing in particular as his mind processed everything. "No, a wife comes before children in making decisions about her husband."

"But Carl, they've never lived together, really," Ed said. "As man and wife. She left him three years ago and hasn't made any effort to get in touch."

Stacey spoke up. "Ed, she's stayed in touch with me the entire time. And always for news on Jack. She loves him very much but just can't get past that every time they are together, people die."

"And right now that damn well might be my only brother," Ed said.

"And I know Jack loves her very much. He was devastated when she left him the last time," Stacey offered.

"And what about now?" Ed asked. "Do we let her into his life? And if he by some miracle survives, what will happen when she leaves once more? And you know she will. Can he then survive his injuries and his wife leaving him again?"

Ed had hit home with the salient argument, and both Carl and Stacey knew it. The passion that Jack and Kotone held for each other always hit reality when something bad happened. And it always seemed that bad things came their way when together. An impasse between the three of them took over as the hospital staff waited patiently.

Finally a decision was made. "I'll tell Mrs. Wesley that at this time no visiting privileges are being extended." She began to walk off. Stacey stopped her.

"This is wrong," Stacey said. "Jack needs Kotone by his side in this fight. We can worry about what happens later. The woman loves him. And if, heaven forbid, Jack doesn't make it, can we live with ourselves that we kept her away?"

Ed spoke first, "I'm going to go get lunch. It's your decision, Carl."

Ed headed off to the elevator and the ride down to the cafeteria. Carl stood looking at his wife and then shifting his gaze to the staff person. She was trained in these type of family issues and knew when to just let the family deal with things.

Stacey's gaze locked on her husband's eyes. They projected the love she felt for him as well as her father-in-law. She knew what a tough call her husband needed to make and she held herself so he could make it without her interference. She knew if she pressed the issue and Jack died, there would always be a resentment between the two of them over this.

Finally Carl looked away from Stacey and at the staffer. "I'd like to meet with her first."

"Of course, Mr. Wesley. She's in my office. I'll take you there and let you two have some privacy."

Carl leaned over to Stacey and kissed her. Then he walked off following the staff person. Stacey went back to Jack's bedside and sat down. He took Jack's hand with both of hers. He continued to lay still, unconscious.

It must have been an hour or so when Stacey heard a small knock on the door. Kotone's face emerged from behind the door as she let herself into the room. She let out a small gasp when she saw Jack lying in bed.

Stacey walked over and the two friends embraced. They held their grip on each other as Stacey heard quiet sobbing coming from her friend. She backed off and smiled at Kotone to give her some strength. Leading her to Jack's side, she helped Kotone sit down in the chair next to Jack. Stacey guided Kotone's hand to Jack's hand and then she left the room.

Carl sat against the wall across from the nurses' station with his head down. Stacey walked over and sat down next to him, taking his hand.

"You left her alone?" Carl asked.

"Of course," Stacey replied. "Whatever kind of relationship they have, it's not ours to judge, Carl Wesley."

By her tone to her husband, Stacey noticed the look she received back from Carl. She knew more thn her husband on how far the relationship had progressed. And if Jack eventually survived, he and his wife needed to finally face things. They had made a commitment to each other and Stacey was one who believed in following through with those commitments. *Too many young people never knew what commitment entailed* she thought. *And these two weren't that young, so they have no excuses.*

The elevator pinged and the doors opened. Ed Wesley stepped off from his lunch break. Stacey saw the uncle returning and decided she needed some fresh air. She kissed her husband, said hi to Ed, and grabbed the next elevator down to the lobby. Once outside, she made a quick walk to the children's play area. She needed to hear the yells of children being happy enjoying life. Hospitals were altogether too depressing to linger in for her.

As she approached the play area, she noticed a woman she knew. She changed direction and moved toward the children's sand pit. Two little boys worked hard on building sand structures which were then summarily destroyed by a bigger boy.

One woman stood up and embraced Stacey. They sat down together on one of the benches.

"How is Jack today?"

"The same, Valentina," Stacey said.

Loud protests caught them staring in the distance, unable to continue their conversation. The bigger boy ran through the sand city the two younger boys had just completed. They cried out their protests at their hard work being destroyed. Before they could interfere, the mother of the bigger boy arrived from somewhere and grabbed his arm.

Crying and protesting, the mother led her son over to the play structure and got him interested in climbing the tire ladder to the tower. Some older children were up there playing lookout and the new arrival quickly forgot his destructive mode and joined in scouting for pirates. The mother walked over to Stacey and Valentina.

"I'm sorry. He usually is better behaved than this," the woman said.

"That's OK," Stacey said. "Look, they are back hard at work."

The two younger boys were busy building again, their laughter evident as they played together.

"Please sit and join us," Valentina said. "Do you have someone in the medical center?"

"Yes, I have a good friend in there. A mutual friend called me and I flew here as soon as I could."

Stacey noticed Valentina giving the woman more than a casual look. The new woman picked up on the evaluation and looked back at Valentina.

Almost simultaneously, they said together, "Do I know you?"

Stacey sat between the two and leaned back. "You two know each other?"

There was a lingering quiet as the two women fought for memories. The new woman remembered first.

"Off the Isle of Capri. What was it now?"

"Three years ago. I remember you. Catamaran," Valentina said.

"You're right. It was three years ago. The woman in the motorboat picking up my friend."

The comment stopped all conversation. All three now knew who they had in common.

"You know Jack?" Stacey finally asked.

"Misty Duran. Jack and I go way back. We met five years ago .. ."

"Sailing around the East Coast," Stacey finished her thoughts. "Jack told me about the trip and the woman he had met along the way. I'm Stacey, his daughter-in-law. And this is Valentina, who you met briefly in Italy I guess."

Valentina greeted the new member of the group. Stacey suddenly noticed Misty's eyes grow big.

"You had just given birth when you picked Jack up," Misty said "Is that your son?"

"You noticed," Valentina said "I don't think Jack ever noticed. We spent three days together and he never said anything. I even had to hide and use a breast pump."

The other two said in unison, "Men."

"And yes, that's my son." Valentina called to her son who stepped out of the sand pit and walked to his mother. She brushed sand off as he stood by her side. "Giovanni, say Ciao to Stacey and Misty."

Giovanni dutifully said "Ciao."

Misty called to her son who slowly left his pirate watch and ran over to his mother. "Jan, please say hi to Giovanni. And this is his mother Valentina. And say hi to Stacey."

The bigger boy spoke clearly to each person. He stood as his mother brushed his hair to one side to make him more presentable. Jan leaned into his mom.

The elephant in the room hadn't been answered after the formal introductions. Misty leaned and whispered to her son. Jan stepped over, took Giovanni by the hand and the two joined the third boy in the sand pit. But this time the older boy began helping the other two build sand castles. Gone was the destructive streak he had exhibited earlier.

Misty turned to Stacey and asked, "How is Jack? They won't give out his condition at the front desk and only family are being allowed to see him."

Since Stacey knew that neither woman was fully informed, Stacey went through the list of Jack's injuries and how the last 72 hours had gone. When she got to the latest doctor news, all three women grew quiet. Stacey knew the prognosis was not good and that the odds of Jack living through his injuries were slim. That these two women had uprooted their lives and family to be here only spoke volumes of the effect Jack had had on other people. She had personally seen that effect as well as experienced it herself.

As Stacey finished her update on Jack's condition, Valentina and Misty sat quiet. The three boys were content to continue their sand castle building as they enjoyed each others company. The three women watched the boys playing, each in her own thoughts.

Chapter 27

Balboa Park, San Diego, California

The wake-like setting was broken by Mrs. Paquette walking up with Stacey's two boys. The added energy level the older boys brought to the park changed the mood. Receiving bare acknowledgment from her own children, JJ and CJ climbed immediately into the tower and began yelling about pirates.

The commotion attracted the younger boys and all three left their sand work and attempted to join the older boys. While Jan at three years old had the motor skills to climb up the short ladder, the two-year-olds were not capable. But they attempted to show they were big boys too and headed upward.

Mrs. Paquette, realizing that the three other women were focused on other things, waved them off and headed over as spotter. While the younger boys struggled climbing, she stood right behind them in case they fell.

"Misty, Valentina, I'm sorry I don't have better news," Stacey said.

The statement caught the other woman staring at their sons and their efforts. Kotone's son John missed a foothold and stumbled, Mrs. Paquette catching him. Valentina jumped up and ran over to him, Stacey right behind.

"I'll take him," Valentina said. She took John and raised him up to the platform where the three older children were playing. John joined in looking for pirates. As Giovanni struggled as the lone boy not pirate hunting, Valentina bent down, picked him up and placed him with the others.

Stacey looked at John and then back to Valentina. The two-year-old hadn't protested a stranger picking him up.

"Valentina, do you know John?" Stacey asked.

"Si, I met Kotone here at the park yesterday," Valentina said. "We chatted and discovered our mutual connection to Jack. She asked if I'd watch John today while she went to see Jack."

As the boys tired of looking for pirates, JJ led the parade of all five boys descending the ladder to find another game to play. The two younger boys waited patiently as Valentina placed each down on the ground. They ran off to join the other three.

They ended up in a large rotating plastic barrel that laid on its side. It would turn as anyone small tried to walk through. The trick was to adjust ones steps to the turning barrel. At five years old, JJ easily mastered the task. The two- and three-year-olds made varying attempts at walking through the barrel. Soon all four younger boys were in a heap rolling together, laughing. JJ worked hard outside the barrel rotating it faster to torment the younger boys. The women just watched and smiled at the fun each boy was having.

The mood suddenly changed when Kotone walked up, her red puffy eyes speaking volumes. Stacey took her and hugged her, the other two women standing nearby.

As the boys seemed to be fine tumbling into each other, all but Mrs. Paquette retreated to a park bench. Kotone sat down between Stacey and Valentina, Misty sitting nearby.

"Oh Stacey," Kotone said. "Jack started bleeding out his drain tube. They are saying they are going to have to take him in for emergency surgery."

Jack had a drainage tube placed in his lung cavity during his first operation. The discharge had been normal up to now which had the doctors thinking that things were progressing fine. Blood indicated that internal bleeding was taking place which needed to be corrected immediately. But a second operation placed that much more stress on his body which was not handling the first operation well.

Kotone began crying again and Stacey held her. As she sat on the bench staring at the other two women, each began to tear up. Soon tears were flowing down the cheeks on all four women. Tissues came out of purses as each one blew their noses and dabbed their eyes.

A loud scream broke the crying as Mrs. Paquette suddenly had mayhem on her hands. Three boys screamed as they held their heads. JJ continued to push the barrel around and Stacey raced to pull him off.

Misty grabbed Jan who held his forehead, crying. She pulled his hand away to discover a large goose egg raising up from where he had knocked heads with someone. Valentina pulled Giovanni out of the barrel and found him holding the back of his head, a large lump forming. John stepped out of the barrel with blood running down from his nose. He was quiet until he saw his mother running toward him. With Kotone's tear streaked face, John let out a scream and began crying.

CJ stood close by rubbing his head with his right hand but held back his tears. He wanted to show he was a big boy and didn't cry like these little kids. As Stacey checked him over, his lower lip quivered, but he didn't cry.

"O.K., I think we all need to take a break," Mrs. Paquette announced. She walked over to a medium-sized cooler and opened it up. She pulled out soft packs of juice with a straw attached. "Come on, everyone take a seat and enjoy your snacks." A package of cookies was offered and soon all five boys were content drinking and eating.

As Mrs. Paquette played the doting grandmother role, the four younger women sat down on a two nearby benches. Across from the park was one of the car parks for the hospital. Cars were constantly arriving and departing as visitors to the hospital came and went. A medium-sized camper turned into the parking lot and fought the congestion to find a place to park. Luckily at the back parking lot away from the hospital three empty spaces together allowed the camper to park sideways.

The side door opened and two people stepped down. Locking the door, the man and woman began the long walk to the front of hospital. It took them along a sidewalk on the west side of the playground. An open grass area between the sidewalk and the play structure held two teenagers playing catch.

Misty sat straight up as she looked at the man. The other three women noticed the change in their friends attention.

"What is it, Misty?" Stacey asked.

"That's Jack's friend LaMarcus walking over there," Misty said.

"You know LaMarcus?" Kotone asked.

"Oh yes," Misty said. "He and Jack sucked me into one of their escapades. I know him too well."

"Who's he with?" Valentina asked.

Once it was established it was LaMarcus, all four focused on the woman. The scrutiny was intense.

"She's at least thirty years younger than him. Where did LaMarcus come up with her?" Stacey asked.

The woman was just a bit shorter than LaMarcus who himself was a big man. The women estimated she was six feet. tall

"Wherever she came from, she's way out of his league," Misty said. "Check out that body. She could pass for a model if she isn't one."

"Check out the bounce in her chest. Do you think those things are real?" Kotone asked.

"Every man's dream right there. She is the total package," Valentina said.

"I'll say," Stacey said. But she was busy working her memory. This woman who was walking past rang a bell to her. But where had she seen her before? The thought settled in as Stacey strained for an answer. That she was heading into the hospital with LaMarcus tied her to Jack. *But how?* she thought.

"But she could lose a few pounds," Misty said. All four women laughed at Misty's comment.

* * *

LaMarcus opened the front door of the hospital for the woman beside him. They walked in together and LaMarcus led them straight to the elevator. He had been to Jack's room before and knew the way.

Stepping off on the correct floor, he looked down toward the intensive care unit.

He knew he wasn't on the official list of visitors that Jack's family had given the hospital. But he had someone with him that he knew Jack cared about deeply. And he was determined that he would get her into his room to see him. He took the woman by the hand and together they walked toward Jack's room.

Not seeing Jack's brother Ed or son Carl, LaMarcus stood in the waiting area outside the room. LaMarcus figured he had made it. He stepped to the window to look into Jack's room and froze. The woman beside him looked blankly at the empty room and then turned to LaMarcus.

"Where is he?" she asked.

"He was here earlier. I don't know what happened," LaMarcus said.

The bed had obviously been occupied recently, by the disheveled sheets. The monitors that had kept track of Jack's condition were still in their place. The few flowers and cards that had decorated the space lingered. There just was no Jack.

Panic hit both of them at the same time as they realized that maybe Jack had died. That would explain the missing body but a room still being used. LaMarcus turned to find someone official even if it meant he would be kicked out.

He stopped a nurse walking by. "Excuse me, Jack Wesley was just here when I visited him before."

"Are you part of the family?" the nurse said. "You don't look like it so I can only give out information to family members. Now you need to leave the unit."

LaMarcus and the woman turned to leave. As they approached the elevator, Jack's brother Ed came down the corridor.

"LaMarcus, hold on," Ed said.

"Oh Ed, I'm glad to see you. Where did they put Jack?"

Ed eyed the woman standing quiet next to LaMarcus. He turned back to Jack's Marine friend.

"They took him in for a second operation. He developed internal bleeding on top of his infection."

The woman broke down and LaMarcus just caught her as she wavered toward the floor. Ed jumped in and took the woman's opposite side as the two men led her to a chair in the waiting room. LaMarcus helped her sit and held the woman as she sobbed, her head down.

As LaMarcus held the woman, Ed gave him the look to ask who she was. The answer would have to wait until she calmed down. When the sobbing subsided, LaMarcus whispered in her ear. She straightened herself so LaMarcus could stand up. He motioned Ed to follow.

A short distance away from the woman where she wouldn't overhear them LaMarcus stopped and turned to Ed. "This is Jack's good friend Katarina. She came all the way from Amsterdam to see him."

Ed knew Katarina by name only. All that Ed knew was that after Jack's run-in with her, Jack had lit out for Thailand to live. *Or escape,* LaMarcus thought. *From Jack's comments I'm not sure of the real reason he came to Thailand. And now she is here in person asking to see Jack.*

The two friends had lived in Thailand until Jack decided to head back to the States. In that time Jack had spoken often of two women in his life; Kotone and Katarina. While there had been others, none had had the effect on him that these two had. And now they were in the same city, both seeking him out.

Ed recognized LaMarcus's strained expression. "What is it?" Ed asked.

"There's something you need to know about Katarina," LaMarcus said.

He proceeded to describe to Ed the dilemma they faced. The two men finished without reaching a conclusion. With Jack undergoing his second emergency surgery, they would hold off on any big decisions.

LaMarcus had Katarina headed back to the camper when she asked, "Is Jack going to make it?" Her lower lip quivered as she asked.

"Sure he is," LaMarcus lied. "He's tough as nails."

"I don't know what I'll do if he doesn't make it. I should have never left him in Wyoming. What a fool I was, LaMarcus."

"Let's get back to the camper and you lie down and get some rest," LaMarcus said. "You had a long flight and now the stress of Jack. You need your rest."

As they exited the front entrance and took the sidewalk leading to the back parking lot, LaMarcus noticed a familiar figure off to the right. The person was obviously trying to catch LaMarcus' attention but not Katarina's. LaMarcus unlocked the camper's door and helped Katarina up the steps inside. He then excused himself after advising her to go lay on the bed and get some sleep.

Reaching Stacey in the children's park, LaMarcus smiled at Jack's daughter-in-law. In reality they only knew each other by photos they had seen of each other. Stacey held out her hand to greet LaMarcus but he went right for a hug.

"I'd know you anywhere," LaMarcus said. "Jack has shown me so many pictures of you I can't believe we've never met in person before."

"I know," said Stacey. "You and Jack have had too many adventures together and none of them included me."

"Ah, that would be a good thing," LaMarcus said. They both laughed at his statement.

"Yes, the only one I was involved in was bad enough."

LaMarcus grew quiet from the smiling banter. "Jack really got involved this time though."

"He wouldn't have wanted it any other way," Stacey said. "Mess with his family and he only knows one way to respond."

"I just wish I could have been there with him."

"And you'd probably be dead like poor Colonel Roberts," Stacey said.

"Yeah, there's that, isn't there."

The two watched Stacey's two kids run through and over the play structure. The others had left before LaMarcus had returned so they had the bench to themselves.

"LaMarcus, can I ask you something?" Stacey asked.

"Anything."

"The woman who was just with you."

"You don't know her?" LaMarcus asked.

"Let me guess. Figure skater from Amsterdam? Met Jack in Europe and stole his heart."

"Katarina, that's her. Flew in yesterday after I emailed her from Bangkok."

"Boy, you sure know how to complicate everything," Stacey said. "Kotone has finally showed up and now this."

"It's more complicated than you could ever imagine."

LaMarcus started to explain himself when the door to the camper opened and an older woman stepped out with a baby stroller. She set the stroller on the pavement and then disappeared back into the camper. She soon reappeared with a baby, placing the baby in the stroller. She adjusted the sheet for sun protection over the baby, shut the door and began walking toward where LaMarcus sat.

"Don't tell me," Stacey said.

"OK, I won't."

Chapter 28

San Diego, California

The next day Stacey rose early from her hotel room and checked the two boys sleeping in the attached room. Her mother lay on the second bed next to the boys. She had slept alone as Carl continued the vigil at the hospital. Stacey had stayed with him until midnight and then retreated to the hotel for rest. She figured one of them needed to be sharp and awake as today might be a critical day for Jack.

She threw on her clothes and headed down to the lobby. She walked the short distance to the hospital through the predawn light. It would be another hour before the sun actually broke out. Stopping in the hospital coffee shop, she ordered for herself and her husband. Carl would be running on fumes by now and would need a jolt to make it.

Stepping off the elevator, she saw the trio of Jack's support. Carl lay asleep in a chair while Ed and Graham sat nearby. Stacey wasn't sure how Ed was keeping the pace he kept but the dutiful brother had been here the whole time.

Stacey set Carl's coffee down on an end table and, after checking through the window that Jack was in his room, sat down next to Ed. She peeled the plastic cover off and took a sip. She realized that she probably should have grabbed something to eat with the coffee but she had been in a rush to get here.

"How is it going? It's a good sign he's back in his room."

"The doctors are guarded," Ed said. "The operation went well and they tied off the bleeder. But opening him up again just knocked him back on his recovery. His blood count shows the infection still battling inside him."

Stacey sat and took in Jack's information. The infection had to be beaten if Jack was to live. That the infection couldn't be suppressed meant bad things would happen. Jack's life counted on his body fighting off the infection. The four people sat quiet.

Eventually, Ed and Graham stood up announcing they were going to go to the cafeteria and get something to eat. Stacey looked at Carl continuing to sleep and asked if they could bring something back for her.

At two nurses walking by pushing a medical cart, Carl stirred. He sat up and looked at his wife. She handed him the coffee.

"Thanks,'" Carl said. He took a sip of coffee. "I don't know how long I've been out. Where's Uncle Ed?"

"He and Sir Graham went down to get something to eat."

"I'm kinda hungry myself," Carl said.

"Before you go anywhere, we need to talk about your Dad," Stacey said.

They were still in discussion twenty minutes later when the elevator doors opened and Kotone stepped out. The conversation suddenly stopped. Stacey rose and walked to her friend. They embraced before walking arm-in-arm up to Jack's window. A sigh of relief came from Kotone to see Jack still in his room.

"I had to go get some sleep last night," Kotone said. "But when I laid down the only way I could fall asleep was to climb into bed with John and hold him."

Stacey knew the motherly reaction to bad news. Gathering up your children and holding them close was also her reaction. And while CJ was young enough to let Stacey lay with him, JJ was too old to let that happen. And it really was JJ she had wanted to hold. Not that both of her children didn't mean the world to her. But at this time in her life, the mother instincts called strongest for one over the other.

"Kotone, you need to go be with Jack," Stacey said. "His infection continues and he needs a miracle to fight it off."

"I don't know what to do," Kotone said. "He just lays there. I hold his hand and speak to him, but there is nothing."

"Then pray," Stacey said.

Kotone acknowledged Stacey's comment with only a look. She walked over and opened Jack's door. Stepping into the room, she let the door go, the swish sound of the door closing announcing their separation.

"That was harsh," Carl said.

"I don't care," Stacey said. "Somebody needs to get Jack to fight. It's his only chance."

"But to dump it all on her."

"She's his wife," Stacey said. "The woman that he committed to cherish in sickness and health. Its time she stepped up to those vows."

Carl gave his wife a glance that told Stacey she was being out of line. The couple sat down and sat quietly, the increased activity of the Intensive Care Unit taking over. The nurses went about their morning rounds and soon doctors began appearing checking on patients. The entire time Carl and Stacey sat mute. Kotone continued her bedside watch and Stacey would walk over to the window occasionally to check if anything had changed.

But Jack's monitors continued their reporting as Jack remained unconscious. Kotone sat beside him holding his hand and Stacey could see her lips moving. Whether in prayer or otherwise, she couldn't make out. But she was making her presence known to the man who needed it. Something inside Jack needed to be sparked to get him back on the healing side. The lingering mode he was in now did not bode well.

As Stacey returned to her seat next to Carl, LaMarcus and Katarina stepped off the elevator. Carl sat up as Jack's good friend walked up. Stacey stood and embraced Katarina, leading her over to the window. Katarina's legs buckled slightly at the sight of Jack in his bed and Stacey led her to a chair.

"Stacey, what is going on?" Carl asked. "Who is this?"

"Carl Wesley, you just sit there a minute and listen," Stacey said. "Your Dad married Kotone and expected to live happily ever after. That Kotone disappeared on him after all she went through wasn't right. And I think she knows that now."

"But, you are going to tell me . . ." Carl started to say.

"I said listen," Stacey interrupted. "Two whole years Jack made the best of a life not knowing where his wife was or even if he had a wife. No news whatsoever."

"But you knew where she was," Carl said.

"You are missing the point. Yes, Kotone and I stayed in touch by email but it was her wish that I not tell Jack. If I had broken that promise, she would have disappeared altogether. That she is now here and attempting to be a wife speaks of the progress she has made."

Carl looked at Katarina and back at his wife. The look spoke volumes to Stacey.

"And yes, your Dad loves another woman. And she's sitting here right now so we have to deal with it. So, Jack loves two women. He may not live to see either one again so I don't think we're risking much here."

"What are you saying Stacey?" Carl asked. "You aren't about to say . . ."

"Carl Wesley, grow up. Your Dad made this world and it just might save him." Stacey stood up and took Katarina by the hand. She led her over to the door to Jack's room. She looked back at her husband who was about to boil over. She opened the door and stepped aside. Katarina walked in.

* * *

Kotone looked up from her praying to see a tall woman walk in. From her looks and build, Kotone quickly surmised who she was.

"Katarina?" Kotone asked to confirm.

Katarina snapped her look from Jack to the woman sitting by his side. She had a shocked expression at her name being spoken.

"Yes, how did you know?"

"Stacey and I stayed in touch all these years. She told me about Jack and of course she passed on information he told her. He was very forthcoming about you to her."

"He was?" Katarina said. "Then you must be Kotone."

"Please come sit down beside me here." Kotone motioned for Katarina to grab a chair by the door and move it beside her. Katarina sat down as Kotone took Katarina's hand and placed it on Jack's undamaged hand.

"He looks so . . ." Katarina stopped. Her words failed her in speaking of Jack.

"I know."

The two women sat silent. The mutual link between them lay quiet. Except for the normal hospital noises, the room was still. Each woman was content to be sitting next to the man she loved, hoping against all odds that he would live another day.

As tears formed in Katarina's eyes, she let go of Jack's hand to reach for tissues her mother had given her. She dabbed her eyes to hold the tears back. Kotone glanced to see Katarina as she took Jack's hand again. Seeing Katarina's reaction, tears began to form in Kotone's eyes. Katarina passed a tissue to Kotone, who took it in one hand.

Katarina placed one hand on Jack's upper thigh to be close. Since his hand was occupied by Kotone's hand, his thigh was the next closest body part. When she gently stroked his upper leg there was a tremor from Jack. Both women looked first at Jack and then at each other. Jack lay with his eyes closed but there had definitely been a slight tremor in his body.

Katarina moved her hand gently across his thigh again and Jack responded again. Kotone tried to emote a similar response by rubbing Jack's arm but nothing happened. Katarina reached over to Jack's opposite leg and brushed her hand against the sheet. She felt his thigh underneath and the action caused a third body tremor. Kotone looked at Katarina. She nodded her head for her to continue her touching. Each time Katarina rubbed Jack's body, he reacted.

"I'm sorry," Katarina said.

"Don't be. Keep going," Kotone said. She knew they could sort out which one of them he loved only if he lived. If Katarina had the touch that could get Jack to fight inside, then Kotone would live with the results.

Katarina had Jack twitching as she touched his feet and lower legs. But his eyes remained shut while he remained unconscious. Kotone leaned over and whispered to Katarina.

"Oh I couldn't," Katarina said.

"It's not like you never did before," Kotone said.

"But you're his wife. You need to try that."

"You seem to have the touch that is reaching him," Kotone said.

"He often spoke of you when we were together," Katarina said. "I was married too and we both talked of our marriages."

"I'm afraid I wasn't much of a wife. I can only imagine what he said."

"That he loved you very much. But that you disappeared on him," Katarina said.

The words hurt Kotone as Katarina said them. That she had agreed to marry Jack only to abandon him after all he had done for her. *But that is the problem* Kotone thought. *He is always rescuing me and I just want it to end.*

Kotone looked at Jack longingly and realized that she had no part of him being near death. She hadn't been anywhere near him in over three years. The other woman who obviously loved him had done so more recently. She now knew that she wasn't a jinx to Jack, but now it was too late. Jack was responding to another woman's touch, not hers.

As Kotone silently said a prayer while watching the man she loved lay in bed, his eyes suddenly twitched. Kotone's heart stopped as she stared at Jack's face for more. A second eye twitch took her breath away.

In her excitement to see if Katarina had seen the same, Kotone turned her head and gasped. Katarina's hand was under the sheets as she slowly massaged Jack's manhood. Katarina stopped her manipulation when she saw Kotone's opened-mouthed expression.

"I'm sorry. I thought it would catch his attention," Katarina said. She began to withdraw her hand from under the covers.

"No, no don't stop," Kotone said. "Did you see his eyes move?"

"Maybe you should be doing it? You are his wife."

"It doesn't matter right now who is what. We need a man who's alive and you seem to be awakening something. Keep it up," Kotone said.

Katarina grew red at what she was about to do, but followed Kotone's instructions. She moverdher hand back to Jack and the sheets began to move. Both women watched intently as Jack's eyes rolled behind his eyelids. Suddenly his eyes opened and snapped to the two women sitting beside him. Katarina stopped her stimulation.

Jack tried to speak, but his throat resisted. His eyes pleaded for some moisture for his mouth as he leaned his head toward the women. He attempted a weak smile for their benefit. He received two beaming smiles in return.

Chapter 29

Missoula, Montana

The Bitterroot Mountain Range continued its grip on winter as the high peaks shown white in the afternoon sun. On the valley floor of the Clark Fork River, spring had arrived three days ago and continued its hold. While the evenings were cool, the past few days were glorious after the long Montana winter.

The warm weather had gotten the ornamental trees blossoming as pink showed on neighborhood cherry trees. In places the white of apple and pear trees offset the bare brown of the deciduous trees just waking up. The early flowering shrubs added vibrant yellow along the local residential street.

This was the time of the year that awakenings of all kinds were in evidence. Part of that evidence was the shorts and light shirts that the university students wore as they played in the sun. While the ground was still too wet for plantings, neighbors were fitting out pots of plants on front porches. Everyone gathered outside to enjoy the first pleasant weather since October.

Jack Wesley sat quietly and took it all in. He knew he was lucky to be alive. Once he had regained consciousness, the tender attention of both Kotone and Katarina gave him the strength to recover. After another week the doctors had announced the infection had been beaten. Jack made steady improvement after that.

Valentina and Misty had made their visits and then flown back home. Carl and Stacey along with Ed had all soon left leaving only the two women to oversee things.

Now back home in Missoula, Jack had been recovering from his brush against death. While his injuries still caused pain, physical therapy and daily exercise had brought most of his strength back. The combination of a local health club's indoor track mixed with cross-country skiing had enabled him to almost regain his former self.

But the scars of his encounter with the Mexican drug cartel were very evident. And not just in his continued limp from his leg injuries. The doctors had said that he should be able to overcome the limp with continued workouts. No, there were more substantial scars that were not easily walked off. And as he sat on the porch swing at his house, the most critical one sat next to him.

His daughter Inez had lost her husband in the abduction. Newly married and just beginning a life together, her Eric had been brutally killed. Jack moved his arm around Inez's shoulders and drew her closer. She instinctively curled up next to her father. As Jack slowly swung the chair suspended from the porch ceiling, the slow rocking motion soothed the pain he knew she suffered.

It had been an even tougher winter for Inez as she fought the loss of her life partner. When Jack returned to Missoula a few months back, he discovered the house across the street vacant and for rent. The illegal Mexican family that had been living there had been deported back to their home country. That they had provided information to the drug cartel on the comings and goings of the Wesley family had overridden any argument for leniency with the U.S. Government.

With an available house nearby, Jack had persuaded Inez to make the move to Missoula to be nearby. When Inez discovered that she was pregnant while in the San Diego hospital, the draw of family only increased. Stacey had done the best job of selling the idea of Inez moving with the thought that the new baby would have cousins close by as well as built-in day care.

Inez moved slightly to get more comfortable as her large belly forced her to almost lay back in the swing. Her due date grew closer and she had shifted to living with Jack most of the time. Being alone did not appeal to her and Jack welcomed the addition to his house.

Sitting across from them, Carl took a sip of water. The men had been doing yard work and the evidence sat in Carl's driveway. Jack's pick-up truck bed overflowed with tree trimmings and other brush cleaned up from the two houses. In front of them the smell of newly cut grass wafted over them as the lawnmower track patterns announced spring. While the grass still had a dull sheen to it from its dormant winter sleep, the first cut of the year evened things out to be ready for the warm weather growth.

"So it looks like the weather will hold one more day," Carl said. "We can get down and recycle our yard debris tomorrow."

"I'm sure they're open on Saturday with weather like this," Jack added. He took a big gulp of his water. The two men had been working hard all day with a brief break for lunch. He knew they should go right now before the recycling depot closed and dump their load. They could wake up to rain. Weather in Montana could change drastically in a mere few hours and unloading in the rain or snow didn't appeal to him.

"You want to go now then?" Carl asked.

"We should," Jack inserted but the energy just wasn't there. And the way Carl looked at his Dad, he knew his son guessed the reason. While Jack seemed to be back, the injuries sapped his endurance.

"Dad, why don't I take it down and dump it? You can just relax."

Jack remained quiet. While Jack would soon be fifty-nine years old, some days he felt like he was eighty. And he didn't want to admit that to his two children. But the slow swinging motion felt just about all he could do right now.

A car moving down their street caught Jack's attention and he stiffened slightly. Inez noticed the change in her Dad and tried to sit up, her legs moving so they hung down. As the black four-door sedan slowed to a stop in front of his house Jack turned toward the street.

"Carl, take your sister into the house and close the door," Jack said. The command style of his voice drew Carl's attention to the new arrival. Without any question, Carl stood up, helped Inez to her feet and assisted her to the open front door. Once through the doorway, the natural wood door closed.

Two men in suits stepped out of the car and met on the sidewalk at the end of Jack's front walk. They teamed up and walked slowly up the walk, stepping onto Jack's porch. They removed their sunglasses and placed them in their suit coat pocket.

"Jack Wesley?" one asked.

"Who wants to know?" Jack asked back.

In unison, the two reached inside their suit coats and retrieved their IDs. Flipping them open, the badge and the picture were held up for Jack's scrutiny.

"FBI," said the taller one. "I'm Special Agent Stoddard. This is Special Agent Miller." Agent Stoddard flipped his thumb toward his partner to make sure the two identities were confirmed.

"And what brings you to my porch, special agent?" Jack asked.

"Mind if we sit down?" Stoddard asked.

Jack would have loved to tell them no, that he did mind if they sat down. While he had plenty of deeds from his past that would warrant a visit by the FBI, he assumed the latest episode would be what they would be investigating. The lull answering became apparent, so Jack relented.

"I suppose."

"Thank you Mr. Wesley," again spoken by Stoddard. Jack make a mental note that he was probably the senior man of the two. But you could never be sure. Jack had spent time around the FBI during his career in law enforcement and had learned to never assume anything where they were concerned. He had learned many other things and shifted his brain to focus. This would not be just a casual visit on the front porch.

"Was that your son and daughter we saw as we pulled up?"

"Yes. My daughter is very pregnant and needed to lay down for a while," Jack said.

Behind him, he heard his pick-up truck door open and slam shut. The engine started and Jack turned to see Carl back down the driveway and drive off.

"Is there a reason your son's leaving?" Stoddard asked.

"I imagine he is going to the recycling center to unload the bed. We've been busy today cleaning the yards."

Agent Miller finally spoke. "Yes, looks good. I hope the weather lasts into the weekend so I can get some yard work done."

Jack noticed the slight look of annoyance by Stoddard at his partner's interjection. Agent Miller didn't pick up on his partner's displeasure as they both faced Jack in separate chairs.

"We might want to talk to him afterwards," Stoddard said.

"I'm sure he'll be back," Jack said.

"First I want to offer my condolences on the loss of your son-in-law. Major Reiner was a credit to the Air Force and I'm sure your daughter misses him greatly," Stoddard said.

"Yes she does. Every day."

"Because he was a federal employee, the FBI is responsible for the investigation of his murder."

"And how is that investigation going? It's been six months now. Surely you have news to give me so I can tell my daughter that you've arrested the ones who murdered her husband."

Stoddard squirmed slightly in his seat at Jack's question. He cleared his throat and leaned forward slightly.

"Actually Mr. Wesley, we are discovering that anyone associated with the case is dead," Stoddard said. He carefully watched Jack for a reaction.

Being a former police detective himself, Jack knew when to hold his emotions in check and when to have a poker face on. And he knew this was one of those times. Jack knew everyone was dead because he or his friends had killed them all. There would be no waiting around for the slow wheels of justice to grind away. Jack's method of solving problems was quicker to resolution.

"Surely someone is still alive that could answer some questions," Jack said. He already knew the answer, but in case these two agents wanted to offer someone he had missed, he was all ears.

Stoddard continued his cold stare of Jack. "We received the report from the Mexican police of a pile of bodies near Islita, Sonora, Mexico. But you know about them already."

Jack knew that Stoddard was playing the game of throwing facts out and seeing if Jack would admit to them. He had used the same technique many times.

"Only by what people told me," Jack said. He kept his body steady and showed no emotion or change in body language to give off any tells. A tell is an involuntary movement that a person makes tohat could give themselves away. Whether playing cards or any endeavor where the truth is hidden, people gave off certain movements or facial expressions that sometimes was opposite to what their mouth was saying.

"But you were in Mexico at the time, I believe. You crossed the border at Islita the day before the compound was attacked."

"If you say so." Jack pushed his hairline back on his forhead to reveal the raw scar of the round he had taken in the head. "Since being shot in the head, my memory of everything is pretty scattered."

"Are you claiming that you have no idea what happened at the drug compound?" Stoddard asked. His facial expression belied his calm composure.

"Special Agent Stoddard, I don't know if you've taken a 9mm bullet to the head before, but I'm just glad to be alive. That I can walk and chew gum at the same time is even better. And that my gum doesn't drool out of my head is the best part. I worked every day in rehab at the hospital with those who were injured fighting for our country. I saw many head wounds and I thank God for watching over me."

"So you know nothing of the attack on the cartel in Las Vegas where five people had their heads chopped off? One of which was a woman," Stoddard said.

"Being comatose for a month in the naval hospital in San Diego limits one's knowledge of events taking place. But people have told me that

Daniel Vasquez and his drug gang had all been killed by a rival Mexican gang. Cutting heads off is a cultural thing down there."

"And you have no knowledge of a LaMarcus Lewis arriving from overseas for a quick visit?"

"Mr. Lewis and I go way back and it was very thoughtful that he would fly all that way to see me."

Stoddard perked up. "So you remember him visiting then?"

"Of course. He had to remind me who he was, though. And that we took a picture for my memory book helps," Jack said. "A memory book is something that people with brain injuries have. You put pictures and label them to help remember who everyone is."

"Well, Mr. Lewis left the country soon after visiting you. If you know where he went to, we would like to question him about his activities while in the U.S. He rented a camper van similar to one we have closed circuit TV film of being in the vicinity of the killings in Las Vegas."

Jack knew that if the FBI had conclusive film evidence of LaMarcus driving a camper van near the murders, they would be doing more than pumping Jack for answers. Obviously whatever film they had lacked conclusive evidence that it was LaMarcus.

"I can't help you Special Agent. But passports are difficult to fake, so I'm sure wherever he went you can obtain his entry information."

"Yes, we have him entering Malaysia but he seems to have disappeared from there," Stoddard said. "You've been in that part of the world Mr. Wesley?"

"Oh yes. You'll have to remind me where and when I was there but I do have images of Asia in my brain."

"A year ago you left Thailand and flew through Europe to Mexico from where you entered the U.S. You were in Mexico when Ernesto Vasquez was killed."

"I was?" Jack asked. "Where did that take place?"

"I think you know full well that Ernesto was killed outside Las Vegas."

"Well, I didn't know that. Or if I did, I sure don't remember it now," Jack said. "So if I was in Mexico and Ernesto was killed in the U.S., in my police days that would be an alibi."

"You didn't have an alibi a year ago when you killed two gang members in Jackson, Wyoming."

Jack grew tired of the game that was being played. The FBI didn't have anything they could pin on him and they were just throwing things out there to see if Jack would slip up. It was the FBI's style these days. Jack called it the 'Martha Stewart' entrapment game. Question someone long enough and when they answered a question differently than they had two days before, arrest them for lying to the government.

In todays FBI, it didn't matter if a crime had been committed. That was irrelevant. If the Feds wanted to convict someone, they didn't need a crime. They just made the process so burdensome on an individual that the person would mess up. Then a process conviction was applied and people went to jail for lying, not for criminal activity. And Martha Stewart was the most obvious example.

The FBI never got her committing a crime. She was guilty of not remembering what she had said at the beginning of twenty-four hours of questioning. The slip of memory was lying to the FBI and guilty of a Federal crime. And Jack was not going there.

"I'm sure you guys checked the record because again I don't really remember it. But let me guess that it was self-defense? Two people trying to kill me and they lost, correct?" Jack said.

"Your memory loss is convenient for you, Mr. Wesley," Stoddard said.

"Well, I sure don't recommend getting shot in the head so you can use that as an excuse."

Again, Special Agent Miller finally spoke, "Come on. I think we've taken up enough of Mr. Wesley's time here."

Jack noticed the glare he received as he said it from his partner. The two stood up to leave and thanked Jack for his time. As they walked down the walkway, Jack relaxed slightly that they were leaving.

Chapter 30

Missoula, Montana

As the FBI agents opened the doors to drive off, Carl and the pick-up returned. Carl swung the Tundra into Jack's driveway and shut it down. Jack's attitude shifted as he noticed the FBI agents slam the car doors shut and walk back up the walk.

Carl walked onto the porch with a nod of his head toward the two men in suits. It was his way to ask who they were.

"FBI," Jack said to his son as Carl sat down next to his dad. The two agents arrived on the porch, introduced themselves to Carl and proceeded to sit down again.

Agent Stoddard spoke first, "Carl Wesley?"

"Yes," Carl said.

"We would like to ask you some questions about the murder of Daniel Vasquez and associates."

Jack held his composure. Part of him wanted to stop it all in its tracks by telling Carl to ask for a lawyer. In all his experience in police work, he knew the truly smart people never spoke to the police without a lawyer present. There were so many ways that the police knew to entrap people. If they were guilty of a crime, that was one thing. But the whole process crime convictions Jack had seen lately were outrageous. Innocent individuals swept up by saying the wrong thing to the police.

But Jack knew if he claimed a lawyer be present, then the FBI would think they smelled blood. And lawyers were expensive. Not that being locked up for years for something you really didn't do was cheap. So Jack held his breath and waited to see what happened.

"I thought a rival Mexican gang had killed them," Carl answered.

"That's what your Dad said, too."

Jack jumped in, "Because that's what we were told." He knew Stoddard's answer was to imply collusion between Jack and his son and that meant they had conspired in something.

"Mr. Wesley, we are interviewing your son here. Please be quiet." Stoddard turned back to Carl. "You didn't sustain a head injury did you?"

"No, Special Agent Stoddard, my head is fine."

"That's good. Maybe we can get some answers then," Stoddard said. "So where were you at the time of the murders?"

"Please be specific. What murders? What date and time did they take place?"

Jack smiled inside at his sons answer. Carl had been around Jack enough times to know some of the techniques cops used in interrogations. But Jack knew that these FBI agents were much more experienced than his son.

Special Agent Stoddard gave the pertinent information as to place and time. Carl sat as though he had to think about the answer.

"Trouble remembering?" Stoddard said to Carl.

"It was six months ago. And my Dad was near death in the hospital in San Diego. So there was a lot going on for me at the time. But I think there were plenty of staff at the hospital that can verify that I was at my Dad's side every day. And when I wasn't there I was at my sister's side as she recovered from her trauma."

"And where were you prior to being in San Diego with your injured Dad?"

"Let me think," Carl lingered on his thoughts, the FBI agents showing irritation at the delay. "Oh yes, I was visiting my Uncle Ed outside Yuma."

"Doing what?"

"My uncle works for the U. S. Senator from Wyoming and he was doing some kind of government work," Carl said.

"And you want me to believe that you just took time off from work to travel all the way to Yuma just to see your uncle?"

"Gee, Special Agent Stoddard," Carl said. "I don't know if you have family, but family is very important to the Wesley clan. He asked that I come to visit him and I did."

"I see," Stoddard said. "So at no time did you cross into Mexico while in Yuma?"

"I think my passport would show that one. Did you check with Border and Customs Agency?"

"We checked. Do you know a Karma Somda?"

"Sure, he was my neighbor."

"And would you know why he crossed the border at the same time as your father and a Mr. Gregory Roberts?"

"No idea." Carl looked straight at Stoddard.

"And no idea why one Karma Somda left the country right after the murders in Las Vegas?"

"Again, no idea," Carl said. "I know he was anxious to return home to his family."

"And where would that be?"

"I believe he was Gurkha. So I guess he would be heading home to Nepal, but I'm not sure where he lived."

"And you knew Mr. Roberts since he was also your neighbor. Might you know why his body was cremated without an autopsy as to the cause of death?"

"I remember the doctors saying he died from trauma to the head," Carl said.

"Not very definitive is it?" Stoddard said. There was a pause and Jack could tell the real question was about to come out. "So do you have any idea what happened in Mexico while you were sitting with your uncle in Yuma, which is nearby, I'll point out. Three men enter Mexico, one is killed, one is almost killed and the lone survivor has left the country. Meanwhile, close to where they entered Mexico, a large compound is blown apart and many people were killed. Would you find all that curious?"

"Are you investigating crimes in Mexico now? I thought you'd have enough to do in the United States."

Jack blanched inside at Carl's flip answer. He knew you had to be careful with Federal agents. They had tremendous power to ruin lives and it was best to not antagonize them. Jack saw the anger rise in Special Agent Stoddard face at Carl's comment.

"Son, we follow crimes wherever they lead if part of them takes place in America. I thought you would want to catch the thugs that killed your sister's husband."

Jack slightly elbowed Carl to not take the bait that was being thrown out. Jack shifted in his seat to disguise the maneuver from the agent's gaze. Luckily Carl took the message from his father.

"And I appreciate your work in bringing them to justice," Carl said. "I'm just not sure I know anything that can help you find them."

"Well, maybe we need to talk to your sister then. She was there when her husband was killed and may be the best source of information."

Jack was out of his seat in a shot, startling the FBI agents. They immediately stood to counter any threat, their hands shifting noticeable toward the guns they carried.

"That's not going to happen," Jack said. Carl joined him as the two Wesley men went into protection mode over Inez.

"Mr. Wesley," Stoddard said. "We've tried to cooperate with you and your family in our investigation. But we have more formal ways to get what we want."

Jack exploded. "Then plan on lots of lawyers because my daughter is still recovering from her ordeal. And with her pregnant, I'm sure any defense lawyer worth his money would be glad to take the case. She will not be talking to anyone anytime soon."

"Calm down, Mr. Wesley," Agent Miller interjected. "We understand the trauma your family has been through. We are just searching for the truth here."

"As you said, everyone connected to this case is dead. These weren't nice people. Some would say they got what they deserved. Maybe the appropriate thing to do is move on and find a case where good people are seeking some measure of justice. I'm sure you have plenty of those to investigate."

Miller wrapped up things finally. "You might be right, Mr. Wesley. We will contact you if we need any more questions answered. And we will make a note that your daughter has requested a lawyer be present at any questioning."

Jack held his tongue as he wanted to say more. But the two agents stepping off the porch let him stay quiet. When they got into their sedan and drove off, he could finally sit back down. Carl took the chair opposite.

Before they could discuss what had just happened, the front door opened and Inez walked out. She sat down next to her Dad on the swing seat. Katarina followed holding Johan. She undid her halter top, placed a towel over her shoulder and began breast feeding the baby.

Her action distracted Jack from what had just happened. He still wasn't used to Katarina living with him, and while he loved her and his baby son, life had been very confusing to him lately. Gone was the simple time of enjoying an adventure out in the world as he lived his retired single life.

Jack had come out of his unconscious state to find Katarina at the hospital with a baby. That the baby was his fit with the fact that they had certainly been intimate nine months ago. And they had been intimate a lot.

They had expedited her immigrant visa application, thanks to his brother's help, so they could be together. Jack was a responsible guy and if he had a son out there to raise, he would step up and be a dad again.

Jack's thoughts were broken by Inez speaking. "Dad, thanks for defending me against those men. I don't want anything to interrupt me having my baby. Its the only thing I have left of Eric and I don't' want anything to take that away."

"Don't worry," Jack said. "I think they got the message.

"So, Dad, do you think they'll be back?"

Jack just stared ahead. That was one question he had no answer for. But all three people were looking at him for an answer. Carl had his family to think about as well. Three young children and one more on the way. The Wesley family needed protection at all costs. They had done what needed doing and maybe the FBI would move on to another case.

But Katarina knew full well that Jack had a history. And a history that went back longer than the Vasquez drug gang. She certainly didn't know all the details and Jack would never tell her, but the FBI had the resources to dig into sensitive things if they choose to.

And now here was his family asking if things would return to normal. There were children to raise, yards to mow, jobs to work and maybe normalcy to enjoy. Jack didn't have the answers to that. But Jack would fight with all his strength to protect those around him.

"Will they be back? I can't answer that question," Jack said. "But if they return, we will be ready. That's our only recourse."

Chapter 31

Bozeman, Montana

The week of nice weather had been invariably followed by a change in the weather. Snow returned to Montana to show everyone that winter was not over yet. And although the official start of spring had happened, everyone knew that snow could happen in any month in Montana.

Jack maneuvered carefully on the Interstate highway through Butte. As the highest elevation on the freeway, Butte would often have heavy snow compared to the lower Missoula. The pickup swung down the grade that led to the flats heading into Bozeman.

Reaching the second Bozeman exit, Jack dropped down onto N. 7th Street and headed south into town. It was rainy here in Bozeman but the surrounding hills were heavy in fresh snow. He turned right onto W. Main Street before turning left at the Bozeman Food Co-op. Turning left onto W. Curtis St., he stopped in front of a white single-story duplex.

A small face in the window said it all. Jack looked at the small boy who was screaming and pointing wildly. With the windows closed he couldn't hear anything but he knew what was being said.

Soon Kotone walked into the room and picked John up. They both smiled and waved at Jack.

Jack sat momentarily and let the love soak into him. That he was married to Kotone but only lived half the time with her was a compromise the two of them had worked out. That Jack loved a second woman and had a son with that woman meant splitting his time between two families. And though this shared schedule had been going on now for four months, he still felt remorse about it. He was old-fashioned enough to know that this was not the way it was supposed to be. But he had been a father and husband before and that had ended in a disaster. At least the marriage had ended. That he lived next to his two children and had a wonderful relationship with them was certainly not a failure.

But these two new families needed him also. He had the means to support both of them financially and he was attempting to support both of them physically. The two in the window had disappeared and Jack scanned the house to see them open the front door.

Kotone walked across the front yard and up to his driver's door window. Jack buzzed the window and she leaned in to kiss him. John grabbed his Dad and Jack pulled him in through the window, placing him standing on his lap.

"Good morning," Kotone said. "Afraid to come in?"

"No, just sitting here thinking what a lucky guy I am."

"Lucky that you knocked me up and that I finally came to find you." Kotone smiled at her dig at him. Ever since they found each other at the hospital in San Diego, this had been her theme, that she had become pregnant during their brief honeymoon but then she had disappeared. Jack didn't know about his son until he met him in San Diego.

"Please don't talk like that, especially around John," Jack said.

"OK, sorry to bring it up. But it's the truth."

"I know, but with the others out there, it's a sore subject."

Kotone knew about Jack's other young children. That four young souls had resulted from his sexual escapades weighed on him. That two of them would be raised by other men and not know the truth helped. But that left Katarina and Kotone sharing him on a two-week basis. Two weeks in Bozeman followed by two weeks in Missoula. To anyone that asked, Jack went out on book signing tours. In the meantime Kotone had her sister Komatsu living next door in the other duplex for support while he was away. In Missoula, Katarina had Carl and Stacey along with Inez. Soon her parents would be emigrating and living in the house next door. When Gregory had been killed and Karma headed home, Jack had purchased the house they had left. Katarina's parents wanted to live near their daughter and Jack would make the house available to them.

But all this family together weighed on Jack. He knew he was paying the price of running around the world and hooking up with anyone that came along. While he thought he was more discerning than that, obviously with four young kids with four different women he had not been too discerning. But he loved each of them in a different way.

And he was just happy he could share the lives of two of them. That one was twenty years younger than him was great. That the other woman was thirty years younger was just as great. That they both were willing to share with the other was even better.

"Come on John. Let's show Daddy our surprise," Kotone said.

"Yes, yes, Mamma." John leaned out the truck window and his mother took him in her arms.

"Come on, you. Time to do your Daddy duties."

Jack grabbed his travel bag and stepped out of his truck. He followed his family into the house and shut the door behind him. The warmth and smells took him away from all his past problems. Here he could be Daddy again. And being retired, he could be Daddy full time.

Kotone had worked with the university to have a schedule that accommodated Jack's arrival every two weeks. She worked part days until Jack arrived and then switched to full time. Jack was left with day care duties for his two-week stay.

He loved it. He could do all the things he had missed doing with Carl and Inez. Visit the park if the weather was good. Go to the children's museum for colder days. Play in the snow and then come into the warm house for cookies and milk. Things that he had missed as he worked his police career.

While it all seemed exciting now, he did wonder if it would grow old. He knew the problem of parents who stayed home full time, and he had two families to parent.

Chapter 32

London, England

Jack's flight from Washington D.C. had provided time to think through all that had happened. It was now a year since the fight with the cartel had left him near death. It had also killed a man. A man who had chosen to stand with Jack in defense of his family even though he barely knew him.

As soon as Jack was out of the hospital he had contacted the British Embassy in Washington D.C.. He wanted to go and pay his respects to the warrior who had fallen beside him. Over the ensuing months of his personal rehabilitation, letters were exchanged that located the burial site of Colonel Gregory Roberts.

Further inquiry of any family of the colonel turned up a sister. Once arrangements had been made, Jack boarded a jet in Missoula headed to Great Britain. He had to turn down numerous family members and friends that had offered to travel with him. Jack declined, saying it was something he needed to do by himself.

Greg had chosen to go into harm's way with Jack and had paid the ultimate price for his decision. That the man had lived through any number of military actions to only die in a doorway in a tumble down Mexican shack spoke volumes. To men who served, the commitment to their brothers-in-arms meant everything. And Jack would keep it between himself and Greg.

The surprise had been upon reaching Washington D.C. Dulles Airport to change planes, he was moved up to first class. Luxuriating in the small cubicle lounges that first class afforded, Jack snoozed in-between watching movies for his seven-hour flight. Now as the Dreamliner dropped down for a landing at Heathrow Airport, Jack pulled on his shoes and readied himself for the landing.

The jetliner taxied up to the gate and Jack received his second surprise. The stewardess announced that all the passengers should remain seated until a special detail had exited the plane. Jack looked around where the special detail might happen and was surprised when two policemen and a man in a suit walked onto the plane. They moved directly to where he was seated.

"Mr. Wesley, please come with us," the man in the suit said.

Jack was taken aback by the three standing in front of him waiting. As he gathered his carry-on and stood, he looked at his fellow first class passengers. He received the look of shock mixed with disdain that someone that had sat with them the whole time was now being escorted off the plane by the police.

Jack followed the one man off the plane while the police officers brought up the rear. He heard the announcement that passengers could now exit the plane. As the other first class passengers filled the jetway, the man in the suit opened a side door and led the four of them through it. As it slammed shut, Jack saw the final look of the others as they headed to immigration.

"Am I in trouble?" Jack asked.

"Hardly, Mr. Wesley," the man in the suit said. As he said it Jack noticed the two policemen drift off and disappear. Now just the two of them, the man continued. "I'm George Wakefield of the Queen's own office. The Queen wanted you met and taken straight through to your hotel."

George opened another door and they walked out into the receiving area of immigration. They walked up to an officer with a 'diplomatic visa' sign over him. No one else stood in line unlike the long lines waiting for the other officers. Asking for Jack's passport, George handed it to the immigration officer. It was quickly returned and the two headed to another private door.

"My men will collect your luggage and arrange for it to be at your hotel. My car and driver are right over here," George said.

Jack was suddenly liking the VIP treatment on entering a country. Over the last year his connection to the Queen of England had been paying off. He climbed into the backseat of the Jaguar as George climbed into the front. He swiveled around to face Jack.

"I've been instructed to make your stay as pleasant as possible. If you require anything, just ask." George then handed Jack a cell phone and instructed him to use it to call. George's number was listed as well as his hotel's number.

"Is Ms. Robert's number in here?" Jack asked. Gregory Roberts's sister was his only living relative. Neither one had married, Greg for obvious reasons related to his military service. Jack didn't know about the sister. But one letter from the British Embassy had stated that the sister had been contacted and had agreed to meet Jack. That would take place in two days in Wales where Greg's interment had taken place.

"Yes, third number down. But only use it in an emergency as she has no car and lives in a small village in Wales. Actually the same one she and Colonel Roberts grew up in."

Jack had been to London before and knew some of his way around the city. The Jaguar maneuvered through traffic as it made its way to Jack's hotel. The British Embassy had made the reservation and Jack had checked the name on the internet. He was anxious to finally see it.

The driver pulled into a turnaround at the front of the hotel and stopped. George stepped out and opened Jack's door before the hotel staff reached it. Being late to their task, the staff took Jack's carry-on as George led Jack inside. The hotel lobby confirmed what Jack had surmised. He had never stayed in a five-star hotel before but this met his imagination at what one looked like. Large chandeliers with gold trim matched the rubbed wood smell of the lobby as George checked Jack in and handed him the key.

"I'll let you relax today. Tomorrow will be your trip to Wales where we will meet Ms. Roberts. I've been instructed to inform you that the Queen has asked you to lunch upon your return from Wales. I hope your schedule will afford her request."

"Thank you, Mr. Wakefield," Jack said. "Yes, I surely can accommodate lunch with the Queen. Thank her for her kindness please. But I might need some advice of dressing for such an event. I'm afraid that what I brought with me won't be adequate."

"Quite alright," George said. "We have staff that can help you out. Until tomorrow then."

Thanking George Jack headed to the elevator with the bellman. Walking into his room, he was shocked that his suitcase was already there, sitting on the little suitcase rack. Jack showered, changed clothes and headed out to walk around London for the day.

The car ride to Wales the next day let Jack focus on his mission. While the Queen's invitation loomed, his immediate concern was finding flowers in Swansea. Colonel Roberts had been buried nearby in a regimental graveyard and Jack wanted something to show his respect. George Wakefield solved the problem by locating a flower shop. Jack purchased a fresh bouquet of flowers after checking that leaving them at the grave would be OK.

The next stop was at a hotel where Ms. Roberts waited. She had taken the train in from her small community and would spend the night courtesy of the British taxpayer before returning home tomorrow. Jack stepped out of the Jaguar and waited while George retrieved her from the lobby. As she came out the front door, Jack walked over and extended his hand. George introduced the two and escorted them back to the car. Jack held the door for Ms. Roberts and then walked around and got in the opposite side.

The car was quiet as they made their way to the graveyard and the driver pulled in. Ms. Roberts directed the driver through the maze of small narrow lanes to where her brother was buried. The car stopped when told and Jack and Ms. Roberts stepped out and closed the car doors.

Sitting on Jack's side of the car was a grave marked with Gregory Roberts. Below his name were his rank, his regiment and the dates of his life. Jack held the flowers and took Ms. Roberts's arm as he walked forward.

"I wanted so much to be here, Ms. Roberts."

"Robbie, please. I understand you were also ex-military, Mr. Wesley?"

"Please call me Jack. And yes. Former U. S. Marine."

"Then you and my brother had a common bond. I'm glad he died with a fellow warrior by his side."

"He didn't have to be there. That's what bothers me. He sacrificed himself for people he barely knew," Jack said.

"Let me say something, Jack. My brother had a long career. Many of his friends did not. He put his life on the line constantly for people he didn't know. His was to serve God and country."

"I just wish I could have saved him, that's all," Jack said.

"Mr. Wesley, you need to know something about my brother," Robbie said. "He was at home with me after his retirement going crazy when he got a call. A call that sent him to Montana to live next to you. He never told me, but I gather you are a very important person in the eyes of the Queen. My brother volunteered to be watchdog over you and your family."

"I got that impression," Jack said.

"What you don't know is he had started having headaches when he was living with me. Complaining about flashes of light in his side vision.

When he got to Missoula he sought out medical care. Tests revealed an inoperative brain tumor. The doctors had given him six months to live."

"I thought there was something wrong," Jack said. "Bright light bothered him."

"So, thank you, Jack. My brother got to go out doing what he loved most," Robbie said.

"We Americans have an expression for that," Jack said. "We call it 'Dying with your boots on'."

"Well, good on ya for that. Yes my brother died with his boots on as all good soldiers should."

Jack bent down and placed the flowers on the grave. He stood at attention and saluted his fallen comrade. As they turned to leave, an army captain in uniform was standing quietly beside the car with George.

"Sergeant Wesley, I'm Captain Lillian, of her Majesty's Armed forces. I would like to invite you to a nearby drinking establishment so that friends of Colonel Roberts may buy you a drink."

Jack was taken aback at the reference to his rank in the Marine Corps. But he knew the sentiment of fighting men. While he didn't really like beer, sometimes duty called. And warm British beer would really require sacrifice.

"It would be an honor, if it's all right with my guide, Mr. Wakefield here."

"Of course," George said. After Robbie declined joining the men, George offered to return her to the hotel and await Jack for the return to London.

Jack walked the short distance to an army Jeep and climbed in with Captain Lillian. They drove the short distance to a pub where about forty of Greg's friends had gathered.

"When we heard you would be here we got some of the lads together to say thanks," the captain said. "We had a full blown bash when the colonel got buried. Well over three hundred were here to do him right."

"I'm afraid I got your colonel killed, captain," Jack said.

"No sir, you saved him from six months of hell from what we've been told. Dying by those bloody bastards in hospital or in battle. No choice there in my mind."

"Mine either, Captain," Jack said. From what Robbie had said and by what he had observed, Greg had a miserable life remaining for him. Jack knew he would choose the same. "Now, let's go meet the lads."

Chapter 33

Orlando, Florida

Jack had decided that lunch with the Queen was rather anticlimactic after his bash with the lads. He had survived toast after toast as he consumed more alcohol than he had in the previous year, and then had to be ready two days later for the Queen. George Wakefield had been there through it all and deposited him back at Heathrow Airport for his flight to Orlando.

Jack was arriving one day late due to his date with the Queen. His family had arrived on Sunday and would be at the Magic Kingdom. Along with his invited friends, Jack had rented three houses near each other to accommodate twenty-three people.

The taxi he had picked up at the Orlando Airport crept through the subdivision of newer homes while Jack searched for the address. A large six-bedroom house rose up among the others and Jack spied the correct street number. Paying off the cab, Jack stepped out into the blazing Florida sun and quickly walked to the covered entryway. He leaned on the doorbell confident that someone would be home. Inez opened the door holding her daughter in her arms.

"Oh look, Grandpa Jack has finally showed up."

"And good to see you," Jack said as he picked up his bag, gave Inez a kiss and walked into the air-conditioned house. Eric's parents were sitting in the family room and Inez's father-in-law rose to greet Jack. After inquiring how his flight had been, Inez passed off the baby to the grandmother.

"Come on, Dad, I'll show you where your room is," Inez said.

Jack noticed a slight exasperation in her voice as she led Jack up the grand staircase that overwhelmed the foyer in true Southern style. Jack whistled at the soaring two-story entranceway as he climbed the stairs.

"Pretty fancy. Not my usual," Jack said.

Inez kept quiet as they walked the short hallway to the back of the house. A large double entry announced the master suite. Inez sat down on the bed and looked at her dad.

"Whose idea was this?" Inez said.

Jack placed his suitcase down on the floor, laid it down and opened it. He excused himself as he stepped into the master bathroom. When he came out his long pants had been replaced by his Big Dog nylon shorts. He unbuttoned his shirt and grabbed a T-Shirt out of his case.

"That bad already?" Jack asked. "Hey, you were the one who wanted to invite your in-laws along."

"But twelve people in this house. Its a bit overwhelming. And the three boys . . ."

Jack had been a little nervous about putting the three young boys all together. Being roughly the same age, they could be a handful.

"But at least they should be out of the terrible twos," Jack said. "It's only for five days, honey. Then you can go home to peace and quiet."

"I know, Dad. And I know how much this means to you."

And that had been why Jack had arranged this get-together. It was a year since he had had his brush with death and Jack wanted to embrace the people who meant everything to him.

"Thanks, honey. If there's anything I can do to make it more enjoyable, I'll try."

"Why don't you go enjoy the pool? It will feel good after your flight," Inez said.

"Come and join me, honey. Like old times," Jack said. "You have your built-in baby sitters downstairs."

Inez smiled at her dad's suggestion. She had wonderful memories of she and her dad playing in the pools of the various motels they had stayed at. She went to her room and put her swimsuit on. They met by the pool at the back of the house.

Jack noticed her wearing a one piece. Gone were the days of bikini suits for her. *At least until she stops breast feeding and gets the extra weight off* Jack thought. Inez was self-conscious of the extra pounds from having been pregnant and wore a towel around her to cover things up. With no one else around, she dropped the towel on a deck chair and dove into the pool. She swam over to where Jack leaned against the pool's edge.

Inez soon excused herself and returned to shower, get dressed, and feed the baby. Jack slid a lounge chair over under the shade and laid down. The entire crew would be arriving and he decided to take a quick nap to get ready.

Jack was awoken by a kiss on his forehead. He opened his eyes to Inez sitting beside him.

"Dad, Eric's folks are taking me out for dinner. The horde should be home anytime and I think they are looking for someplace peaceful."

"No worries. I told you that except for Thanksgiving dinner, everyone should do their own thing," Jack said. "Have fun and don't worry about me."

Jack closed his eyes and relaxed while he could. He was half asleep again when he was jolted awake by the screams of boys followed by a geyser of water hitting him as the three boys all cannonballed him. Jack snapped up to see the horde standing watching the action. He jumped to his feet, located his tormentors, and jumped in next to them, his splash in retaliation. Three boys immediately jumped on him and attempted to push him under the surface.

"Hey boys, leave Jack alone right now," Misty said. Having the oldest boy of the three, she took charge of the trio. Kotone and Valentina stood next to Misty as they put their motherly control on the situation.

"Oh Mom," came a chorus.

"Play nice with Jack," Valentina said with her Italian accent.

"We will be watching," Kotone added.

The three moms all sat down together in the shade on the pool deck. The boys were together by the edge of the pool plotting their next attack on Jack when they were covered in water. Two older boys completed their cannonballs and surfaced near Jack. Now with five boys in the pool, Jack knew when to retreat. He climbed out of the pool and took a seat next to Kotone.

"I thought they'd be all tired out after all day at the Magic Kingdom," Jack said.

"In your dreams," Kotone said. "You should have heard the complaints when we dragged them out of the park before the big nighttime light show."

"You didn't want to stay?" Jack asked.

"As we decided, we have a week here and we need to pace ourselves," Kotone said. "With three-year-olds that means shorter days at the parks. We saw some families that were going all out. Kids throwing themselves on the ground and screaming. Total melt down."

"That's what I read online. Assume you're going to come back so don't try to see everything at once," Jack said.

Stacey and Carl walked in followed by Stacey's parents who were enjoying the family time. They had a smaller house across the street.

Misty and Valentina were staying in Jack's house, their husbands choosing not to join the fun. A third house two doors down the street had Katarina and Johan along with her family from Amsterdam. They all soon showed up in bathing suits and joined the pool party.

Jack took little Johan from Katarina and walked over to the steps into the pool. Just one year old, Johan was just walking and this was his first pool experience. Jack placed him standing at the edge of the pool and knelt in the shallow end. Johan immediately jumped, trusting Jack to catch him. Placed back on the pool edge, he repeated his jump. While the five other boys swam by, Jack focused on the one-year-old.

Soon other adults joined in the fun and the pool was alive with activity. Jack focused on his charge as Carl seemed to attract the attention of the bigger boys. Stacey pulled off her cover-up, revealing her baby bump. She wore a two piece and still had the figure Jack remembered, having done a good job getting rid of the extra weight after each baby. Kotone stood and pulled off her loose shift. Her baby bump stuck out on her bikini. She had also retained her slim figure that Jack loved.

But it was when Katarina showed up and pulled the loose shirt over her head that got his attention. Jack knew she had worked hard all summer in Montana to get her trim figure back and now it showed. Her breast feeding had just ended as Johan turned one year old. And her breasts still overshadowed everything.

Jack looked at the group gathered for reactions. Especially Kotone's reaction. This was the first time the two had been together since the hospital in San Diego. Both women had been content to live separate lives while Jack traveled between them. This week would be the test of how their lifestyle was going to work. Jack wanted his family to know each other no matter how that family was constituted.

While Stacey's parents were the only ones that seemed to react to Katarina stepping into the pool, Jack let Katarina take over Johan's jumping drills. He moved to take a seat on the steps so he could observe. He hoped to make this a semi-annual event and how this one proceeded would decide if it would even happen at all. Kotone slid over beside him and took his arm.

"You sure know how to throw a party," she said.

"Are you OK? This is all pretty crazy after your simple life in Bozeman."

"I can handle it, Jack," Kotone said. "Komatsu is having fun. It's good for her."

Kotone's younger sister Komatsu had traveled from Bozeman with the group. While she lived next door in Bozeman to Kotone in her own duplex, her experience of being kidnapped and assaulted still affected her. And this was the first time she had left Bozeman in four years.

"I'm glad she came with us," Jack said.

Kotone leaned into Jack and whispered, "So do you think James Bond experienced this?"

"What? Why ask that?" Jack asked.

"Well, I've been thinking since seeing all of this. You know, James Bond slept with a beautiful woman on every mission. But they never show the aftereffects of those romps in bed."

"You mean sex has consequences?" Jack asked. He smiled as he said, "And you think I'm like James Bond?"

"Well, you certainly have had a lot of adventures," Kotone said. "And you've certainly bedded your share of beautiful women. And you've certainly procreated a lot."

"I always felt like I was reliving Mr. Pennypacker's life," Jack said.

"Who the hell is Mr. Pennypacker?"

"From the movie 'The Remarkable Mr. Pennyacker' starring Clifton Webb," Jack said. "Mr. Pennypacker owns two factories in different cities and he has a family in each city that he visits one week at a time."

"And how old is this movie?"

"I suppose its from the 1950's. Quite shocking for movie audiences in those days, but seems natural to me."

"It would. Jack Pannypacker huh?" Kotone asked.

Jack turned to look at his wife. She matched his gaze before adding. "Its OK, Jack. Your taking responsibility for your actions."

"You know?"

"Well yeah. You live half the time with another woman." Jack continued his stare at her. "Oh, you mean Misty and Valentina. I figured that out in San Diego."

"And you are still OK with that?" Jack asked.

"They have their husbands and they live a long way away, so that's fine," Kotone said. "But Jack, are there any others I don't know about?"

Jack had to think about that question. There were a couple other partners out there somewhere in the world. But no children that he knew of. But who knew? He looked at Kotone with an expression announcing that he didn't know the answer to the question.

"That's OK. We can deal with that if they come up," Kotone said. "So as of right now, this is it. Because if you want to share your time traveling among them I'd have a problem."

"No, no. Two are enough for me," Jack said. They sat together watching the whole crowd having fun. That Kotone knew that Misty's son Jan and Valentina's son Giovanni were both Jack's children took Jack aback. That she tolerated him having a life with Katarina and their son Johan meant everything to him. That she went even further and accepted two more women in their life with his other children was even better.

"Uncle Jack," Jan called.

"Si zio Jack. Come swim with us," Giovanni yelled.

Kotone leaned in close. "Yes, Uncle Jack. Go swim with your nephews."

Jack looked back as he stood. He received a smile over his Uncle Jack role in life. "You know, I'm a lucky guy," Jack said back to Kotone.

In response, she moved close and shoved Jack under the water. She climbed on top and pushed him down. Five boys all swam hard to help Jack with his tormentor. Kotone soon surrendered and swam alone back to the steps, climbing out to safety.

"Thanks, boys, for rescuing me," Jack yelled so everyone could hear.

The next day was a rest day for everyone. For the kids it was a swimming pool day. Five boys had much energy to burn, especially when the multiplier effect was added by the five being together. The adults took shifts in leaving for other locations for peace and quiet even if it was only to one of the other two houses they were renting.

Wednesday was taken up with a park day. The willing all loaded up in three rental cars and headed for an early start at Universal Studios. While the children were all too small for the big roller coaster rides, Misty led a contingent of adults on a whirlwind ride feast. The other adults were content to have fun in the smaller kid area where the Woody Woodpecker Roller Coaster kept them all entertained.

Jack found the ball pit and soon had five kids blasting away with the nerf balls and the cannons provided. A two-story building holding balconies and nerf guns kept the boys enthralled for the afternoon. With the high afternoon temperatures and their time in the park winding down, Jack got all the boys out in the courtyard for the tank dump.

They had watched all day as unwitting tourists wandered into the courtyard outside the nerf castle to have a giant tank dump hundreds of gallons of water onto them. It was all Jack could do to save the wet stuff till the end. Now he stood as they awaited the bell that announced the tank turning over. He held little Johan so he could experience the thrill with the bigger boys.

The other adults had all begged off and were sitting in the shade by Woody. The bells started and the gathered all started jumping up and down in excitement. As the tank emptied, it hit the building's roof and thus spread out the flow to avoid injuries.

The force of the water falling in such a large quantity from the second story roof still knocked down John and Jan. Both were up in a shot as if nothing had happened as they joined the other wet victims. Once wet, they all wanted to wait for the next dump. After four dumps, Jack announced it was done. Dry clothes were pulled out of backpacks as Jack took them all to a nearby restroom to change.

The next day was Thanksgiving and Jack had planned dinner for twenty-three. He had much to be thankful for and he wanted the time to share. To make life simpler, he had ordered dinner to be prepared at a local restaurant chain. Dinner arrived on time and everyone helped carry it in from the delivery truck. The smell filled the large home as everyone gathered in the kitchen in anticipation.

Part of the deal Jack had set was that everyone would dress for dinner and he arrived in his British-made suit. While a little warm for Florida, the air conditioner helped keep him comfortable. When he described that the suit had been a gift of the Queen, everyone wanted to inspect it.

Stacey's Mom noticed the tag. "Savile Row. Wow, very classy."

"What, you didn't think my father-in-law wasn't classy?" Stacey fired back.

There was an awkward moment before Stacey broke out laughing. Everyone joined in the fun. A single table had been cobbled together by pushing two tables into one.

As everyone sat down to dinner, Carl stood and offered a toast. "To a very lucky family. And to my Dad who lived through everything to bring all these friends and family together today."

"Here, here," a chorus said in reply. Dishes were soon being passed around as everyone dug in. Moms helped the little ones sitting at the table cut their turkey. Grandparents gazed at the collection of people gathered.

Jack just sat and took it all in. He wondered if the six grandparents present had a clue as to how the group all was related. The story that some were good friends kept the myth alive and Jack wondered if they really believed. Or that they wanted to believe it and it was best to ignore any other tale.

He didn't really care. He loved all these people at the table and didn't care if the world knew how he was the father to four of them. And soon to be five with Kotone pregnant. And Katarina speaking that she wanted another would be six. Add in his two older children and Carl and Inez brought the total to eight.

The table kept busy as everyone carried on chatting. Being at the head of the table allowed Jack to observe all. He let the others chat as he looked over everyone. He was too emotional at what had almost happened to really talk at the moment and everyone seemed to sense that.

As the eating slowed Jack announced since everyone was dressed in their best he wanted some pictures. Carl produced a camera and a tripod and soon pictures were taken. Different family groups were snapped as people moved in and out of the seating area. Carl used the timer to snap an all-inclusive picture and then went back to work on getting other shots.

As people drifted off to the family room Jack unobtrusively called to Jan, John and Giovanni. Picking up little Johan, he sat down with the other three boys. Carl snapped some shots before anyone noticed that Jack had singled out those four boys to take a picture. Kotone looked on smiling.

Jack looked over to the opposite side of Carl and saw Katarina smiling. *So she knows too* Jack thought. *I haven't talked to her about all of this.* Jack noticed Stacey standing nearby also with a smile. But her smile seemed different than Kotone's or Katarina's.

Soon the dress clothes were replaced with swim gear as another day at the home's pool was called for. Tomorrow those that wanted would head to the Kennedy Space Center on the east coast of Florida.

After another fun filled day and when the children were finally shoved into bed, Stacey found Jack sitting in the family room. She made a motion for him to follow and Jack rose and left the house with Stacey. As everyone else was in their bedrooms relaxing from a full day, the two stepped out to the sidewalk.

"It's a beautiful night for a walk, don't you think?" Stacey asked.

Jack knew something was on his daughter-in-law's mind. But he had been around women enough to let her lead.

"Beautiful. And quiet too," Jack replied.

"Yes, Jack Wesley, you know how to throw a party."

"Well, after Hawaii, I can afford to," Jack said.

"I saw you sneaking in a picture with Jan, John, Giovanni and Johan," Stacey said. Jack noticed a certain tone to her comment.

"And you know why I did?" Jack said. "We got the other pictures with JJ and CJ so this isn't about that is it?"

Jack was confused over what Stacey was talking about. *Why does she seem upset about me taking a picture with my four sons?* he thought. *I know we are not broadcasting that fact to everyone, but what's the problem?*

Stacey walked along not saying any more. Jack decided to join her just walking. She would raise her issue when she was ready. They walked around the block and were quite a ways from the three rental houses before she spoke. She stopped and turned to face Jack.

"Jack, we go back six years. Hard to believe," Stacey said.

"Yes Stacey, a lot has happened."

"I think about our bike ride every once in a while."

Jack cringed at the comment. He and Stacey had been riding partners for a few months as they crossed the United States on bicycles. And now she was married to his son and Jack didn't care for those memories to surface.

"Those were good times for sure," Jack said.

"But when I saw you gather the four boys together, I just wanted to say something."

Jack's heart raced and his chest tightened. Whatever Stacey was about to say, he really wanted to tell her to keep it to herself.

"To include Carl and Inez next time?" Jack said. He held his breath.

"And JJ, too."

Jack's mind exploded at the news. *What was she saying?* he thought.

"JJ, I should include him?" Jack said. A bead of sweat rolled down his back, the warm Florida night and the walk adding to his stress level.

"He's your son, too."

Stacey began to cry, tears rolling down her cheeks. Jack looked around to see if anyone was watching. He reached out and took Stacey in his arms.

"Does Carl know?"

"He'd have to be a complete moron not to know."

"So you've never told him?"

"No, never."

"But how?" Jack said. The two pulled apart.

"Jack Wesley, if you don't know how, let me explain it to you."

"Well, I know how it happens, but how did it happen?"

"We were riding through Colorado after we got back together. And I knew you had Kotone on your mind when we were together."

Jack cringed at hearing of his actions. He remembered him, and Stacey and the wonderful time they had together. But Kotone certainly had stolen him away.

"I'm sorry," Jack said.

"Oh, Jack, grow up. I'm a big girl. But we separated when we hit Kansas. Kotone and I got chased out of town by Sheriff what's-his-name."

"I remember," Jack said. "Carl and I were riding across Missouri together when we heard from you that Kotone was in jail. We rode to the rescue."

"And you left for Oregon with Kotone and I left for Virginia with Carl."

"All true," Jack said. "So . . ."

"So everything, mister. When you add in the month crossing Kansas and Missouri with the month Carl and I took to get to Virginia, that's two months of no sex but baby growing. You don't think I jumped Carl the first night we were together?"

Jack was silent in response because he certainly didn't know the answer to that. That Stacey and his son hooked up was sufficient for him. He didn't really want to think about the details.

At his non-answer, Stacey added, "Well, I didn't. We didn't start you-know-what until we had turned south on our bikes. So imagine Carl's surprise when after a month doing you-know-what with his new girlfriend, she starts showing a baby bump. Never mind puking on the side of the road from morning sickness. I don't think he considers he has super sperm."

Jack cringed at Stacey's explanation. "And he's never said a word?"

"Just acted like it was his all along. What you don't know is by the time of our winter layover in Mississippi, I was too far along to pedal. We bought a cheap car and I drove shag wagon across the southern U.S. while Carl finished cycling back across to California. We showed up in Montana just in time for me to give birth."

"And no one else knows?" Jack asked.

"No, its something I don't broadcast," Stacey said. "Not that I'm not proud of JJ and who his father is, but considering the situation, having Carl be Dad makes better sense."

"Yes, lets keep it that way." Jack and Stacey started walking again toward home. As they came around the block, Jack broke the silence. "Stacey, thank you for telling me. I'll always be Grandpa to him, but deep inside I'll know."

"So, I hear Katarina is pushing for a second baby," Stacey said. "With Kotone already along in that direction, what do you think about having nine kids?"

"Feels great. As Mark Steyn, my favorite social commentator says, 'The future belongs to those who show up'."

"And you are determined the Wesley clan is there?" Stacey asked.

"Damn straight I do. All raised right. Freedom-loving individuals all."

"God help us," Stacey replied.

The End

Acknowledgements

First I would thank Timothy Johns, my tireless editor. Though he works hard that my writing is presentable, place no blame on him for the final product. That all rests with me.

My proofreaders offer valuable feedback at different phases as my draft is put together. Dick Martin, Marsha Wiles, Larry Stoddard, Tiffany Martin, Barbara Foster, and John Briggs have all kept me from straying too far off on tangents.

John Ewing was an early supporter who didn't get to see the final product. His wife Bertha Ewing was invaluable as a listener as I read out loud to her on one of my many edit jobs.

Finding Morwenna Rakestraw to do the cover layout was a relief and I appreciate her sticking with me.

Mitch Press of World Book has offered his wisdom from his family's years in the book business. While not all encouraging, his guidance as publishing transforms in the digital age has been invaluable.

Finally, I need to thank my wife for her support of my writing. She means everything to what I do.

Dear Reader,

Thank you for your selection of reading material. I hope this book measured up to your expectations. The most critical part for a new author is getting the word out to other readers.

I would appreciate your help in spreading the word. There are three important things you can do. You need to understand the importance of the first one to my becoming a successful writer. Amazon.com is huge in the new book publishing era. So please:

1.   Go to Amazon.com and leave a review
2.   Tell a friend about this book
3.   Tell your social network about this book.

The more positive reviews that are made in various places, the more it will help readers find me.

Again, thanks for your support.

W.B. Martin

And check out my website at wbmartinauthor.com

Read an excerpt of the original Jack Wesley thriller
from W.B. Martin.

Trouble Leaves Too Slow

Available from Amazon.com

Chapter 1

Eugene, Oregon

Jack Wesley sat on his Lane Transit bus as he rode home from his novel writing class at Lane Community College. His class got out a 9 PM each Monday night and he rode the #66 VRC/Coburg bus toward his apartment off Goodpasture Island Road. It was almost the end of spring term and he was ready for his class to be over.

Retiring six months earlier after thirty years on the job, he was looking forward to a new challenge. Novel writing had intrigued him for a number of years and he was sure that his life time of work would provide him with countless plots.

He had plunged into his new calling upon starting school in fall term, yet his first novel was progressing slowly. And now summer was coming and he was anxious to start another new adventure. But that would have to wait a couple more weeks while he wrapped up his life in Eugene.

He sat back as the bus headed into the Downtown Bus Terminal. This was where things could get interesting. Being the center of the anarchist movement in the country, Eugene had any number of strange characters and they all seemed to ride the bus at night.

Jack watched as the bus driver wheeled to a stop in the transit center. Three people hit the rear doors and exited the bus. Jack looked around at the five people remaining. He noticed he was the only person over thirty years of age.

And he was the only person without any unusual piercing or tattoo showing, except for one young woman whom he had noticed previously riding from the college. She was dressed conservatively and sat toward the front of the bus where the seats were reserved for the old and handicapped.

Jack typically sat just behind these seats himself so he could hit the front door when he exited. The back seats had steps up to reach them and Jack figured he didn't need the extra challenge. Not that he was old or infirm, it was just that riding the bus wasn't his favorite task. But since his job gave him a free bus pass and it was good for the rest of the year, he figured why not. It saved him wear and tear on his truck and parking at the college was limited, even for the night classes. And it kept him in touch with the other side of Eugene. He smiled at the conservative woman as she acknowledged his look. They had shared the same bus after class each Monday evening but had never spoken. *Two students riding the bus home dealing with the riff-raff of the city,* he thought.

Jack turned and looked at the new riders as they got onto the bus. It was the typical strange crowd joining him. Some of the riders were familiar to him as he recognized some of the Monday night regulars.

He surmised that they must work downtown. Considering how they were dressed and adorned, he assumed they must work at the many alternative establishments that lined Eugene's downtown streets.

But two of the new riders were noticeably stranger than the rest. Jack had never seen them before, and the way these guys looked, he would have remembered them. The two walked up the center of the bus with a decided attitude. He watched them walk by and got the stare down in return. Jack's innate antennae for trouble vibrated as they walked by him.

One was above average in height but very skinny. The tattoo up his neck had a less-than-polite nature to it. The second guy was average height and stocky. His three nose rings were his most noticeable feature.

Jack shifted in his seat so he could watch them from the corner of his eye, but they didn't head to the back of the bus to join the others. They both slid in the seat right behind the conservatively dressed young woman. *Not good,* he thought.

The bus driver closed the doors and headed out. The bus moved into traffic and the driver dimmed the interior lights to reduce the glare on the windshield. That's when the trouble started.

"Hey, keep your hands to yourself," the young woman said.

"Hey bitch. What you saying? Nobody's doing nothin'," the tall one said.

Jack turned so he faced the two trouble makers. They were one seat behind his row but across the aisle. His shoulder bag twisted with him and he shoved it onto his back so it was out of his way.

"What you looking at old man? Get you face back forward or I'll move it for you," the stocky one said. He added as much threat to his gaze as he could muster.

Jack stared back then glanced forward to see if the bus driver had noticed any of the exchange. The driver leaned forward, ignoring the developing confrontation.

The woman said more emphatically, "I said keep your hands off me."

Jack noticed the tall one reaching around the seat back with his left arm. The young woman stood up and walked forward to one of the handicap seats. She sat down and stared straight ahead.

The two guys looked as if they were deciding to join her as they stood up to move. Jack decided that was not going to happen and stood up quickly, blocking their way.

"Move, asshole, or you'll wish you had," the stocky one said.

"Sit down, boys. Those seats are reserved. You don't look handicapped to me," Jack answered.

The stocky guy moved close to Jack so the tall one could get out of the seat. He moved behind his buddy and looked over his head into Jacks' eyes. The two six-footers stared each other down while the short stocky one mouthed off.

"You don't know who you messin' with, hombre."

"Sit down now, or I'll sit you down," Jack said.

That was enough for the shorter guy. At the challenging words he instantly drew a knife from his coat pocket, but before his hand was halfway out, his forehead was crushed by a head-butt from Jack. The guy dropped like a sack onto the bus floor. He didn't move.

His buddy wound up for a right cross to Jack's head. Jack recovered from his head-butt and jabbed his straightened fingers into the tall guy's solar plexus, just below the ribs.

The tall guy staggered from the blow and forgot all about his roundhouse arm swing. He stumbled backwards and regained his breath. He stood upright just as Jack hit him with a high kicked boot to the chest.

The man flew back as the force of the kick transmitted to his body. Jack knew how to apply the full weight of his 215 pounds to a swift kick. As he fell back his head banged on one of the bus poles. He moaned and rolled onto his side.

"Hey, I'm calling the cops," the bus driver finally yelled as he pulled the bus over to the curb.

About time, Jack thought. With both of the perpetrators prone on the floor, Jack sat down and waited for law enforcement to arrive. *No one was getting home early tonight,* he thought.

"Thank you," the young woman said.

"No problem. Sorry Eugene tolerates these guys. Makes life difficult at times," Jack said.

"Well, I appreciate it. My Dad can't understand why I ride the bus in this town but I just can't afford a car while I'm in college."

"You shouldn't have to apologize. The city should apologize to you," Jack said.

In the distance sirens were rapidly approaching the bus. Jack waited patiently. His charges lay quietly. The bus driver sat passively like he had been through this before.

Finally one cruiser arrived and stopped behind the bus, lights flashing. Right after, a second patrol car swung across the front of the bus. *Well, we're blocked in now for the duration,* Jack thought.

The two police officers stormed onto the bus from two directions. With their hands on their guns, they swung their heavy mag lights. The one coming in through the front door reached the aisle and stopped fast.

"Oh, it's you Jack. I should have known."

His partner scrambled up the back stairs and stepped over the stocky guy on the floor. He looked at Jack.

"Well, Detective Wesley, I thought you were retired," he said. "Are you responsible for this?"

"You have to ask? If Jack is around trouble, we know who resolved it," the first officer said.

The bus driver finally spoke. "You need to arrest this man. He caused the whole thing. I saw him beat these two boys up."

"Damn straight. I saw the whole thing. That old dude caused all the trouble," one of the pierced guys in the back of the bus yelled.

"That right, Jack?" the officer with three stripes on his arm asked. He smiled slightly as he gave his friend a hard time.

"Officer, this man saved me from those two molesting me. I'll be happy to serve as a witness to the whole thing," the young woman said.

"Yes ma'am. I believe you were the victim then. I'll take your name and a detective will contact you. Don't worry about Mr. Wesley here. Things will be all right," the officer said. Turning to Jack, he added, "Come on Jack."

The two stepped off the bus. The officer put in a call for an ambulance on his shoulder-mounted radio. While the younger officer took down details from people on the bus, Jack stood and waited with his friend.

"So, you still got your trip planned?" the officer asked.

"Yeah, in two weeks. This whole thing better not mess up my plans," Jack said.

"Shouldn't be a problem. You know the routine as well as I do. These two perps will sit in jail tonight and be arraigned tomorrow. They'll be released since there's no room over at County. They might show up in a month for a trial, but most likely the DA will offer them a deal, probation with community service. It's a joke."

"I know. That's why I'm getting out of here. Go see some other parts of the country. Maybe find a decent place to retire," Jack said.

"Well, be careful that these two don't file a civil suit against you. Some ACLU lawyer would love to tag you after some of the arrests you've made in this town."

"They'll have a hard time serving me. I don't plan on leaving a forwarding address," Jack said.

"Kathy still going to babysit your apartment?" his friend asked.

Kathy Moore was a fellow Eugene police detective who had recently separated from her husband. She needed a place to live until things were sorted out. Jack didn't see much hope in the two of them reconciling. Her husband was a philanderer and everyone who knew the two of them never understood why Kathy had stayed with him so long.

But Jack was glad to have someone sublease his apartment. He had a nice location near Valley River Center and the bike paths along the Willamette River. While he didn't intend to stay much longer in Eugene, one never knew. He could afford to pay some towards the rent so he could shove his personal things into the second bedroom.

With a fellow police officer living at his place, it was more secure than renting a storage unit somewhere. And Kathy should have her life worked out in the six months he planned on being gone. A win-win for both of them.

The ambulance pulled up behind the bus and lined up with the police cruiser sitting there. The two EMTs walked up. They acknowledged Jack and the officer.

"Another of your jobs, Jack? I thought you were retired," the EMT who had been driving asked. His partner smiled at the jab.

"Very funny. You two guys better shake it and attend to our 'victims'. You might end up attending multicultural training so you'll be more sensitive next time," Jack threw back.

"Yeah, yeah. I'm gonna miss the overtime you provided me picking up after you though," the driver said as he stepped onto the bus.

One of the 'victims' awoke and the EMT checked him over before escorting him back to the ambulance. The younger police officer stood watch at the back of the ambulance as he returned with the gurney to retrieve the second 'victim'.

"The other guy may have a concussion. And what's with the boot print on his chest? You step on him in a hurry to exit the bus?" the EMT asked.

"My heart bleeds. No, he walked into my boot as I defended the young woman in there. But nobody seems to care about people like her around here anymore," Jack said. His anger grew. The black police humor could only cover so much of the rage he felt about the thugs who were slowly taking over his city.

The EMTs loaded up the second 'victim' and wheeled him to the back doors of the ambulance. Jack started to climb back on the bus.

"You're not arresting that guy?" one of the pierced bus riders yelled.

"You want a ride home?" Jack's friend said.

"And leave the young woman alone in there? No, but thanks for the offer. I'll be all right," Jack said.

"I wasn't worried about you."

The ride across the river was uneventful. Jack glared once towards the back to shut the riff-raff up. He suggested to the young woman that she get off at his stop and he would give her a ride the rest of the way.

The two finally introduced themselves as the bus trundled along the freeway towards the Valley River Center exit. With only one more class for this term, they agreed to look for each other the next week.

Chapter 2

Astoria, Oregon

The Astoria Bridge towered over the Columbia River where it ended its race to the sea. The green lattice work of steel girders rose over the city that sat along its banks. Once a bustling seaport, the years had seen hard times fall upon Astoria.

Starting in the 1800s, Astoria was the fur and fish trading capital of the Pacific Northwest. Beaver pelts as well as other furs brought wealth to the new city. When the California Gold Strike hit, San Francisco became the market of choice as fish and timber headed south.

Astoria continued its growth into the 1900s as fish and timber ruled the city docks. Then the fish started dropping off. The gigantic salmon runs that had sustained the Native American tribes that lived along the Columbia for generations collapsed.

The huge fish wheels that sucked every salmon from the river made sure that new salmon were never born. After decades of overfishing, the salmon run became regulated and limited. The old days of fish canning factories lining Astoria's waterfront were gone.

Then in the late 20th century, timber took a hit. Environmental concerns soon tied up the Federal forest lands to the point that logging essentially ceased. Only private timber lands still cut trees, and these had more restrictions than ever.

Astoria's golden years were behind it. Lately, the city tried to rely on tourism to keep the economy alive. The old waterfront factories were turned into shops and restaurants. The many old Victorian houses were converted into Bed and Breakfasts.

It was at the Sand Island B & B that Kotone Butler found herself on a foggy Tuesday morning. She had arrived from Portland Airport with a small duffle bag and two sets of bicycle panniers. After a night's stay, she headed downtown to the local bicycle shop to pick up her bicycle.

Kotone had shipped her Cannondale road touring bicycle a month ago from New York City by UPS. A New York City bike store had disassembled her bike and boxed it up. She had checked the week before by phone that the bike had arrived safely. The store confirmed that her bicycle would be assembled and ready to ride upon her arrival.

As the store clerk handed her the bike, she said, "Looks like it survived the trip. Anything out of sorts?"

"Nope," the clerk replied. "UPS delivers all our new bikes. One out of fifty might have a problem, but yours was fine. Nice bike. You hitting the Trans Am?"

"All the way to Virginia. Can't wait to get started. I've been riding my old bike to stay in shape. I missed my Cannondale."

"Well, you're starting right in the rush. End of May is typically our peak time for Trans Am riders. Too much rain in April and if you start in June, you hit the Midwest in the really hot weather," he offered.

"I watched the weather report last night on TV. It looks like it will be nice for the week," Kotone said.

"Don't pay too much attention to Oregon weather reporters. They do a lot better than they used to, but still only hit it half the time. The old saying here is, if you plan on rain, and get a dry day, enjoy it. Until you cross the Cascade Mountains, you can expect rain anytime."

"Thanks, I'll remember that. Any other advice? I've read a lot of the blogs. I know about the log trucks, the tunnels, and the winds. Northerlies this time of year, right?"

"Yep. The winds can be wicked. But you can catch a southerly once in a while. Enjoy the moment if you do," the clerk added.

The two finished up their transaction and Kotone walked her bike out the door. Climbing on, she started pedaling back to her B & B. *Feels good to be finally hitting the trail,* she thought.

Two blocks later a Monaco RV with California plates cut her off as it came out of a parking lot. Kotone hit her brakes and the disc brakes did their work. She stopped just short of the side of the forty foot camper as the two oblivious occupants looked forward. One had blue hair, the other white. *It might not be New York City traffic, but Oregon had its own challenges,* Kotone thought.

Kotone lived on the Upper East Side of Manhattan Island. A short two blocks from the United Nations building, she had a one bedroom apartment that faced 49th Street. If she moved all the way to the west in her living room and craned her neck, she had a glimpse of the East River.

She loved living in the city, except for riding her bike. A new convert to triathlons, she took the subway out to Rockaway where she kept her road bike at a fellow competitor's house. They would ride their training circuit near the shore where the traffic was tolerable. She also enjoyed running on the beach for her conditioning.

Swimming was accomplished at the 46th Street YMCA. The pool sat on the 22nd floor. She enjoyed walking over from her flat and seeing the green glow of the pool high in the building. It made her marvel at the city and how everything was constructed. That a swimming pool could be located so high up in a building with regular offices below it amazed her.

She had been planning this trip for two years. Ever since her second divorce, she had felt that she needed an adventure. Originally, a female friend was to accompany her, but her friend got cold feet and had made excuse after excuse until Kotone stopped asking.

It only made Kotone more determined to start. At thirty-five years of age, she knew she was in the best shape she'd ever been in her life. Kotone wanted to test herself both physically and mentally. But her friends soon became concerned that she was heading into the wilds of America unescorted and began pleading with her to reconsider.

The more they argued, the more Kotone focused on her goal. Finally she was ready to start. Tomorrow would be her first day on the road.

She awoke to the B&B shaking. Her bedroom window rattled in its track as the wind buffeted the glass. She got out of bed and looked out the window. Her view of the Columbia River made her heart sink. Whitecaps blew spray inland as the river rolled west toward the Pacific Ocean.

Reaching the dining room, the B & B owner greeted her warmly. "The wind is kicking up today," she said. "Still plan on leaving this morning?"

Kotone walked out onto the front porch. It was all she could do to close the front door behind her. Her hair instantly swept back on her head as she surveyed the city. She caught a flag outstretched on its staff down by the waterfront. It was flapping east and that meant a cross wind if she headed out today on Highway 101 South.

As she watched, the flag suddenly moved to the south. She could feel the wind shift against her face. Now her hair wanted to fly over her left ear. She waited. Would it stay southerly or shift again?

The flag remained flapping south. She headed inside.

"Have you seen a weather report for today?" she asked the owner.

"I checked for you earlier. Should be northerlies all day which means it'll be blowing south for you. And clear too."

Kotone raced up the stairs and threw her gear together. She pulled on her Lycra bike shorts and Trans Am bicycle shirt. She snapped her front and rear panniers together and shoved her bike shoes through one of the loops.

Placing her bags by the front door, she headed to the dining room for breakfast. The owner brought her a steaming plate.

"I put some extra on for you. The bikers we get here all seem to eat more than anyone else we have. If you want more, just ask."

Kotone looked at her plate. *I can't possible eat all that,* she thought.

She cut into the ham and cheese omelet and took a bite. It tasted wonderful. She broke open a blueberry muffin. *Marvelous,* she thought. Next was a bite of a Belgian Waffle followed by coffee. She worked her way through the various items. She knew that she needed to carbo-load for her ride today, but this was ridiculous.

Finally, the plate was pushed away. She couldn't eat anything more.

"Those blueberry muffins were to die for," Kotone said as the owner came out of the kitchen.

"Huckleberries. They grow up in the Coast Range. My husband and I pick them every year and freeze them. Wonderful treat."

"I'll say. It was a great breakfast. It'll keep me going today," Kotone said.

"Well, I've packed you some snacks while my husband got your bike out of the garage. Have a safe trip. And come back to see us."

Kotone thanked the woman and stuffed her snack bag into a rear pannier. She opened the door and headed to her bike. As she hooked all her gear onto the racks, the husband and wife watched. She snapped on her helmet and slid her sunglasses under the straps onto her ears. Her camera was passed to the husband for the obligatory 'before' shot. Stuffing the camera away, she pulled on her gloves and waved goodbye to the owners as she pedaled off.

Riding down the modest hill, Kotone felt the Cannondale flex from the load. She had done some weekend bike trips in Vermont as a warm-up to this trip, but she had forgotten how weight changed the feel of her bike.

She quickly calculated that she had more weight on her bike today than on any of her short trips. All those little extra things she'd packed for the long trip. *It sure adds up,* she thought.

Reaching the bottom of the hill, she turned left onto Highway 101. The wind buffeted her as she pedaled through Astoria. Whenever a cross street came up, the wind hit her with full intensity. She leaned right into the wind to compensate for the force trying to push her into the traffic lane.

Passing each intersection, the buildings then blocked the southerlies and Kotone found her lean suddenly carrying toward the sidewalk. Straightening the bike vertical stopped the swerve, at least until the next intersection, when she would adjust her lean once again.

Finally she was through the main part of town and the highway curved left. Now the wind hit her in the rear and she felt the pedals go easy. A tail wind to a bicycler was a gift from God. Kotone laid into her pedals and the Cannondale sprinted down the road.

Soon, she crossed the Warrenton Slough on a long narrow bridge, her first experience with tight Oregon roads. She checked her mirror and saw a car coming up from behind. Kotone stuck to the white fog line as the bridge had no shoulder. With just two lanes of traffic, it was tight quarters.

Kotone looked up and saw a log truck coming towards her. Checking her mirror again, she realized that the car was gaining rapidly on her. All three were going to meet at the same spot on the bridge. She pedaled harder to change that dynamic.

The log truck grew closer as Kotone pedaled hard. The tail wind was helping and it would be close. The wind from the log truck hit her just as the car sped by on her left. She fought to control her bike from the buffeting.

She saw the cars fender streak by just inches from her leg. The driver hadn't moved over at all and had nearly clipped the bicycle. With her panniers sticking out, Kotone figured she'd find white car paint on their sides when she had a chance to stop. She pedaled on, checking the mirror again.

Another car passed her, but this one rumbled over the reflectors in the center of the road. With no approaching traffic, the driver had moved over half a lane to give the biker some room. *Thank you,* Kotone thought.

The end of the long bridge arrived and Kotone could move over onto a nice wide shoulder. She sighed in relief. She loved cycling, but fighting the bad drivers made the experience a little unnerving at times.

The highway continued south and she maintained a relatively fast pace. With the wind at her back, Kotone could make good time. The view she had been expecting of the Pacific Ocean hadn't materialized yet, though. She rode through a mixture of small developed properties interspersed with forest.

She looked down at her handlebar bag and the map she had placed in the plastic sleeve. It appeared that she wouldn't see the ocean until she was down by Cannon Beach. She pedaled on.

After a stop at a roadside rest area to eat some of her prepared snacks, she began to hit some hills. Small ones, but ones that slowed her progress. But her tail wind assisted her, pushing her up and over each hill.

At Seaside, she pulled into a convenience store for a break. She leaned her bike against the wall and pulled out her cable lock. She wound the cable through her bike frame and attached it to the newspaper box sitting in the front. That would keep anyone from running off with her bike while she was in the store.

But it didn't protect her valuables. Those she had placed in her handle bar bag. She pulled the bag off its wire rack and slung it by its shoulder strap over her shoulder. In the store, she selected a large water bottle and a bag of peanuts for later. She walked to the counter to pay.

In front of her were two large men, one in a police uniform. She checked out the front pages of the gossip magazines as she waited for them to finish. The clerk rang up the bill and Kotone fished through her bike bag for her wallet.

Grabbing her purchases, she pushed the door open and turned toward her bike. The two large men were standing in front of a pickup truck, staring at her bicycle.

"Good morning," the policeman said.

"Morning," Kotone replied.

"Starting out on the Trans Am I see. You alone?" the large uniformed man asked.

Kotone had already thought through this question. She knew it would be the first thing people asked. And being a good New Yorker, she wasn't about to admit that she was solo.

"Alone? No way. My friends are behind me. They're still working on getting in shape for the ride. There's six of us. Been planning this for a couple years," Kotone lied.

"Good. Not right for a woman to be out here on the road alone. Too many bad things can happen," the policeman said.

"I figured that you being a policeman and all, you'd have a good handle on it," Kotone said.

"No, no. I'm a Deputy Sheriff. Clatsop County, ma'am. You're not from around here, I take it. Must be an East Coaster. Not too many deputies back there from what I hear."

"I think we might have sheriffs, but I don't know what they do," Kotone said. "So, out West, I'll see lots of Deputy Sheriffs?"

"Just like in the movies," the other big man said. He grinned with a rather stupid looking leer. The smile revealed a missing tooth. It dawned on Kotone suddenly that these two men were related. The size and looks revealed that they must be brothers.

"Well, nice talking to you, but I better get moving. Don't want to chill down too much," Kotone said.

"You're not going to wait for your friends?" the stupid-smiled one asked.

"Oh no. We'll all meet up at our campsite later. We've done this lots of times." She unlocked her bike and put the lock away. She slid the handlebar bag back onto its wire rack and secured it. Climbing onto her bike, she nosed it into the parking lot.

"Have a nice day," the deputy said. The two men checked her out from behind as she pedaled across the parking lot. Their stares were unnerving, as they watched her thighs move up and down with the pedals. She watched them in the mirror as she stopped to check the highway traffic. They seemed to be saying something to each other as she pulled onto the highway.

Men were always watching her backside when she rode. The combination of her long legs and tight Lycra shorts made her butt very revealing. Sometimes she didn't mind the opposite sex checking her out. She worked hard to have a tight athletic body. These two, however, creeped her out.